THINGS THAT NEVER HAPPENED

ALSO BY SCOTT EDELMAN

The Gift (1990)

Suicide Art (1992)

These Words Are Haunted (2001)

What Will Come After (2010)

What We Still Talk About (2010)

Liars, Fakers, and the Dead Who Eat Them (2017)

Tell Me Like You Done Before (2018)

THINGS THAT NEVER HAPPENED

SCOTT EDELMAN

CEMETERY DANCE PUBLICATIONS

Cemetery Dance Publications
132-B Industry Lane, Unit #7
Forest Hill, MD 21050
www.cemeterydance.com

ISBN: 978-1-58767-794-6

CONTENTS

THINGS THAT NEVER HAPPENED

When Barb, for the first time in years, visited the woman who had raised her, she assumed, after all of their tumultuous history together, that she'd see in that wrinkled face—

—a hint of fear—

—or possibly even some barely suppressed anger—

—or a trace of irritation at being interrupted—

—and would remorse have been too much to ask for after how she'd been treated?

But instead, the reaction Barb received was as if she'd been a stranger.

As the woman in the bed looked up, and saw who'd come into her private room, her expression didn't change. Not at all.

Barb had arrived at the nursing home too late.

"Eleanor," she said. "Hello."

She was unable, even after years of therapy and especially after the things that had recently happened in her life, to speak the word "mother" to this woman, to even use it in her thoughts. But then, because all she got in return for her greeting was a nod and a slight smile and no apparent acknowledgement of the minefield that stretched between them, Barb forced herself to dig deep and say a word she'd banished from her vocabulary long ago.

"Hello, Mother." She said it as flatly as she could, her lips barely moving, but Eleanor didn't seem to mind. Or even appear to notice.

Barb dragged a chair to one side of the bed, momentarily thinking she should ask, "Mind if I sit down?" But she was beyond asking her mother permission for anything anymore. Those days had passed. Were past.

She placed herself between her mother and the window, wanting the glare of the sun in her mother's eyes so she'd have to squint during their conversation. A petty desire, perhaps, and one her therapist wouldn't have been happy to hear about it, but even small paybacks had their pleasures. Besides, Eleanor still had the upper hand in the relationship, even if the Eleanor Barb knew was long gone, and she needed every advantage she could get.

"We have a lot to talk about," said Barb.

And Eleanor, continuing to smile, asked "And *you* are?"

There was even a twinkle to her eyes. Barb couldn't believe it. Where was the damned twinkle when Barb needed it growing up, when it could have saved her? But no, Eleanor had been storing up all of her smiles and twinkles until now, when it no longer mattered. How was it possible she could be happy, happy to see *her*? But then she was probably happy to see anyone and everyone who bothered to visit her.

That wasn't what Barb wanted. That wasn't what Barb expected. That wasn't what Barb needed.

Too late.

Much too late.

But she had to try.

"I'm your daughter," Barb said, trembling. So many of

their conversations had taken place with Barb trembling, and as she looked at Eleanor, even in that deteriorated condition, she was brought immediately back to all of them. "It's Barbara. Don't you remember your daughter Barbara?"

"I have a daughter?" Eleanor asked.

"Yes, you have a daughter," said Barb.

"How about that?" she said. "I have a daughter."

"But you never acted like it," said Barb. "You never treated me the way a mother should. Surely you still remember at least that. You've got to."

Eleanor's smile faded, but only enough to make her look slightly confused, rather than unhappy. Barb wondered whether a person could even *be* unhappy over a past she no longer remembered. And Barb needed her to be. She so desperately needed her to be.

"If I…" Eleanor started to say, then stopped, then started over. "Then I'm sorry for that. I'm sorry…what did you say your name was again?"

Eleanor saying she was sorry? Barb had never known it to happen before.

She'd hoped for an apology, but not one like this.

She wanted whimpering, she wanted begging for mercy and pleading for forgiveness, she wanted to see the stoic face she remembered crumple and fall in on itself, she wanted to hear the words "I'm sorry, I'm sorry," repeating over and over again as tears streamed down the face of the woman who'd raised her, and then, when Barb finally told her exactly what it was she had just done as the end result of all the abuse she had been handed, she wanted to hear some shrieking as well. She wanted to see Eleanor fall to her knees and cry out to God.

As if there was a God.

Instead, all she got were empty words, a reflex of a response—like an automatic "bless you" after a sneeze—

from a woman who didn't know to whom she was apologizing, who didn't know who *either* of them was anymore.

Not good enough.

"Do you remember me, mother?" said Barb. "Do you remember when I was a little girl?"

"You were a little girl," said Eleanor quietly. Her voice was not so much blank as astonished, as if anything but this moment, with Barb before her in this state, was inconceivable to her.

"Yes, Mother, I was a little girl," said Barb. "Your little girl. I'd come home from school crying because the other girls were making fun of me, and do you remember what you'd say?"

"What would I say?" asked Eleanor.

"Actually," said Barb. "At first you wouldn't say anything. At first you'd laugh. I hated that laugh. It hurt so much I'd rather you'd slapped me. But you'd just laugh, and take another puff on your cigarette, and tell me that I didn't have it so bad, that when you were a girl, you'd had to hide in basements from soldiers. You told me *that's* something worth getting upset about, not being teased by classmates. What I felt…to you it was nothing."

"I said that," said Eleanor, continuing to be amazed.

"Yes, you said that," said Barb, shouting this time. This wasn't the way she had planned it. Barb told herself to calm down. Just calm down and get to the point. *Tell her.*

"And how about high school?" said Barb. "Remember high school, and how miserable I was? Binging. Purging. Cutting. Hurting myself in so many ways. I'd laugh all one day and cry all day the next. And I asked you for help. Do you remember that? Even after all the years of belittling, of mockery, I still reached out. Do you know how hard that was? Do you know how desperate I was? But it was pointless. I should have known I would be. And again, you told me that nothing that ever happened to me could ever be as bad as what had happened to you. I wasn't allowed to be sad, and I wasn't allowed to be depressed. I wasn't allowed to be *me*."

Barb leaned forward in the chair, almost reaching out to grab Eleanor, to shake her until she understood. But what would be the point of even trying? She knew it would be useless.

"You wouldn't *let* me be me," said Barb.

A stocky woman, her blouse covered with pastel flowers, walked into the room just then, carrying a fresh set of bed linens.

"And how are we doing today, Mrs. Asher?" she asked.

"I'm fine today, Patrice," said Eleanor, brightening.

Patrice gently placed a free hand on Eleanor's shoulder.

"Lean forward a bit so I can change your pillowcase, won't you, dear?"

As she guided Eleanor to sit up, Patrice stepped back, bumping into the chair by the side of the bed.

"Now how did this get here?" she asked. Frowning, she pushed it back into a corner, then continued changing Eleanor's sheets. Patrice moved her from one side of the bed to the other, keeping up a constant comforting chatter until she had the woman tucked back under her blanket again. When she was done, she patted Eleanor on the back of one hand.

"You have a good day, Mrs. Asher."

"You do the same, Patrice," said Eleanor.

Barb was by the bed again the moment the nurse left the room. This time, she didn't bother with a chair. She was too angry to sit, and so loomed over Eleanor, her shadow touching her in a way she never could.

"Her, you remember?" said Barb. "Her, but not your own daughter?"

Barb was so angry she had no idea what to say next. Her

entire script, so carefully rehearsed, had fled. Her mother peered up at her, lifting one hand to shade her eyes against the sun.

"Have we met?" she asked.

"Yes, we've met," shouted Barb, dropping to her knees. "We've met, we've met, we've met."

She flung herself across her mother's lap and cried. What more was there to say?

Eleanor reached to comfort her daughter, but hesitated before touching the unfamiliar flesh. She turned her hands palms up and looked from her arms to those of her daughter and back again.

"Your wrists," she said, both statement and question. "What happened to your wrists?"

Barb raised her face from the blanket and looked at the twin gashes which ran lengthwise up her arms, fresh cuts ripping through her skin alongside numerous older scars.

"What do you think happened to my wrists?" she said, watching Eleanor's expression for a sign, a sign that someone was still home. "I killed myself, mother. I killed myself because of you."

Eleanor's eyes widened, and she pulled away, pressing back into her pillow. But there was nowhere further to go.

"No," she whispered.

"Yes, mother," said Barb. "And now I'm back to make you pay. Why else do you think I would finally visit you after all these years? But how can I haunt you if you won't remember?"

"I won't remember," Eleanor said flatly, but regardless of the emptiness of her tone, her forehead furrowed, and she turned her eyes away.

"See these scars?" said Barb, thrusting her arms closer to Eleanor, forcing her to bear witness. "This one is from when I cut myself after I broke up with Billy, and you told me you always knew it would happen because I wasn't good enough for him anyway. This is from when I didn't get that part I wanted so badly in the school play, and you said my voice wasn't right for the lead, that if I'd gotten it, the audience would only have laughed. And this one here—you see it? That's from after Harry left me, and you said it wouldn't have happened if I'd been a better wife. These aren't scars, these are my life. I'm wearing my history. I'm wearing *your* history, mother."

"I don't understand," said Eleanor, but Barb knew differently. She could see from her mother's eyes that perhaps she was finally, finally beginning to understand.

"You taught me that whatever happened in my life was my own fault," continued Barb. "Then on top of that you told me I had no right to feel whatever it was I felt about my life. And you belittled every attempt I ever made to find help. You broke me, mother. Broke me so badly each day was agony. I couldn't take it anymore. So I ended the pain the only way I knew how. I killed myself, mother, and I was cursing your name as I did. I want you to know that."

"You killed yourself," said Eleanor, the flatness gone from her voice, replaced only by horror.

"*You* killed me mother," said Barb, looking down at her wrists, and then back to her mother, her eyes filled with contempt. "*You* did. And you started doing it the day I was born."

"No, no, no," shouted Eleanor, slapping her hands at Barb, trying to push her daughter off the bed. But it was no use. Instead, her hands passed right through. She gasped, and held those hands to her chest. "Why are you telling me these lies? Stop it. Stop it!"

Patrice ran into the room and rushed to Eleanor's bedside.

"What's wrong, Mrs. Asher," she said. "Why were you shouting?"

She looked at Eleanor, saw there would be no answer, and quickly ran off.

"You remember me now, mother, don't you?" said Barb. "I can see it. You remember."

"Of course, I remember you, Barbara," said Eleanor, sitting up, all confusion and uncertainty gone, suddenly able to push her daughter away. "How could I possibly forget? I don't think I've ever known anyone to complain as much as you did."

Barb held a hand to her face as if smacked and stumbled back into the chair on the other side of the room. Her mother had returned, the mother she remembered. What was she thinking, expecting closure? All she was in for was more pain.

"Mother, how could you?" said Barb, whimpering, the words catching in her throat.

"How could I?" said her mother. "How could I not?"

Eleanor stood, towering over her daughter. Now Barb was the one trying to get away, pushing her chair back until it banged against the wall. This wasn't the way it was supposed to be. It wasn't.

"Compared to my life, yours was a fairytale," said Eleanor. She held a hand to her mouth as if expecting a cigarette, then looked surprised because none was there. "I was the one with a hard life. But did you ever hear me complaining? No! Your father abandoned us both, but did I bitch about it? No! All I ever wanted was to give you a better life than the one I was handed, the one I learned to live with. And I did that for you. But it was never good enough. Nothing could ever be good enough for you."

The words landed like blows, and Barb curled smaller in

her chair. But there was no escape. Even after what she had done, how could there be no escape?

"How can you do this?" Barb said. "How could you speak to your daughter this way?"

"You're no daughter of mine," said Eleanor, kneeling down so that Barb was forced to look her in the eyes. "You have my blood, yes, but my spirit? I've yet to see it. You're weak. Strong enough to complain about your life, but not strong enough to do something about it."

"I *was* strong enough," shouted Barb, her voice trembling with both fear and rage. "Strong enough to do *this*!"

Barb pushed her hands forward to once more show off her wounds, and this time, when Eleanor slapped out at her, she made contact, knocking them away.

"Only your cowardice was strong," said Eleanor. "You were too afraid to live. You've always been too afraid to live. So what if you finally did what you'd already been doing bit by bit each day?"

It was as if Barb had never died. Was this what life—or whatever it was that came after life—was going to be like? Eleanor opened her mouth once more, ready to continue the abuse Barb thought she had ended, when the room suddenly filled with doctors and nurses, shouting at each other, wheeling carts with machinery that blinked and beeped. Barb looked to the bed and saw her mother lying there, a doctor already pressing paddles onto her chest.

"Clear!" he shouted, and as the others pulled away, Eleanor jerked. The doctor waited in silence, watching a monitor until its flat line began to dance. "She's back. You saved this woman's life, Patrice. If you hadn't heard her shouting…"

The doctors and nurses left the room, leaving the machinery behind, and soon Barb was alone with her mother once more. She moved slowly to the bedside.

"Mother?" she asked. "Mother, are you there?"

Eleanor opened her eyes, eyes which told Barb nothing.

"Mother?"

"Hello," said Eleanor, smiling weakly. "It's nice of you to come. Am I supposed to know you?"

"Yes," said Barb. "Yes, you are."

"Who are you, dear?" said Eleanor.

"Don't you recognize me?" asked Barb.

"I'm sorry," said Eleanor. "I have trouble remembering things these days. I've had trouble remembering things for awhile."

"That's all right," said Barb.

Eleanor smiled. It was an honest smile. Barb had made her happy.

"Good," said Eleanor. "So, who are you?"

"I'm...I'm your daughter," said Barb.

"I had a daughter?" said Eleanor.

Barb held her breath, which felt odd, as she no longer had any breath to hold. Breathing had been left behind, abandoned to the world of the living, along with so much else...except for what truly mattered, except for what she'd been trying to escape. That, apparently, was inescapable. Even though life could be extinguished, her lifelong struggle would know no end.

When Barb woke in the bloody bathtub—was "woke" even the right word, she thought, to use about one who was dead?—she knew she'd have to make her way to this place, to put a period at the end of the sentence of her relationship with...Eleanor.

With her mother. (It was somehow easier to call her that now.)

But the closure she sought was no longer even possible. How could it be? How does someone who no longer exists find closure with someone else who is herself only a shadow?

Staring into her mother's childlike eyes, finding the woman she'd known both there and not there, Barb realized…there *was* another way. A way that could give her more than mere closure. What she had been seeking during her long, agonizing life but had never found was finally within her reach.

"I had…a daughter," Eleanor repeated with wonder.

How much time had passed while Barb was lost in deciding what to say next? She couldn't tell. She sat slowly on the edge of the bed.

"Yes," Barb said finally. "Yes, you did. And you loved her. You loved her very much."

"That's nice, dear," said Eleanor. "Tell me about her."

And Barb decided she would, taking what she could get, telling of things that had never happened to the mother she'd never had, over and over again, until she could almost believe them.

PETRIFIED

Our therapist suggested that Elaine and I, instead of getting a divorce, should try taking a vacation first. While it would certainly be cheaper, I wasn't completely sure that it would end up being any more pleasant. Not considering the company we'd each be stuck with.

Someone once said that Hell was other people. Well, marriage is other people, too. Put those two thoughts together and I guess you could say that marriage is *also* Hell, right?

And after a disastrous three years with Elaine, I wasn't looking forward to a vacation from Hell on top of that as well.

But Futter kept playing up the potential benefits, preaching in our therapy sessions how our time spent alone could perform miracles, telling us how it would save the sinking ship of our relationship, dazzling us with his endless psychobabble...and what can I say, he eventually wore us both down. I don't think Elaine wanted to be here any more than I did, not really, but we tried to pretend this thing we had was worth one more shot.

Who can be sure, though? If not for the frequent-flier miles, we might not have bothered.

Things went bad right from the beginning. And believe me, if you'd ever seen the two of us in action before, you could have predicted that.

I'd wanted to spend our week away camping in the mountains, rising early on crisp mornings for hiking and fishing. Elaine wanted to spend our time together at the beach with mojitos in hand, baking in the sun. We split the difference, which meant that we ended up with a plan to spend seven days together driving through a desert.

How stupid was that?

I don't care what Futter says, how many times he tried to indoctrinate us that meeting in the middle was the only way to go. Compromise is *never* the way to go. Whenever the two of us would try, neither of us ended up happy, both of us ended up resentful. So what's the point? We already knew how to achieve misery on our own *without* his advice.

As we drove straight from the airport toward Petrified Forest National Park our first day in Arizona, I looked sourly at the endless blinding nothing which surrounded us. Our rental car's air conditioning sputtered fitfully as I sped through the badlands. Red sand split in two by an endless ribbon of black road. Nondescript mesas to the left, mind-numbing buttes to the right. Or was it the other way around? I glanced from the vista framed by the windshield to the smaller one displayed in the rearview mirror. Where we were heading didn't seem so different from what we had left behind.

"Would have been nice to have seen something green," I grumbled.

"Would have been nicer to have sat by something wet," she whined.

Grumbles and whines, those were our usual methods of

communication. We were a thousand miles from home, and yet it was as if we'd never left. That wasn't quite the result Futter promised when he proselytized about the power of compromise. Compromise was one of those touchy feely tools of his that was supposed to pull us back from the brink. It sure didn't feel that way so far. Instead, it looked like it might just push us both over the edge.

"Can we make it one day without sniping at each other?" I said. "Can we make it one just goddamned day? Do you think you could do me that favor, Elaine? I'm trying my best here, I'm really trying."

Elaine tilted her head to look at me over her sunglasses, which were all I'd seen of her since boarding the plane. She peered at me over the lenses. I couldn't make out any trace in those eyes of what I had once long ago made out, whatever it was that had first brought us together, a quality I could barely remember. She snorted, sliding the sunglasses back up her nose to hide her eyes from me again. She turned away to the window and toward the endless wasteland outside.

"One day," she said in a voice drained of compassion. "Give *you* one day? I doubt you could even make it to the goddamned visitors center."

I'd show her. But I knew of only one way that we could possibly do that.

In silence.

WITH THE WELCOME center far behind us and a stack of pamphlets on the car seat between us, I figured it was safe to start up the conversation again. But I was wrong. With Elaine, there's no such thing as safe.

"So, how was that?" I said, pleased with myself, and

trying hard to suppress a smile. We'd gotten in and out of the place without a scene, and for us, that was something.

"You don't get credit for your good deeds if you crow about them," she said.

As I drove, Elaine sat pressed up against the passenger-side door, staying as far away from me as she could get considering the circumstances. Her sour expression let me know that she wished she could retreat a heck of a lot further. I was glad I couldn't make out the eyes beneath her sunglasses right then, because her look might have burned me.

"If I didn't, I wouldn't get credit either, and what's the point of that?" I said. "I figured I might as well go ahead and say it myself."

"Whatever," she said. "Considering your track record, taking credit is something you won't get much opportunity to do in the future anyway."

"Give me a break, will you?" I said. I slammed my palm against a wheezing air conditioning vent. "It's too damned hot to argue. I'm here, aren't I?"

"So you're here," she said. "Whoop-de-frickin'-do."

"Hey, this whole thing was your idea," I said. "Aren't you going to at least try? *I'm* trying."

"Oh, no," she said. "No way. You're not going to put the blame on me. This wasn't my idea."

Damn you, Dr. Futter. Maybe this vacation exercise worked for your other clients, but if it did, it only meant that they were probably amateurs at this kind of thing. Elaine and me, we're rotted meat. We're too far gone to be made palatable again.

"I wasn't blaming you, Elaine," I said. "I was just saying—"

"Sure sounded like that's what you were doing," she said. "You used that tone of yours again."

"I keep telling you," I said. "I don't have a tone."

"Don't give me that," she said. "There it was again."

How can you tell when Elaine and me are fighting? Our lips are moving.

"Look, should we just turn back?" I said. "Clearly, this isn't going to work. If I floor it, maybe we can make it back to the airport in time to get flights home tonight. And if we're *really* lucky, maybe they can be separate flights."

"Don't you dare," she said. "You're not going to get the satisfaction of pinning this one on me. I'm sticking with this thing all the way to the bitter end, so when we tell Futter it didn't work out, it'll all be on you."

"Like that makes much sense," I said.

"As much sense as anything else you've done during the past three years," she said.

I suddenly noticed a sign retreating in the rearview mirror and realized that Elaine and I had been going at each other with such determination that we'd missed the entrance to the first trail site. Wouldn't be the first thing we'd missed that way, but this time, instead of keeping on keeping on, I squealed to a stop and shifted the car into reverse.

"This would be a Hell of a lot safer if you just turned around," she said.

"Let me do this my way," I said, backing up the quarter of a mile, and even managing to stay on the road most of the time.

"Maybe that's been your problem all along," she said. "Maybe you've always been doing things your way, only your way is ass backwards."

I hit the brake sharply, and it didn't bother me one bit when her head banged back against the seat. Her can of soda flew out of the dashboard drink holder, but she managed to catch it before it could spill all over her lap.

"You're a jerk, you know that?" she said.

"Yeah, I know that," I said. "You've told me that one often enough."

I stepped out of the car, instantly regretting it. So it turned out the groaning air conditioning had been working after all. Looked like that was the only thing that day which *was* working. Elaine joined me, pamphlets in one hand, her soda in the other.

"So what are we doing here?" I said.

Elaine glared at me. I knew that look. She could accuse me all she wanted of having tones, well, she had looks, and they were all variations of "Go to Hell, you moron."

"That isn't what I meant and you know it," I said. "I meant, what are we doing *here*?"

Elaine unfolded one of the pamphlets and spread it across the hood of the car. She leaned forward to hold down two of the corners and put the soda can at a third to keep the warm breeze from snatching it away.

"According to what it says here, we're standing in the middle of what once was a tropical forest," she said. "That's what this whole area was like. There were rivers once, lined by 200-foot tall trees."

"How long ago was 'once?'" I said.

"More than 200 million years ago," she said.

"Doesn't look like it was worth waiting for," I said. "Might have been something to have seen back then, though. Let's get it over with."

I took off down the path, not looking to see whether Elaine would follow after. I already knew that she would. She could bitch all she wanted about what a bastard I was, but I knew that she couldn't keep away.

I didn't have to go far before I came across the first fallen log. Only it wasn't a fallen log. Something looked off about it, as if it had been replaced with a jeweled replica. It looked manufactured somehow. Parts of it appeared to glisten in the sun, like that opal ring I'd given Elaine for our first anniversary.

The ring that she'd later that same day ripped from her finger and flushed down the toilet. She'd been laughing at the time. It was a laugh I had heard many times, and had long since memorized.

"It's beautiful," Elaine said.

"So what happened?" I said.

"I don't know," she said, scanning the pamphlet, frowning while she tried to comprehend. "I'm no scientist. Water…water mixed with the wood to become quartz, I guess. The trees, they got crystallized. They were once alive, but then they absorbed chemicals and became brittle."

"And beautiful, you said."

"Yes," she said.

I had an idea. I continued down the winding path, gazing left and right while trying to see the world as Elaine saw it. Which could be a dangerous thing, but I thought I'd give it a shot anyway. I eventually spotted a short, stout log a dozen feet off the path, one end seeming to flicker as I moved. I stepped off the path and circled it, studied it, pausing by its widest end. Elaine was right. It *was* beautiful. I knelt and slid the car keys from my pocket.

"What do you think you're doing?" she called out from where she'd remained on the path. Elaine had never been comfortable breaking those kinds of arbitrary boundaries, no matter how I'd egg her on.

"You should have a piece to take home," I said, figuring that was one way to make her happy. Figuring I owed her a compliment as well. "It's beautiful. You're beautiful. You belong together."

I pressed the point of one of the keys against a narrow groove running vertically through the log.

"Stop it!" she said. "You're not supposed to do that!"

"Why not?" I said. "Other chunks are missing. See? It's pockmarked. We're not the first visitors who wanted to take a souvenir. What difference will one more piece make?"

"You're not being funny," she said. "You *know* you shouldn't do that. You *always* know you shouldn't do what you do."

"Who's it going to hurt?" I said. "Besides, we're alone out here. No one will ever know."

"I'd know," she said. "And besides, they'll search us on the way out. That's what the pamphlet says."

"I'd figure out a way," I said. "It wouldn't be the first time I snuck something past a guy in uniform."

"Enough," she said, stamping a foot. "If you ever loved me, don't you dare."

"Sure, sure, whatever you say," I said. I stood up, opening my arms wide to show her my empty hands.

"I'm heading back to the car," she said. "Jerk."

Once she had turned away, I bent over quickly, pried away a small fragment of petrified wood, and shoved it in my pocket. Later, when we got home, she'd thank me. I was sure that she would.

Who knows? Maybe someday, I'd thought, we'd both look back on that moment and realize that it had been the turning point for us. I suddenly felt hope after all.

By the time I reached the car, Elaine was already inside. Her arms were folded tightly against her chest, telegraphing to me just how pissed she was. Somehow, with that chunk of crystal in my pocket, I was anything but.

Whistling, I pulled back out onto the road.

"I DON'T SEE what you have to be so happy about," she said.

"And if you have to whistle, would you find yourself another damned song? I'm sick of that one."

I stopped whistling. Might as well contain myself. The surprise could come later. I'd recognize the right moment. I rested my hand over my pocket, which contained the ragged piece of petrified wood.

"I never could fake happiness the way you do, you know," she said. "It could all end here. Do you realize that? This could be it for us."

"If it works out that way, well, it'll be your damned fault," I said. "You've always been too negative. Even on our wedding day. You refuse to look on the bright side. Hell, you refuse to even admit that there *is* a bright side."

"You want a bright side?" she said. "Here's a bright side for you. At least we never had any children, so our divorce won't screw them up. Oh, and another bright side? I'm still young enough so that when I get remarried, I can still have children with someone who actually cares about his life."

"I care," I said. "I came. I'm here, aren't I? I'm right beside you driving the damned car."

"Here in body, maybe," she said. "I'm not so sure you've ever really been here in spirit."

"Screw you," I said.

The desert stretched on, doing little more than remind me of the desert inside the heart of the woman who sat next to me. The woman I had chosen. Now why had I done that again? Someone please remind me.

"I could have split plenty of times," I said. "I didn't."

"And can you really say that we were better off for that?" she said.

I spotted the next trail site coming up. Good thing. Because if I were trapped next to Elaine any longer, I'd be tempted to test the airbags. I pulled to the side of the road, but was too riled up to get out of the car just then. So I sat there, flexing my fingers on the steering wheel, feeling the sweat trickle down my back.

"Boy," I said. "If it all ends here, we sure picked a good place for it."

"What do you mean?" she said.

"We haven't seen another car all day," I said. "We're the only people stupid enough to want to be here. That sure says something, doesn't it?"

"Oh, we don't have to be here," she said. "'We' don't have to be anywhere. You were right. A week was too much, too long for us to try to hack it alone. A day was all we needed to find out that we're dead."

Elaine got out of the car and slammed the door. She then leaned back in the window, but all I noticed of her face then was my own face, two of them in fact, staring back at me from out of the lenses of those damned sunglasses.

"Whatever we had," she said, "It's gone. I admit defeat. So let's just take one last look at this place and head back to the airport."

I couldn't seem to muster the energy to follow her. I continued sitting there, watching as she vanished down the path. I took the chunk of wood from my pocket and balanced it on one knee. I'd thought the silly thing was going to be a reminder of the time and place we came back together. Instead, it would only come to symbolize the day we fell completely apart.

Our love had been a lush forest, too, once. I could pretend all I wanted to that it had never been so, because somehow, when I was able to do that, it hurt a little less, but I had to admit that, yes, it had been. Only that was a long, long time before. Now we had turned brittle ourselves, and we didn't have the beauty to make up for it. Well, maybe Elaine still did.

Then there she was, rapping at my window. I quickly

placed one hand over the fragment and rolled down the window with the other.

"What do you want?" I said wearily. I still just sat there. There didn't seem to be much point in seeing one more grove of dead trees. I got it. You seen one, you've seen them all.

"Something weird is going on," she said. "Come. You've got to see this."

Now she was using *her* voice, the serious one. The one that said, "I'm not playing around this time." I got out of the car and looked off the road into the patch of desert beyond the mouth of the path.

"So what am I supposed to be seeing?" I asked.

"Just keep walking," she said. "You'll know."

I meandered along as the path weaved around logs that weren't even actually logs anymore. Some forest. The whole thing seemed like false advertising to me. How many other couples had come here expecting something more, something greater? Something to save their lives? And then to get…*this*? I kept thinking that maybe the mountains could have turned it all around.

But really, even I knew it was far too late for that.

"So?" I said. "I still don't get it."

"Oh, come on," she said. I knew I was frustrating her, but then, I was used to that. Only this time, I promise, it wasn't intentional. "How can you not see it? Doesn't it feel a little too familiar?"

"It *all* looks a little too familiar," I said. "It's all looked a little too familiar all day. Sand, sand, and more sand. Some rocks. Occasionally some dead trees. What am I supposed to say? Shoot me, okay? I can't see what you want me to see. It wouldn't be the first time. Are you happy now?"

"You can't be that blind, damn it!" she said, kicking up a cloud of sand. "Not even you. This is just like the place we left behind. No, more than 'just like.' It's the same. *Exactly the same.*"

Once she mentioned it, I could see what she was talking about. The path followed the same arc, with logs strewn around in the same places. But she was getting worked up over what had to be a coincidence.

"So what?" I said. "This doesn't mean anything. You think these paths just grew this way? People made them. Maybe some desert geek figured out an optimal design for this sort of display, and then they just dragged the logs into position. You're getting stirred up over nothing. There are probably lookalikes all along this road. Get a grip."

"Maybe you're right," she said. "But I still don't like it. Let's get out of here."

"That's the first sensible thing you've said to me all day," I said.

She headed quickly back to the car. I took my time, measuring each step, matching every bend in the path to the earlier path in my memory until I could see a large log just like the one from which I'd swiped my sample. When I knelt, I could see this one also had a fresh gouge. I took the souvenir from my pocket and held it against the open wound.

It seemed as if it would fit perfectly.

"Damn," I whispered.

I ran to the car in a straight line, ignoring the winding of the path, outpacing Elaine, who continued playing by the rules. Probably just to show me up, which is why she usually did it. I'd started the engine before she'd even made it to the road. I honked the horn and tapped the gas so that the engine roared.

"What's gotten into you?" she said. "Did you pop something when I wasn't looking? Should I be letting you drive?"

"It's nothing," I said. "Just get in the damned car."

But would she? No, the faster I wanted her to move, the slower she got. Same as it ever was. She stood there, making a show of sipping slowly at her drink. She made a horrible squeaking sound as she sucked up the dregs through her straw.

"Don't rush me," she said, turning her back on me. "I'm taking one last look."

"Get in!" I shouted.

"When I'm ready," she said. "I want to remember this."

I swiveled away from the steering wheel, stretched out my legs, and kicked the passenger-side door open. It hit her in the ass and made her drop the can. She spun, leaned into the car, and started screaming at me.

"What the Hell was that?" she said. "What do you think you're doing? You could have—"

"Get *in*!"

There was only one way to make her listen. I reached over, grabbed her by a wrist, and pulled her into the car. Her sunglasses flew off and hit the sand. She yelped as a shoulder hit the seat. I knew that I'd probably bruised her wrist, even though I'd promised never to do that sort of thing any more. But she'd left me no choice. She never leaves me any choices.

I floored it out of there, which made the door slam shut on its own. As we drove, the only sound was Elaine weeping. I turned up the air conditioning in an attempt to mask it out, but it didn't help.

"You'd better be heading for the goddamned airport," she finally said through gritted teeth once her sobbing had stopped.

"I am," I said. "Believe me. I want nothing less."

But it was starting to dawn on me that it was no longer a certainty that I could make it there.

"OH, NO," I said, as another trail site came into view ahead. I slowed the car, but I wasn't sure that I could bear to bring it to a stop. "This isn't happening."

"That's what I've been telling myself for the past three years," she said. "What are you slowing down for? I don't want to do this with you again. This is not my idea of fun anymore."

"Like it was fun before?" I said.

I shut the engine about a dozen yards short of where the trail began.

"Look at that," I said softly, pointing through the windshield at a bit of flattened metal glinting in the sun.

"So?" she said. "Someone left their trash. What do you expect me to do about it?"

"Not just someone," I said. "Us. That's *your* can out there. I crushed it as we drove away. I left it behind us, and now…now it's ahead of us. We're back, Elaine. Back in the same goddamned place. And what do you think that is next to it? Those are your sunglasses, for God's sake!"

Elaine looked from the things we'd left behind over to me and then back again. She wiped the tears from her cheeks with the backs of her hands.

"You're just screwing with me, aren't you?" she said.

She flung the door open and leapt from the car. By the time I'd caught up with her, she was on her knees, turning the can over and over in her hands. I could see traces of lipstick on the crushed metal.

Elaine's lipstick.

She reached over to pick up the nearby sunglasses and wiped them clear of sand. They fit perfectly.

"What's happened to us?" she whispered, a look of horror and confusion coming to her face. I would have enjoyed seeing that look had I not been feeling those same emotions myself.

She turned her back on me and staggered away leadenly. I followed a few steps behind her as she stumbled down the trail. I could sense what was coming, knew what I would have to say, and did not want to be within her reach when I did so. Her jaw hung slack as she surveyed the slabs of wood that surrounded us. This time, she ignored the marked path, wandering as if dazed.

"We're back," she said. "Back where we began. So I was right the last time. It's all the same. This is the third time we've been here. We're…trapped. What the Hell is going on?"

"I think I know," I said quietly, almost hoping that she wouldn't hear me, but knowing that she must. I took the chunk of petrified wood from my pocket and held it out so that she could see it.

"Is that what I think it is?" she said. "What did you do?"

"I was only trying to help," I said. "But I guess I must have…I don't know…"

I knelt by the same log again, and fit the piece snugly back into place. It stayed there when I pulled my fingers away.

"See?" I said. I held my hands out, palms up, as if that would make it all better.

"What did you do?" she said. "What did you do? Didn't I tell you that you shouldn't take anything? Didn't I? Are you insane? You've trapped us in a nightmare. This is all your fault!"

She ran at me then and leapt onto my back. As she began to beat me about the head, I stood and shook and flung her to one side.

"I only did it for you," I said. "I thought that it would help us."

"You always do it for me," she said, backing away while throwing handfuls of sand at me. "All the pain you inflict, it's always for me. If it's for me, then why does it hurt so much? Nothing is ever your fault. All the fights, all the cheating, all the lies, all the bruises—"

"You gave as good as you got, babe."

"—it's always someone else's fault. Always! Well, I'm sick of it. Go do things for somebody else from now on."

She jumped up and ran away, and watching her back, I figured, let her go. She'll calm down. She'll get over it. But I could see, as she neared the car, that there was a sudden flash of sun in her right hand, and I realized what it had to be— the car keys, snatched from my pocket during our struggle. I took off after her, but unfortunately, she had too long a lead. The door had already slammed and the engine had roared to life before I could reach the car. I could only stand in the middle of the road and watch as she vanished in the distance.

I didn't bother running after her. I knew she wasn't going to stop, and all the sight of me in the rearview mirror would have done was amuse her. I didn't want to leave her with that as a parting gift.

I shielded my eyes from the blistering sun, but it didn't help me see any farther down the road. She was gone. Gone for good. I looked down at the crushed can that was all the remained of Elaine, and my memories of her drinking all morning suddenly made my tongue thick in my mouth.

Based on the traffic we'd seen so far, another ride wasn't going to come along anytime soon to rescue me. I might be there for a while. I tried to remember all of those nature films I'd been forced to sit through as a kid. Could a person really eat a cactus? Would that be enough to let you survive?

I prayed for the sun to set, so perhaps I'd have a shot at making it through the night to see another day, but who was I kidding? The damned thing wasn't going to move. Once I thought about it, I realized that it hadn't seemed to move the entire day. It taunted me now as it taunted me then.

I was screwed. Screwed with Elaine and screwed without her.

But then the silence was broken by the sound of an engine growing louder behind me. I turned away from the direction toward which Elaine had escaped, abandoning me, and saw, in the distance, back from where we had come, a speck that was surely a car. I burst out laughing. Rescue was at hand, and a miraculously quick rescue at that. I danced on the center line of the road, waving my arms high over my head so that the driver would see me and have to stop, whether he'd meant to take a break at this particular stand of fossils or not. Only as the car drew nearer, behind the wheel, I could see…

Elaine.

She slowed to a crawl, and lifted up those sunglasses. Our eyes locked. She looked away, and stopped the car. She unlocked the passenger door without bothering to turn to me.

I got in, grateful for the shade. I had a feeling that it would be a long time before I'd ever get to feel grateful for anything else again.

"I thought I left you behind me," she began, pointing back over her shoulder. She closed her eyes, refusing to look at me, refusing to look at anything. "I thought I'd escaped you."

"I don't think you can," I said. "I don't think I can either."

I leaned back against the headrest and closed my eyes, too. We sat there, silently, waiting for the sun to set.

But it never did.

THE HUNGER OF EMPTY VESSELS

The world had become too abrasive for Christopher Portobello. Events, people, things—they all conspired to scour him raw, stripping away what few fragile defenses he had left as if his sanity had suddenly become nothing more than old skin gone clammy beneath a bandage. The gentlest touch of life could bruise, forcing tears to bleed through him like the spring thaw of a frozen waterfall, that first unexpected melt nearly always followed by an explosive cracking, with great chunks of his former self falling off at every bout of weeping.

It didn't used to be that way, his morning commutes treacherous minefields. But that morning as he'd driven to work, he'd discovered a lounge singer crooning ecstatically on the radio about sitting on top of the world, and since Portobello himself was not, it was as if that world had reached out to mug him yet again, just as his ex-wife had done, just as the courts had done, just as they all had done. He'd had to swerve to the shoulder, rush hour traffic honking in disgust, and sob until the windows had steamed and he had no more tears to give. Other mornings yielded different threats. Thanks to Angela, thanks to Joey, arriving at the office on time these days, or arriving anywhere in an emotional state similar to what it had been when a journey began, seemed beyond him.

Later, at midmorning, the world reached out to strike him once more. Pausing for a moment from hours of wheedling out stock market secrets with his computer, he rested his eyes by looking out the window toward the school playground across the highway from his office park. Recess had just begun, and from that distance the roiling mass of children gave the impression of an anthill that had recently been kicked over. At the base of a ladder leading up to a slide, two young boys pushed at each other, neither willing to let the other go first. While they were distracted by their arguing, a third boy slipped by laughing.

Portobello began to cry, and until he looked down to see his palm slashed open by the split plastic of his mouse, broken when he had gripped it too hard, he did not remember where he was or what he had been doing. The ridiculousness of his empty office washed over him, and it became too much to bear. He had to see his son.

Feeling himself being watched, he turned to the door, expecting to find his boss checking up on him again. This business with Joey had tampered with his performance on the job as much as it had anything else. Instead, Portobello only saw family photos from better times, reprimanding him with their datedness. They made him need Joey even more desperately. That was suddenly all he could think about. The computer, the stock trades, the job, all of them were gone, switched off by the thought of his son.

He had to see Joey that afternoon, he just had to, no matter what his ex-wife said.

PEERING through the tall chain-link fence that surrounded the private school for which his wife insisted they had to shell out, Portobello felt the barrier radiate an aura of imprisonment, but gripping the cool metal, he was unsure for a moment exactly who was trapped and whether he was gazing out or gazing in. He looked across the manicured lawn to the empty yard where the students had worn the earth bare, hoping to spy a student, any student, someone who could allow him to feel even a slight connection to Joey, however tenuous. Lately, he'd begun feeling more and more as if he carried an invisible fence around himself wherever he went, a barrier tightening smaller about him with each passing moment, until he feared that soon there would be no room at all in which to move. The walls would match the confines of his flesh, and he would choke from lack of air, from lack of life.

He was locked away from Joey. Angela had locked him away, blaming him for it all, for the entirety of their long, ugly story, making him the cause of it, forcing him to feel like a thief when all he wanted to do was see his own kid from time to time, goddamn it. He watched the forbidding brick front of the school, and waited, pushing his face so close to the fence that its links vanished at the edges of his vision, and he could pretend it wasn't there at all.

A bell sounded, and before its echo had faded, children began to pour from the ivied building. He struggled to pick out his son, but it was hard to distinguish faces from this distance, and he dared not cross the line of the fence, dared not go even a single step closer. The school had been warned about him. The security guards who wandered the halls were armed not with guns, but with his picture. *Warned!* About *him* of all people! He had hurt no one, could hurt no one, but Angela had made sure no one would believe him on that. As he scanned the crowd, his fingers hurt from squeezing the fence so tightly. He lifted a hand to his lips and sucked a bloody palm. Then he saw Joey and forgot about the pain, any pain, all pain.

His son stood with a dozen of his peers in a ring while a soccer ball bounced along, apparently randomly, from boy to boy. Their gangly bodies, wrestling with the worst torments of puberty, were garbed in those godawful uniforms. Those jackets, the parents were promised, were supposed to make their children look refined, and ready to tackle the demands of the real world—at least that's what the school catalogs had always said—but to Portobello the clothing made them seem less like adults in training and more like a gathering of midget used car salesmen.

The students bounced the ball lazily back and forth among them in a game Portobello did not recognize. Joey, when the ball finally got to him, put a stop to the rhythm of the game. He did not pass the ball, instead choosing to bounce it at his feet accompanied by a great many dramatic gestures. Even at this great distance, even though Portobello had never seen the other boys before, he could read their body language, and could tell that they were not happy with Joey. His son did not appear to notice this shift in the level of tension, continuing to bounce the ball repeatedly in front of him. Portobello wished he could gauge the boy's expression, but Joey's face was just a blur. Would there be any recognition of the situation? Portobello thought not. It had always been that way with Joey. The boy seemed oblivious to even the most profound of the social cues which gave hints others were starting to lose their tempers. It had never seemed to Portobello to be a deliberate blindness, in that Joey was always more bewildered by the aftermath than defiant.

Portobello didn't want to have to see that sadness blossom in his son now. It seemed more important to him than usual. He begged and pleaded as if lost in prayer, please, not today, not this time. Let it just pass. It felt remarkable to Portobello, him, of all people, praying.

But prayer was not enough.

Joey only had the time to give the ball one more bounce before he was on the ground, one of his larger classmates having charged from the opposite side of the circle and knocked him down. Though he was spewing curses, the boy didn't take advantage of the moment, didn't punch or kick Joey after he was down, just bent to rip the ball from his son's fingers, because Joey still, even from his stunned vantage point looking up at his peers, didn't want to let go. Baffled, he studied his empty fingers.

The circle, now one child smaller, shifted raggedly a dozen feet to the left, and then reformed. The game resumed as if nothing had happened. His son looked lost, still not understanding the outcome he himself had created. Portobello knew he could not go in to help his son up from the hard-packed earth, not without great consequences, but still, something inside of him demanded action, and he suddenly found himself perched at the top of the fence, about to tumble over.

Nearby laughter froze him in place.

It was a nasty laugh, the sort of unthinking, uncontrollable sound that burst out of a gleeful combatant in the moment after he's successfully beaten down an enemy, and is about to deliver the final blow. It was not a sound that Portobello had ever heard before, relief and ecstasy and mockery and triumph all rolled into one, and without even knowing its source, he felt an irrepressible urge to make the utterance stop. Portobello turned towards the evil sound, down the line of the fence and into the low bushes that lined the outer perimeter, and at first saw nothing, but then, leaning into the laugh, he discovered a pair of bright and frightening eyes.

He was momentarily disoriented under the bright sun, because at first, all he could discern of the intruder were those eyes, as if they possessed a disembodied life of their own, but then he squinted, and the rest of the body came into view.

He was a thin man, wrapped in a dingy suit that had an expensive look, and from the way he was sunken into the fabric, Portobello imagined they had once fit him well, but now hung loose as if the man had only recently begun to recover from a long illness. The suit was now so infused by dirt and dust as to be beyond color. Portobello thought he understood now why he had not at first been able to make the man out against the nearby foliage.

The laughter continued on without pause, washing away what little restraint Portobello had left, and his fingers tightened on the fence's top rung that he still straddled. He imagined those fingers gripping the man's throat. Who was this stranger? How dare he laugh at Joey? He had to stop this laughter, as if that could erase all the laughter from before and all that was still slated to come. Portobello grunted as his hand slipped in blood, and he almost spilled from the fence. The man turned silent for a moment, and looked toward Portobello. Portobello found the sudden silence to be almost as painful as had been the laughter. Their gazes locked for an instant in the stillness, startling Portobello, and then, before he could summon up any response, the man exploded in movement.

"Hey!" shouted Portobello as the man bolted away from him, but his cry had no effect. The man continued to recede into the distance. "Get back here right now. Talk to me!"

Portobello dropped to the grass and dashed after, but though he ran in the correct direction as quickly as his legs could carry him, he could find no further sound nor sign of the man. Pausing at the foot of the long driveway that led up to the school, Portobello saw that his anger at the intrusion was still flaming within him. His rage was so great that by the time it was pierced by a memory of his downed son in the schoolyard, and he returned to check on Joey, all of the children had already gone back to their classes inside, and he'd missed his chance to comfort the boy.

THE SCHOOL BUSSES, short and squat, annoyed Portobello as he sat in his car watching them pull onto the curved drive at the end of the school day. Angela was sure that this school was what Joey needed, but those busses just ate at him, even though Portobello knew that going to a normal school wouldn't mean it would all be normal again. Waiting for the students to begin their trips home, he would normally turn on the radio to occupy his time, but now he was afraid. He couldn't chance the fit of sadness that might be waiting for him curled within the speakers. Too much mattered now to risk being distracted from what he needed to do.

He hadn't intended to end his day this way when he'd arrived there late that morning. He'd thought, understating his need, that he'd take one hungry glimpse at Joey and then, sated, go back to his office. Back to the weary numbers. Back to make excuses for yet another unexplained absence, knowing even as he stole the time that he was running out of the ability to make his boss accept those absences. But what he could not predict was that after such a long separation, seeing Joey had acted upon him like a drug—one taste, and he needed another fix. He'd felt that aura of intense need before, just as the marriage had begun to fall apart, but on this day, confronted with the distressing sight of an odd man enjoying far too much the sight of the student tableaux that so unsettled Portobello, he particularly wanted more, and damn the cost.

Hours passed, hours during which Portobello stared at the exits and was afraid to let himself blink. When the children finally stormed out of the school, loud and chaotic in their freedom, he staggered back as if slapped. There was so much raw, unconfined life to them that their energy left him breathless, and while his own life had a rawness to it as well, beneath it all it was as if there was no...no life to it. He searched ravenously for his son's face bobbing in the roiling sea of students. With the flood out the door fallen to a trickle without Portobello having found Joey, he feared that perhaps he had missed him. It only occurred to him just then that perhaps Angela had picked the boy up earlier after having received a call about the midday incident Portobello had witnessed. That possibility brought on an overwhelming feeling of emptiness which lasted until he saw Joey through a bus window. He had somehow managed to already get to his seat, having snuck by Portobello's watchful eye, and seemed lost and contemplative. No kid should have to be either, not yet. Portobello could see movement through the other windows of the bus as kids raced up and down the narrow aisle and roughhoused with their friends, but none of that camaraderie spilled over to Joey, chained to his seat by a force Portobello could not comprehend. Joey had made himself into the eye of a hurricane, ominously gravid in his silence.

As Portobello watched helplessly, the storm clouds opened once more.

Joey's face brightened as one of the other students threw himself across the empty bench immediately in front of him. The kid was scowling, even Portobello could see that, but Joey was once again oblivious, with even the obvious turned impossibly subtle through his eyes. Innocently, Joey leaned forward to tap the boy on one shoulder. There was a broad smile on his face as he spoke to the boy, who responded by shrugging Joey's arm away. Rather than accepting this message as others would have done and settling back against the hard cushion for a long and lonely drive home—a home where Portobello was no longer allowed to live—Joey replaced his rejected hand on the boy's shoulder and tried to cheer him up once more.

This time, a shrug was not enough for the boy. He leapt over his seatback to land on top of Joey with a shower of punches. The punishment which had escaped Joey earlier in the day rained down on him now. Portobello rushed towards the bus as he saw his son vanish beneath the window frame in a flurry of fists.

Portobello leapt up as he reached the bus and slammed his fist against the window. The pimply face of Joey's attacker appeared, snarling, but not that of his son, and when the boy swung and vanished once again from view, Portobello sprinted to the front of the bus where he forced open the door and pushed past the startled driver. He shouted his son's name, and in response the sounds of pandemonium trailed off as most of the kids turned to look at the invading adult presence. The boy wrestling with Joey paid him no mind. Portobello was forced to peel him away from Joey and toss him aside. The bus driver came up behind him to chastise him, but Portobello could not hear his words—the sight of Joey crumpled there wiped those words away. Slumped on the floor of the bus, Joey slowly opened his eyes and peered around nervously, hands still raised to ward off the next expected blow. Seeing his father there instead of his attacker, the boy beamed. If only all of them, the cops, the lawyers, and the school administrators, everyone who sought to keep them apart, could see that look exploding on Joey's face.

That would teach them. That would show them the way things should be.

"Come, Joey," said Portobello, reaching down a hand. "Why don't we skip the bus today? I'll get you back home."

Joey's face soured as if he was suddenly confronted with a difficult math problem.

"Does Mom know?" he asked, brushing candy wrappers from his knees.

Portobello's face burned. He was glad his son was looking the other way and would not notice, trying to forget at the same time that Joey might not have been able to interpret the sign even if he had. Why did his cheeks have to go ahead and do that? No matter what Angela said, there was nothing wrong here. All was at it should be.

"It's fine, Joey," he said. "Let's go."

He placed an arm across his son's shoulders, those shoulders slightly higher than when he'd last had an arm around them, and guided him towards the exit, glaring the bus driver into silence.

"Before we go home, though" said Portobello, stepping down out of the bus, "why don't we make one small stop. I'm sure your mother wouldn't mind."

―――――――

FOR AS LONG AS EITHER OF them could remember, Joey had loved the zoo with a passion beyond explanation. Whenever he worked himself up into one of his agitated states— and these disruptive times arrived more and more frequently as the years went by—a visit to the zoo was one of the few things that could restore him to his better self. It worked so well to bring him back to peacefulness that he and Angela started to take Joey there often, hoping the place would empower their son to remain calm in advance of stress, to build up a reserve that would forestall those daily disasters, but it had not proven effective. After a time it no longer mattered whether or not it worked. It just made Portobello feel better.

Once father and son passed through the wrought iron front gate, Joey dashed off, and Portobello quickened his step. His son was fast, so he wouldn't be able to shadow him, but he didn't worry. He knew where he'd be able to find the boy. Ever since Joey could walk on his own, his first steps at the zoo were always the same—towards the elephants, stately and peaceful. Though he'd often tried, Portobello had never been able to get Joey to talk about the meaning of what he experienced at the zoo, so he never knew the nature of the attraction beyond question, but during those moments when he tried to comprehend his son, he imagined it was because the elephants seemed to him as Joey himself would like to be —powerful and in control.

And even in a cage, at peace.

Portobello caught up to buy Joey a bag of peanuts, then fell back to sit on a nearby bench. He was content to watch Joey enjoy himself. His son calmly offered them only to the smallest of the elephants, slyly shifting the bag behind his back whenever the adults approached. His school jacket made him look far overdressed, but though Portobello had tried to get his son to ditch the thing, the boy insisted on wearing it wherever he went. Joey somehow managed to take pride in his school, even though Portobello knew that the school rarely took pride in him. They felt him to be an embarrassment in a school full of embarrassments. They cashed his checks quickly enough, though.

Joey did not feed the elephants in the nasty way that seemed common to most other children, teasing the beasts by making the peanuts snake in and out of reach, forcing their trunks to dance. No, in his best moments, Joey seemed kinder and gentler, and somehow better than the rest. He just wanted them to be happy. Portobello marveled at his son's patience as he held out a still hand and waited for the beasts to shamble over and feed. If only the control Joey effortlessly embodied here could carry over to the other venues of his life. Portobello knew all too well the fruitlessness of such a wish. It was wearying to walk through each day never knowing when someone he loved might step on a landmine. With that daily struggle so exhausting to Portobello, he could not imagine how unbearably grueling the days must feel to Joey.

The last peanuts gone, Joey folded the small bag into a neat square, pressing the corners smooth. He slid the paper into his jacket's lapel pocket and looked around for his father. Portobello stood from the bench as his son skipped near.

"Now it's our turn for something to eat, son," he said, peering past his son to the elephant house. "I don't know about you, but I'm in the mood for something a bit more substantial than peanuts."

Portobello wrapped an arm around his boy and gave a gentle squeeze before they began to wend their way through the late afternoon crowds to a nearby concession stand. Portobello was startled to find himself happy, an extremely rare occurrence for him. He felt good this way, good beside his son, and goddamn his wife, Joey felt good, too. Any fool could see that. Well, no

…there were some fools who couldn't, and that was the problem. This horror had to be fixed. They needed each other in their lives, and everyday, too, not just during the brief moments the courts allowed. Even with the constant threat of having to bear witness to all of Joey's horrific missteps, Portobello comprehended that when they were together there was a peace present that was beyond compare.

Joey yelped, and suddenly all Portobello held was empty air. He spun about, confused, not immediately finding his son and not knowing where to look, until a high-pitched chittering behind him demanded his attention. He turned towards the frenetic gibbering to see Joey grappling through the bars with a capuchin monkey. Its teeth were bared, and its eyes were as mean and nasty as any he'd ever seen.

For some reason Portobello could not at first discern, Joey had engulfed the monkey's wrist with one meaty hand. The answer to the mystery was in the monkey's other paw. Deeper within the cage, as far from Joey as the creature could thrust it, was the neatly folded paper sack.

"Give that back," shouted Joey, grunting. "Give it to me now!"

The monkey's lips peeled back even further to show additional pointed teeth. As Portobello rushed towards his son, it ducked its head in an attempt to bite Joey's fingers. Joey moved his hand quickly up and down between the bars, tossing the monkey about so it could not reach its target.

"Let it go, Joey," shouted Portobello, as his son shook the monkey. That's all he needed to have to tell Angela, that he let his son get bitten or fracture a monkey's wrist. He didn't know which news would sound worse. "It's only a bag."

Joey bared his own teeth, keening in response to the monkey's own wild sounds, but neither the noise nor the expression made an impression on the creature. While the two of them wrestled, the other monkeys spun around the corners of the cage, but none dared approach. Portobello grabbed his son by the shoulder and pulled, but his son could not be moved.

"You don't need that, Joey, I can get you another. Let go of it."

"Let go," echoed Joey, his eyes wide and the monkey tight within his grasp. "Let go."

At the rear of the cage, a small door opened at the base of the wall, and though Portobello did not feel he could take the time to look away to view it directly, he felt a sense of relief. Help was on the way, and he had to have faith that a zookeeper could do here what he alone could not. As he muttered in his son's ear and pulled weakly on his son's arm for fear of injuring the monkey, he expected a hand to reach down upon them from the other side of the bars to help disentangle his son.

With the crowd standing about them in a ring, he felt more fear than shame at the sorry spectacle of which he was a part: him grasping his son, his son grasping a monkey, the monkey grasping a bag. A worthless paper bag! *Trash*! What could Joey possibly be thinking? He always tried to ferret out Joey's way, made allowances for Joey's logic, but this time he was lost. Portobello hoped the zookeeper would hurry, and that this could end with neither boy nor monkey hurting each other before the struggle was over. Working in a zoo, they'd surely seen everything by now, they'd had to, maybe even something as stupid as this. The wait for rescue was agonizing, and Portobello's frustration grew. Sensing no motion within the cage since the door had opened other than the roiling sea of monkeys, Portobello risked looking away from his son for a moment to peer through the bars, seeking a human form, but there was no salvation there.

All he saw at first were eyes.

Hungry eyes, sharp and strong and gleeful, and horrifyingly familiar. They were the same eyes into which Portobello had stared earlier that day at the school.

Anguished words rushed to Portobello's mind, coming from just where he did not know, found in a place beyond conscious thought.

"Get away from my son!" he shouted.

Showing surprise for the first time, the cool eyes turned

momentarily from Joey to Portobello, and then they were gone before he could even register the face in which the eyes were set. The small rear door slammed shut, and the monkey, suddenly silent, released the bag, which fluttered and fell to the bottom of the cage. Seeing this, Joey released the monkey and lunged for the bag, then tumbled back with his prize into his father's arms. Portobello grunted from the sudden weight of the boy, so much heavier than he'd remembered, and fell to his knees. He'd caught him. Maybe he hadn't been able to prevent it from happening, but he'd caught him. At least he'd been able to do that.

The crowd surged forward, helping them to their feet, and Portobello, not taking the time to thank them, instead looked quickly from face to face. He did not find what he was looking for, what a part of him was hoping to find, even as another part of him knew it would be insanity to find.

He hugged his son tightly, and spoke softly to him as they rocked together on the rough paving stones.

"Joey, are you all right? Are you all right, Joey?"

The boy nodded, and studied the paper sack, but Portobello knew that his son was not all right.

Seeing those hungry eyes once that day had been disturbing enough. But to see them twice, that told him a terrifying but undeniable truth.

Joey was being hunted.

And only Portobello could save him.

When Angela's shrill phone call collided with Portobello first thing the next morning at the office, neither its arrival nor its tone surprised him. It had been years since he'd heard his wife's voice in a manner anything but shrill.

As he held the phone a few inches from his ear, he tried

to listen as she spoke once more of lawyers, and indicated that this would be the last time he would ever hear her voice. It would all be lawyers from now on. Her counsel had insisted on it. He was to stay away from Joey except during those times when she had been ordered by their separation agreement to let Portobello see him, and she intended to pay the lawyer whatever it took to eliminate those. Joey was not going to be a part of his life, not anymore. Did he understand?

She wanted to know if he understood.

Yes, he understood, which is why he hung up the phone without bothering to make any response. He knew the way she thought. Her life was not the life they'd promised each other, all those long years ago. She didn't have Portobello all to herself and never had, their marriage had not worked out that way—and for that at times he was genuinely remorseful—but why should that have anything to do with Joey? What right did she have to insist that this time, she would at last have something all to herself? A boy was not a pet, and she should know that.

So he understood her. He understood better than she thought.

He understood that Joey was in trouble.

He loved Joey, but the boy had always been what medical professionals and school administrators seemed to take delight in calling "special," an offensive euphemism if ever there was one, as if there was something to be celebrated about the difficulties he was having, as if the torturous nature of his life might sneak by uncommented upon by others if masked by such an ineffectual term. But the truth was that the world was a wilderness, and Joey hadn't seemed to come equipped with a map. Academically, he excelled; athletically, he was adequate; socially, he was bewildered. Tell him to assemble a science project and he was in heaven. Tell him to decipher the dynamics of his peers and he was in hell. Lately, hell seemed to have gotten even hotter for him.

Teacher requests seemed cloudy. Parental desires seemed bewildering. Friends, well, when there had been some, before they withered away one by one, their words were scripted in a foreign language. As bad as it had been before, recently, bad had become worse, and what Portobello had to wonder, what Portobello had to struggle to understand was—could the owner of those eyes have been to blame?

Someone had been watching Joey during all of his defeated moments. More than once now, Portobello had caught the man while he was spying. Could that be why Joey's fits were happening, that the two facts were more than coincidental? Had something happened in the past between Joey and that man, something that could only have occurred because of Portobello's absence in his life? Had Joey become aware of the man's presence before Portobello had, and had the stress of being watched set him off?

What could possibly have happened? Portobello did not want to think long on the answer to that question, could not possibly endure it, but he knew that he had to speak it to stop it.

That much Portobello understood. That's what Angela could never understand.

He had to stop it.

And so that was the only way he could answer her, by hanging up the phone. He knew that she might go on for minutes before she noticed that he had done so. He stared at the playground across the way, knowing what was next, waiting for the intercom to buzz with a voice telling him it was time to see his boss.

His own time had run out. But Joey's would not.

AND SO THAT night he found himself sprawled out on his stomach, the smell of mulch strong in his nostrils, hiding in the darkness between the bushes outside his own home. At least, he still thought of it as his own home, though Angela would dispute that. He was still paying for it, after all, though he wasn't supposed to even so much as step on the street except for a few brief moments before and after those limited court-ordered visits.

It was disconcerting to see the house from this odd angle, privet hedges slashing at his cheeks. He felt distanced by the unfamiliar view, as if he was present at the filming of a burglar alarm commercial that used some stranger's house. The dull yellow porch bulb and the weak light trickling from the front windows would dispel no one. There was far too much darkness where it should be bright, and Portobello decided that the next day he would see whether Angela would allow him to improve the place by buying some exterior lights. She tended to look on all such offers with suspicion, but as long as there was money flowing in her direction, she would usually give in. Besides, it would at the very least give him a chance to call. Perhaps she'd exaggerated earlier, and she would be willing to talk to him. Perhaps there really wouldn't be a need for more lawyers. Right then, though, the darkness suited him well. As he listened to the voices of what used to be his family floating through the open windows, he imagined the gestures and expressions that accompanied every word.

Joey was telling his mother with great enthusiasm how much fun he'd had playing with the monkeys that day. Portobello smiled to hear that Joey could still be like that at times, alive with joy. As usual, once clouds had passed, Joey could barely remember that there had ever been a storm. The adults were always a different matter, however, unable to so easily shrug off the worst of it. Joey sounded happy as he discussed his trip to the zoo, while Angela's responses were strained. Portobello just knew she had that look on her face, the one that made it seem as if she'd just eaten a bad piece of fish. Be happy for him, he thought, can't you, just this once? But she could never see the boy like that, not once the topic of her ex-husband had gotten involved in the matter at hand. Portobello tried to be rational about these things. He knew he had not been a perfect husband, had never tried to fool himself or her into believing that he was. So he could understand why Angela couldn't bring herself to be happy when *he* did the things he did, but he wished she could at least give that space to their son. It should somehow be allowed to be different. Instead, life moved forward the same as always, and he was forced to listen as she told him, her voice quivering, that if Portobello ever came to pick Joey up again, the boy was to ignore his father unless his Mom was there with him. His son was to turn and walk away.

"After all," she said, "that's what he did to us."

Her stony words filled Portobello with rage. Of all the lies he'd ever heard her tell, that one was the worst.

"But he's my father," Joey wailed.

Portobello's anger overcame his common sense, and his legs pushed him from his hiding place before he even knew that he was going to move. He crawled across the grass on his stomach until he reached the dining room window. Slowly lifting himself up to peer in, he thought that perhaps keeping the house shrouded in darkness wasn't such a bad idea. If Angela got her way, this wouldn't be the last time he'd have to do this.

Though his son and ex-wife were fuzzy silhouettes through the thin curtains, he could definitely see the two of them together. As Joey continued to plead with his mother, his voice didn't sound quite the same to Portobello. It was duller somehow than he remembered it, less full of life. It was a voice that Portobello was not used to hearing. He's different, he thought, Joey's different with each person he's with, a thought that had not occurred to Portobello until then. He could not leave him to become the person that Angela would cause him to become.

Watching them that way, spying in the night, seeing them the way God must see them, he could tell storm clouds were gathering, sense the thickened air within the room. He knew Angela's darker moods, knew them all too well, knew that all he'd needed to do when a situation verged toward the ugly in this way was to remain silent, and eventually Angela would run out of energy. He hadn't been able to remember that all the time or maybe they'd still be married, but most of the time, he'd remembered. If you could avoid the temptation to return the volleys of her rants and raves, Angela would eventually feel too drained to continue. The next day she would be hung over from it all, barely able to put her finger for sure on whatever had stirred her up previously. The air would be clear again for a while.

All Joey had to do now to see his way through was stay quiet. The boy had lived with Angela for fifteen years, he should have learned by now how to dodge the worst of the fights. But no, he had not, not before, and certainly not since, no matter how earnestly Portobello offered silent prayers for rescue.

Instead, Joey had objections to everything this day. No matter how irrational Angela's threats, no matter how obvious it seemed from Portobello's vantage point that she regretted her excesses and wished she could recall them as soon as they came out of her mouth, Joey still sputtered and spun, stoking her vituperative powers, insisting with his tongue that she continue to speak even as she wished she could fall to silence. Finally, Joey could take it no longer, and broke down, spitting out the same blunt syllable over and over again.

"No," he shrieked, "No, no, no, no!"

Portobello leaned close to peer through a crack in the curtain just as Angela stretched across the table with terrifying speed, and slapped Joey hard. Portobello could not say which of the three of them was shocked more by this explosive anger. She had never slapped either of them before, even though Portobello was sure that he'd deserved slapping at least a half a dozen times during their marriage. She slowly studied her fingers, a stunned look of disgust on her face. Portobello wished Joey would act as most kids would do, would get up and run to his room in tears, then it would all be over, but his wishes were ineffectual, and the ragged words continued to pour out of Joey.

"No," he bellowed, tears in his eyes and the red mark of his mother's hand across his cheek "No, no, no, no!"

She rushed around the table to hit him again and again, trying to knock the words out of Joey, but no matter how hard she banged on him, they would not stop. Portobello stood and pressed his palms against the windowpane, ignoring the dangers of being seen. He had to go in. There was no other way. He could not stand there, hoping and shaking and taking no action. He had to go in and end it all. And he had no doubts that the response he contemplated *would* end it all. It would end everything.

He was not sure exactly what a judge would say about a husband who broke into his ex-wife's house, but he imagined that the stakes would raise uncomfortably. It would be his word against hers. Bars would slam shut, making his imprisonment final. But that no longer mattered, not when confronted with this tableaux. He had to make it stop. His son was worth any sacrifice.

Starting to turn to sprint towards the front door, Portobello felt a warm puff of breath caress the back of his neck. He jerked, and spun, and looked for a third time that day into those same, horrid eyes. Though the eyes were wild and alive, the face beneath them was without affect. The eyes did not look back at him, they did not even seem to register that Portobello had turned. They continued, undeterred by anything Portobello had done, to watch with deep satisfaction his wife and son, an intrusion which left Portobello feeling more violated than if he'd discovered he had been spied on himself.

"Get away from us," snarled Portobello, springing at the man. "Damn you, you're the cause of all this. You're the cause of everything!"

The man backpedaled away so quickly that all Portobello caught between his outstretched fingers was an edge of the man's jacket. The cloth was strong, so rather than tear, it held to jerk the man to his knees. Portobello growled and dropped atop him, bending him backwards, pinning the man's bony shoulders to the grass. He placed his hands so tight around the man's throat he could not have answered even if he'd wanted to, and asked him the question he had been asking the universe for years, the question to which the universe up to then seemed to have no answer.

"What have you done to my son?"

Portobello was pleased the man's face no longer seemed so triumphant. The words the man tried to utter could not get past his fingers. Portobello reluctantly loosened his grip.

"We haven't done anything to your son," the man said, his words raw and breathy.

"Then why?" he asked, shaking the man, realizing even as he was doing it that it was in much the same way Joey had earlier shaken the monkey. "Why is Joey like this? You've been there lately when he's screwed up, every time. It's you, I know it's you."

The face into which Portobello looked down softened for a moment, and he could see a compassion there, a compassion which he could tell seemed foreign to the man even as it coursed through him. He seemed to be at a loss for words, and Portobello had to give him another shake to get him started talking again.

"I am sorry," he finally said. "Sorry you have to live this way. But we are the cause of nothing. Life happens, and it happens on its own terms. When we get hungry, we watch. And that's all."

"Hungry? What are you talking about? What are you trying to get me to believe?"

Portobello had always prided himself on being a rational man, someone not given to fanciful theories. Yet as the watcher responded to Portobello's growing anger with both a rising smile and a rising strength, bending Portobello's fingers back with little effort, he had to admit that perhaps there could be something more. Portobello had not at first thought this man to be anything more than a common child abuser. He had hoped he was wrong, but as he rose from the lawn with a force that made Portobello's resistance little more than a slight wind, he realized now exactly how wrong he had truly been.

"You're a vampire," said Portobello softly, falling back to the grass as the man loomed above him. "An emotional vampire. That's what you are. You create our distress so you can feed off it."

"You mustn't blame us for it," the man said. As Portobello stared into his eyes, the rest of the man's body seemed to grow more ephemeral, as if a demonic Cheshire Cat which slowly disappeared to leave only the most terrifying fragment behind. Portobello wanted to attack again, but those eyes pinned him down so that he could not continue his struggle. "Your pain, your complex, delightful pain, is there whether we feed on it or not. Your people cannot help but produce so much of it. It would seem a shame to let such delicacies go to waste, don't you think?"

With one blink, the man was gone.

"You're wrong," said Portobello, crying, finally able once again to rise to his feet. He shouted at the sky, since there was no longer anyone present at whom to bellow his anger. "Do you hear me? You are wrong. You cannot be anything but! You only think you are watching, but I know, I *know* you are the cause. You lie! You made us this way. You make our hearts ache so you can feast on them. Stay away from my son! You can't have him. Stay away from my son!"

His anger spent, Portobello fell to a gentle weeping. Still at last, he could hear a weeping behind him that overpowered his own. When he spun towards it, towards his house, he could see Angela framed by the open front door, with Joey peering out from behind her. Their expressions were the same.

They were both looking at him in horror.

———

WHEN THE KNOCK came at the door to the apartment where Portobello had been living since he had been asked by Angela to leave, all he could think was the same thing about which he had been obsessing since his failed struggle on his wife's front lawn: that the man had used the word "we."

He was not alone.

Looking through the peephole at another strange face, he wondered if this was one more of the bastards come to gloat over his despair. Even when the stocky man calmly but firmly identified himself as a county police officer, Portobello could still not be sure, not even after their strained introductions were followed by the display of a badge. This was not the first time Portobello had been visited for such a talk, and though the dance by now had become routine, it had never become more comfortable. Portobello did not ask the officer to sit, and so they spoke, standing, in the middle of the living room, surrounded by unpacked boxes that still contained the few possessions with which Angela had allowed him to leave. The dirty dishes in plain view through the kitchen doorway hadn't seemed so noticeable to Portobello just a few moments before, when he'd had a beer in one hand and a remote control in the other, and had been trying but failing to keep his mind on anything but his own life.

"That wasn't a very smart thing to do, sir," the officer told him in carefully enunciated syllables. Portobello found himself wishing he'd shut the TV off rather than simply muting the volume. It was difficult enough to pretend he was interested in the message that was to be delivered with all of that movement flickering off to one side. "Showing up like that where you know you aren't supposed to be. Shouting at your wife. You shouldn't raise your voice at her, you know."

Portobello knew he should say nothing, look repentant, and let the officer go on his way thinking that he'd gotten through. But instead he felt compelled to speak, to attempt to make another understand.

"I wasn't shouting at my wife," he said. "There was someone else."

"Who else, sir? Neither your wife nor son saw anyone but you."

When the officer followed Portobello's gaze to the screen, Portobello found himself shifting his gaze to stare instead at the officer's gun snug in its leather holster.

"Do you have children, officer?"

"Not yet, sir," said the officer, his eyes narrowing back on Portobello. "Hope to someday."

"Then you'll learn. You'll learn that what we have to do for our children doesn't always seem…nice. No, not nice at all."

"That's fine with me, sir, because, you see, I'm not concerned at all with whether what you do is nice. Only if what you do is legal. That's the difference, you see. That's the time that people ask us to get involved. That's the line you have to worry about crossing. Not 'nice' or 'not nice.' But legal versus illegal. I'd stay away from them for awhile if I were you."

Portobello wished he could stop himself from continually returning to stare at the gun, but he was helpless. He felt like Joey all of a sudden, always doing exactly the wrong thing, whatever it was, that authority figures would find challenging. Even here, even now, he understood it wasn't the wisest thing to do. But that didn't mean, as he tried to keep his eyes from wandering, that he could stop.

"There was this man, you see," said Portobello. "The things that were happening around him, he thought they weren't all his fault. But they were. He thought he was only watching, but he wasn't. There's no such thing in this world as just watching. He was really making things worse. He thought he wasn't the cause of the misery, but he was. That's who was out there with me last night, officer. That's the man I was talking to. I don't know why Angela didn't see him, but he was there. You'd never believe what he's doing to the boy, officer, just with his eyes, just by watching. He's hungry, and he has to be stopped. I have to be the one to stop him."

Portobello took his eyes from the gun then, just as the officer's hand came to rest on the holster. He turned and looked up at the state of the apartment about him. A portrait hung on the wall of the three of them, he and Angela and Joey. They looked happy. All of them. He knew that they had been happy. The officer crossed his arms, and took a step closer to stand behind Portobello to study the picture.

"Actually," the man said softly, "your wife would very much prefer it if you didn't do anything. That's why I'm here, sir. To remind you that there's no need for this to get ugly."

"That's where there's a problem, officer," said Portobello, staring helplessly at the gun. "It's too late for that. It's already gotten ugly."

PORTOBELLO SLIPPED like a ghost through the dark halls of Joey's school, determined that morning to do the thing he had to before Angela was successful in turning him into little more than a ghost in his son's life. Once that happened— and he saw no way to prevent it—it would be too late for him to save his son. He knew that he had to end this today, or he would fail to end it at all.

And so, before dawn, he climbed in an unlocked window, unsure of his next step, uncaring of his personal future, knowing only that his son could not endure much more. The watcher had tried to convince him he was only feasting on the agony Joey was already forced to endure by nature of his own poor choices, but Portobello could tell the truth was far different—he would have been willing to swear the man had actually been creating Joey's misery, and gaining his own sick joy from that. As Portobello headed for his son's homeroom, he hoped the morning would proceed as he'd intended so that Joey would soon know no more pain. In the back of a dark classroom he made his way to an even darker space that was more alcove than closet, where he stood and waited among the stacks of pens and papers.

Wrapped tightly around a gun, his fingers did not feel as cold as he thought they would be.

Once the officer had decided that it would be better if their conversation continued down at the station—and Portobello could tell that was the way the officer's thoughts were tending—Portobello realized he couldn't let that happen. He was too close to solving it all. There was too much at risk. Who knows what might have happened at the police station, what on their own turf they then would have been able to look at and see in him. He could not let the officer feel his suspicions had been confirmed, because this was not a time when he could allow himself to be confined.

The officer, when Portobello did what he had to do to get away and free himself to act, did not seem in the least surprised. He looked sheepish, a little foolish maybe for having made the wrong choice and allowed himself to get on the wrong end of such a situation, but not surprised. No, that was not an expression that Portobello saw him wear.

And then, suddenly, the officer didn't have any expression at all.

The light in the classroom came on, bright enough even through the narrow slats of the closet door to blind Portobello. He did not have to act quite yet. It was only the homeroom teacher moving quietly about to prepare the room; the students had not yet arrived. Portobello wondered if it would do either of them any good to begin a conversation with the man, to ask him if he had ever seen what Portobello had only just recently seen—the eyes of a hungry soul peering into the classroom during Joey's lowest moments, the presence of an instigating and uninvited audience—but he sensed there would be little point to such questions. He hoped he had sensed rightly. What had to be done he felt had to be done in front of his son, for it would do little good to take any action any other time.

Joey was their target. He was the one whose emotions these creatures desired. He took a short step back to lean against the shelving at the rear wall of the closet and tried to breathe more slowly as he continued to wait, the cool metal heavy in his hands. That's one of the things he was surprised to discover he never got a true sense of from movies and television shows, how heavy guns were. He hoped to be able to stop carrying this one soon.

The students arrived like sudden thunder. As they took their seats, desks shrieking as they were slid across ancient floorboards, Portobello was nearly blind to action in the room. Because of the angle of the slats, he could only make out the backs of the students' heads in the very last rows. If Joey was out there, which Portobello assumed he was, the nature of his hiding place would not let him see the boy. He should have anticipated that, but he knew that it wouldn't matter. The obstruction didn't change a thing. He knew all he had to do was wait, and likely not very long, and he would certainly hear Joey stand out from the crowd. Portobello knew Joey's class routine far too well. Before Angela had asked him to leave, when he had still been an embedded part of his son's life, each day would bring at least one teacher's call, each day a different teacher. Often they were asked to come to the school to pick up their son before the day had barely begun. Portobello wished it could be otherwise, but he doubted he would have to wait long there until something went terribly wrong, and he would have his fragile chance to set it right.

The teacher tried to quiet the class down, and failing to do that, began to take attendance. Portobello closed his eyes to block out everything but that which mattered. He listened intently, and in response to the teacher calling the boy's name, could hear his son call out in a piercing voice that he was present. The students kept up a murmuring that grew louder with every attempt of the teacher to keep order. Occasionally, Portobello picked out Joey's voice slicing through the din. Joey kept sallying forth tentatively from his solitude to offer up remarks that none of the other boys were willing to build on. His efforts tumbled into silence each time, Joey falling quiet until he worked up the courage to try again. He could not start a conversation, and if he tried to enter an ongoing one, his words were sure to be met by a lull.

Portobello cradled the gun, wondering when he would be given the opportunity to use it. His son's behavior so far had been awkward, but not disastrous, not falling to the recent depths the boy had known. At the ringing of a bell, the class began to leave for their first period of actual instruction. Portobello's mood fell at this. He assumed he'd have to wait, that he'd need to slip away to yet another classroom unseen, but then, instead of the silence that would give him his chance, the tumult of dozens of moving teenagers gave way to the soft sounds of Joey and the teacher talking. Portobello doubted those sounds would stay soft for long.

"I'm sorry, Joey," said the teacher, each syllable a blunt weapon. Portobello had made no impression of the man from his voice alone up until then, but the voice suddenly sounded small and mean. "Now's not the time. I have to get ready for my first class. You'll just have to come see me later."

The teacher's tone was one of exasperation and despair, and Portobello was surprised by his ability to maintain that. After all this time, he had to know how Joey was, how he would react to such treatment. The boy would not be able to bear any of that well. Couldn't the man show some patience? He was a teacher, for god's sake!

"But I have to talk about it now," said Joey.

"You know that isn't possible. Please come back later. I'd be glad to make time for you then."

Portobello's limited point of view was maddening. All he could see from the closet were rows of empty chairs. He could hear the teacher move papers about his desk, but was forced to only imagine the suit of disdain he wore. Joey began to cry, and it was difficult for Portobello to remain still when all he wanted to do was burst from his place of hiding, show the snotty teacher the gun and ask in a firm voice that he try to be just a *little* more civil to his son. That's all it would take, Portobello was sure of it. Maybe later, if there was to be a later. The more important work had to come first.

"But it's not fair," said Joey, his voice cracking.

"Later," said the teacher. His words had become even more clipped.

Joey's words grew angrier and angrier through the sobs, and Portobello could imagine the man's face reddening.

"No, *now*. Later's not good enough. *Now! Now! Now!*"

"There aren't going to be any special privileges for you. We've discussed this before. So, please, Joey, please move on to your first class. I've warned you of the consequences."

"But we have to talk about this now. You promised. You gave me your word."

"Don't be silly, Joey."

"*Now!*"

The teacher sighed, and the sound of shuffling papers vanished.

"I'm afraid I'm going to need help up here again."

Portobello realized from the change in the teacher's tone and volume that he had just spoken not to Joey, but into an intercom. The man had abandoned Joey, and was turning him over to the security guards, who would bring with them even less understanding. Joey, realizing what was coming, began pounding the teacher's desk with his fists. The teacher repeated Joey's name to no avail. Each utterance of his son's name sliced into Portobello like a razor. When he raised the gun to place its barrel against a door slat, he heard a faint rustle like fallen leaves behind him. Before he could turn, the watcher had stepped up beside him in a room that had no place where he could have been hiding.

The closet door opened without either of them seeming to have touched it, and they had an uninterrupted view of a nightmare. Joey tossed shredded paper in the air, while the teacher stood helplessly beside him, calling once more into the phone for help. They were too caught up in their own intense drama to notice their witnesses. Portobello turned in horror to the watcher, whose eyes were filled with glee.

"You enjoy this, do you?" said Portobello, slipping quickly sideways to press the gun barrel into the man's back. "You've done it again, haven't you? Look at what you did to him. This is going to stop. And it's going to stop now."

"Now!" echoed Joey, continuing with his entreaties.

"It can't stop," said the man, licking his lips, not bothering to turn to look at Portobello, not able to tear his eyes away from Joey for an instant. "Ever. This is who I am. This is what I do."

"Please," said Portobello, nearly whimpering. "Stop creating misery."

The man's only response was a sigh, as if absorbed in embracing perfection.

"I'm sorry," said the watcher, but Portobello could find no regret in his eyes, only a continued ecstasy, and with his finger on the trigger, Portobello could not help but cry out his son's name and pull.

The gun jumped in his hand, and a bullet passed through the watcher's back and out his chest. Portobello could follow its trajectory as if it was moving in slow motion to where it struck the homeroom teacher in an arm. Joey finally froze in his ranting, but whether he was stunned to silence by his father's anguished cry, the sound of the gunshot, or the teacher's high-pitched scream, Portobello couldn't say.

At first there was no reaction from his voyeuristic target, but then he clasped both hands over his chest, took a small step towards Portobello, then fell back into the closet, collapsing against a shelf and pulling down reams of paper that thudded around him. Portobello followed him back into the closet as he fell, and knelt in the pool of light that spilled over into the dim room to watch the deadly eyes finally deaden. It was over.

The room exploded chaotically as students and teachers entered, shouting and screaming. The children stopped a few feet away from the fallen teacher, unable to approach even as they were fascinated by the scene, forming with their hesitation a ring that the adults must break to reach him and examine his wounds. As they turned to Portobello with questioning eyes, he pointed them towards the closet.

"He's in there!" Portobello shouted over the shoulders of a security guard as the uniformed man rushed to the small alcove. He and the men in suits who followed examined the closet, but no sign of any intruder could be found. There was only Portobello, gun still warm in his hand.

The security guard barreled back into the room and tried to rip the gun from Portobello's hands, but Portobello refused to let go. He could hear his son wail from a distant corner of the room even as he was shoved to the floor. He stretched the gun out before him towards the adults who would dare to try to take it away from him, and the open circle that had previously been around the fallen teacher now formed around him. As he held them there, his arm straight out before him, unable to stop himself from shaking as it moved in arcs that kept them all at bay, he noticed on the fringes of the crowd a half-dozen others who did not seem to belong. In their ragged clothing, they could have been brothers to the watcher whom Portobello had shot. Though their body types differed, in one aspect they were exactly the same: The eyes were joyous. One of them stepped through the circle, uncaring of the erratic way in which Portobello was moving the gun.

"Look at your boy," he said. "Look at what you have done. Look at him."

"He's free now," said Portobello, unsure even as he spoke, wanting to look to his boy but unwilling to look away. "He's free."

"You didn't set him free. Don't you get it now? There was nothing to set him free *from*. Don't you see? We were never the cause. Never. You should have believed the first of us when he tried to tell you. We never prepare our own meals. We've never had to. You were always the cause. Always."

Portobello's terror grew as the other watchers stepped closer to him. He saw their eyes leap with delight from Portobello to Joey to the teacher whose arm was being bandaged, and their smiles grew even wider as their gazes danced the circuit again and again.

"This is as delicious a flavor as we've tasted in many long years. Thank you for preparing the feast."

Portobello stared up at the other expectant faces that surrounded him, and turning from their hungry faces, he looked over at Joey, the way he was cowering in a corner at the sight of his own father, and he realized that they were right. They always had been. Joey's ills were his own fault. He could not push that responsibility onto the shoulders of others. As that realization washed over him, pointing out to him how stupid and foolish he had been, he could see that the watchers too were washed by new emotions invading their being. His agony was bringing them ecstasy.

"Yes," the closest one whispered, tasting the misery of Portobello's despair and Joey's distress. "Such glorious pain."

"You're disgusting," Portobello cried out, his whole body shaking, his hand unable to keep the gun straight as it shifted from one watcher to the next. "Leave us alone."

"But we can't help ourselves," said the next, taking a step nearer to him. Portobello could barely see anyone else in the rest of the room through the wall the watchers made. "This is who we are. This is what we do. You could have helped yourself. But you didn't when you had a chance. We're sorry. But you didn't."

Portobello sobbed, and his son wept, too, but neither moved to get closer to the other. Painfully self-aware in his grief, he could parse their emotions clearly now. It was as if the emotional webs that had bound them together since his son's birth had been made real, and he could see exactly why they were frozen. He could see Joey's fear and disappointment and doubt, and his own anger and shame and denial. He knew in that instant of clarity that whatever manner of men these were, they had been right all along.

Portobello pulled the gun in close to his chest, cradling it as he once had his son, and turning its barrel inward, fired.

The students and teachers shrieked with the terror of dying animals, but the watchers exulted. A frenetic applause broke out of them which seemed to explode uncontrollably, just as a child cannot resist clapping when overcome by happiness. They pulled tighter together then as they stood at the front of the crowd, forming an inhuman fence between Portobello and the rest of the room. Through a crack between their bodies, he could see Joey squirm in an attempt to reach and comfort him, but his son could not breach that fence. They were holding the boy back from him. They took delight in that as well, and their gleeful laughter darkened, its joy tainted with malice, its satiation with scorn.

Portobello realized only then, as the world grew tinged in red, how horribly they had lied, that they had only made him think they were the cause, had manipulated him at every turn because that was what they needed to say to do their job best. And he had believed them. That was their power, that they could make him believe. They were indeed the cause, not only the drinkers of human pain, but the distillers of it as well. They had tricked the two of them into providing the greatest dessert of all.

Portobello knew just what he could do to protect Joey, it came to him then, he knew it as surely as he'd ever known anything . . . .

As he struggled to speak to his son to tell him this and to make what would be a final goodbye, he could not move, pinned by the endless hungry eyes of the strangers who watched him watch Joey's face, and then, as the watchers sighed in unison, that face was stolen away forever.

A TEST OF FAITH FOR A COUPLE OF
TRUE BELIEVERS

The chaplain ducked when I threw the bible, which meant that instead of hitting him, the book arced over his head and bounced off my hospital room's pale green wall. As it landed at his feet, I laughed in a way I hoped he'd find insulting. If he'd truly been a believer, wouldn't he have tried to catch it?

"I'll come back later," he said, bending carefully to pick up his bible.

"Don't bother," I said, as he hurried out into the hall. Once he was gone, I collapsed, gasping as I sank back into my bed pillows. I wanted to berate the man further, but the effort of throwing the bible had worn me out.

As I trembled from rage, exhaustion, and the sickness which had brought me to this place, Shelley came slowly back into the room, balancing a cafeteria tray carefully in front of her. My wife still needed to eat, even if I couldn't.

"So what did you say to him this time?" she asked, tilting her head back at the doorway.

"This time it wasn't so much what I said."

She sighed, but as with all of Shelley's sighs, it was accompanied by a poorly suppressed smile.

"I know how you feel about religion, Seth," she said, sitting in a chair at the foot of my bed. She balanced the tray on her knees and tucked a napkin into the collar of her shirt. "But you don't have to go out of your way to be so obnoxious about it."

"If not now," I answered, "then when?"

I eyed her sandwich as she began to raise it to her lips, and wished I could eat it, but that was only my brain and not my stomach speaking. Truthfully, even the smell bothered me, though I wouldn't tell her that. She saw my sadness and, though she hadn't yet taken a bite, returned the sandwich to her plate and settled her tray onto the linoleum. She dragged her chair closer, and opened her mouth, then remained silent. I could see she was having difficulty speaking. That had been happening a lot lately, considering.

"Do you have any regrets?" my wife finally whispered, as I lay dying.

Her eyes were damp and unfocussed. I wasn't even sure she could see me through her tears and her despair.

"Just one," I whispered.

That made her lean in more closely. My words, I knew, could be difficult to hear over the workings of the machines which I would soon ask to be turned off.

"I regret that when I tossed that bible across the room, it didn't hit the chaplain in the head."

I smiled weakly.

"My aim isn't what it used to be. My *arm* isn't what it used to be."

Shelley smacked the back of one of my hands and laughed as she'd once done quite frequently when she'd thought I'd been outrageous. I wish I'd been able to make her laugh more often lately, but a hospital wasn't the sort of place conducive to it. So I was glad she'd done it. Our last moments should be real ones, not the artificial, automated routines it would be so easy to fall into as death approached.

"No," I said, as the laughter faded. "I have no regrets."

"That's a good thing," she said, tears rolling down her cheeks. She lifted up the corners of her napkin and dabbed at her face, then pulled it from her neck to ball up the cloth in a trembling fist. "A very good thing for you to be able to say…at a time like this."

In the past, when Shelley had cried, I had always blubbered, too. But this time, I was dry-eyed. Maybe I just didn't have the strength left for tears.

"I had a good life," I said. "You know that."

"I know that," she said.

"And that should be enough," I said, unable to hide my anger. But I wasn't angry at her. Never at her. "There doesn't have to be anything more. Why can't the life we've been given ever be enough?"

"How could there ever be enough you?" she said.

I attempted to reach out and touch her, but I was suddenly much too tired, caught by a fatigue that had been visiting me in waves. I couldn't lift up my hand. All I could manage was a few listless wiggles of my fingers. Shelley saw my frustration and wrapped her hands around my own.

"I wish there could be something more beyond this world," I said. "I really do. But there isn't. There's no God. There's no afterlife. No Heaven. No Hell. Listen to me, Shelley. Listen carefully. This is it, the only world we've got. I can't pretend, not even now. *Especially* not now. We don't get anything more. It would be wrong for me to give you false comfort. So please…"

My voice died away, and then Shelley had to speak for me, speak, I hoped, for both of us.

"I know," she said, her words punctuated by sobs. "Don't

go looking for you in the clouds, because you won't be there. Don't be listening for voices in the night, because they won't be yours. Don't waste time seeking ghosts, because there is no such thing. You won't be trying to reach for me, because this is all we have. And all we have...all we had..."

This time it was her voice that died away.

"All we had was beautiful," I whispered, with what I had decided would be one of my last breaths. And then, finally, "It's time, Shelley. Let them know it's time."

She left me then, left to tell the doctors that my torture by machines and medicines was over.

They didn't understand. They never would. They'd even tried to use my own beliefs against me. Why, they asked, would someone with no faith in an afterlife be so willing to abandon the one he knew? Why wouldn't I fight for every additional moment with the woman I loved, fight the pain, the misery, the exhaustion, the depression? I couldn't make them see I'd already gotten all the rewards out of this life that mattered, and one day more or less was meaningless, unless I could be restored to a condition in which I could enjoy it. And with no punishment waiting for me on the other side, in fact, with no other side at all, I had nothing to fear.

When Shelley returned, she was accompanied by an army in white and green. Expressionless, the doctors and nurses fell into their usual places around my bed.

"Are you sure?" one asked. I no longer cared which one had spoken. I no longer had the energy for jousting. I couldn't talk, so I only nodded. They fiddled with dials, pushed buttons, scribbled on those ridiculous, endless forms. Shelley slipped once more into the chair beside me and took my hand.

"I wish we could have had more," she said.

I also wished we could have had more. I tried to remember, now that I wasn't able to tell her anything more, whether I had told her that enough. I hoped that I had. As the machines released their hold over me, and my chest tightened, I stared into her eyes. My throat constricted, and I gasped for breath, but there was no pain. That much I was willing to let the doctors keep doing for me. I just kept looking at Shelley, wanting those beautiful eyes to be the last thing I saw, until everything I saw became tinged with red.

And then it all went black.

I OPENED MY EYES. And then I remembered when and where and why I had closed them, and realized I shouldn't have been able to open my eyes. Death, evidently, had not come as quickly as I would have thought.

I was horrified to see that the hospital chaplain was sitting beside Shelley, a bible in his lap. It was probably even the same bible that had taken my last bit of strength to toss at him earlier. I hoped so. Maybe that would be a reminder to him that we weren't all believers.

Shelley wasn't looking at me. Her head was down, and she was weeping into her hands. I called out her name, suddenly once more strong enough to speak. But she was so lost in her tears she seemed not to hear me. But I needed her to look up at me. If she didn't, how would those eyes end up being the last things I ever saw? The chaplain moved his chair closer to Shelley and slid the bible from his knees to hers, an action which filled me with rage.

That was *not* going to be the last thing I saw before I died. Even though I knew I surely no longer had the strength for it, I forced myself to attempt to reach out for the bible. The movement surprisingly came more easily than I'd expected, but then, instead of knocking the book from my wife's lap, all my fingers did was pass through the cover, continuing on to pass through Shelley entirely.

As I yanked my hand back, my wife lifted up her head. She looked toward me, but by the tilt of her head and the way her eyes were focused, I could tell she wasn't seeing me anymore. She was looking...where? I twisted around, and there, in bed beside me...was me. My body had bifurcated above the waist, with one me still laying down, motionless, and the other me, the conscious me, folded in half, sitting up. Shouting, I leapt up from the bed, peeling my legs away from myself. I stood between Shelley and the chaplain, neither of whom had paid any attention to my cry, and looked back at myself.

I was dead.

But I couldn't be dead. If I was, I certainly wouldn't be around to know it. Because there was nothing after death, no place from which you could realize you'd just lost your life. There was no God, no ghosts, no angels, no miracles, no... no this.

"I'll leave you alone with him now," said the chaplain, rising. "Let me know if you need to talk."

"Yes, leave her alone," I said, going nose to nose with him and shouting into his face. "She doesn't need you."

"My number's in the book," he said, smiling, pointing at the bible on her knee, acting as if I wasn't there.

He left the room, and I took his place in the vacant chair by my wife. Even though I had been proven insubstantial before, I was able to sit. It didn't make sense. But then, none of it made sense.

I spoke Shelley's name, but no matter how many times I repeated it or what I said, I wasn't able to get her to turn her head and look at me. She would only look at the me that was.

She stood, and bent over the body that lay in the bed.

My body. She placed her hands on my cheeks, and sobbed, and leaned in closer to kiss me. I reached out again to see whether I could touch her, but it was useless. I felt no resistance from her flesh. I was dead to her.

I didn't care. I still needed to comfort her, or at the very least, *act* as if I was comforting her. I let my hand hang by her shoulder in an imitation of a caress. It wasn't enough, it could never be enough, but it was all that was left to me.

Shelley backed away from the bed and moved to the door. I was horrified to see that as she passed the chair, she took the bible and tucked it under one arm. It bothered me to see her holding it. Because even if she hadn't tried to brain the chaplain with it—since she was, after all, a much nicer person than I was, and not eager to cause offense—she still should have recoiled from it as from a hot flame. We'd had many long talks about this. She knew how I felt. I thought I knew how she felt. Perhaps it was ridiculous to be denying religion from a place to which a God I denied may have brought me, but my beliefs were consistent, whether the evidence was or not.

"No," I shouted, so repulsive was the sight. At that instant, Shelley paused. Had she heard me, or had she simply turned back at that moment by coincidence for one last look? There was no way to tell. "Shelley, please, leave the bible here. You don't need it. It's just a book of lies. Fairy tales for those who can't live without fantasies. Leave it here for someone else who doesn't know better."

"Goodbye, Seth," she said...but not to me.

And then she was gone.

I should have followed her immediately. I knew that, but letting go of my body proved difficult. So I watched as the nurses returned and detached all of the tubes and wires which I had allowed only long enough to make my goodbye. As they transferred me from the bed to a gurney, they treated me far more gently than I would have expected. I didn't want to see me go, but when they wheeled me from the room, I chose not to follow. I knew what was going to happen next, and there were some things for which even I didn't have the stomach.

Besides, Shelley needed me. I had to go to her. Because I could tell that unless I helped her, she was going to fall prey to faith.

MY WIFE BEAT ME HOME. I really hadn't been thinking. I'm not sure what I'd expected from this surprise of an afterlife. I guess I thought I could arrive there first by simply closing my eyes only to reappear where I wished, but death's rules turned out not to work that way. Since I'd lingered at the hospital instead of moving quickly enough to slip into my wife's car, I was forced to take the bus.

But first I had to wait for other passengers to arrive at the stop, because no bus would pause for me alone. By the time I reached home, Shelley was already planted at the kitchen table, an ashtray with a lit cigarette by her right hand, the bible near her left. She'd broken her smoking habit years before, so the sight unnerved me. But given a choice between nicotine and religion, I knew which one was the least dangerous, which of the two I preferred her to reach for to seek comfort.

As I circled the kitchen table to face her, my wife's hair obscured her face. Head bowed, she chewed a thumbnail. It was a pose that made me uneasy. I was afraid she could slip too easily from sorrow to prayer without realizing what she was doing.

My death had put her at risk.

"Put the book away," I said, as if saying it was enough to make it happen. "Just push the book away."

She lifted her head, revealing how puffy those beautiful eyes had gotten. She took a puff of the cigarette, and I relaxed for a moment. But then she reached out her other hand, beginning to lean to the left, and I shouted, even though I knew she could not hear it. I flung myself at the table, tossing myself between her and the bible with such an urgency I might as well have been protecting her from a grenade.

Before her hand could complete its journey, the book slid from the formica and bounced off the hardwood flooring. Shelley jumped back, startled. But no more startled than me.

I'd just discovered that I could affect the world of the living. *I* had been what had swept that book away from her hands. It may have been done by accident, but having done it once, however unconsciously, I knew that I could learn to do it again, deliberately. I could learn to speak to Shelley once more. I could send her a message. I could bring her comfort. I could…

Yes. I *could*. If I chose.

But it would be terribly, terribly wrong.

Shelley dropped to her knees to retrieve the bible, and then threw herself back into her chair. She placed the bible on her lap and gripped it tightly. She looked around the room, eyes wide. I could tell that she was looking for something I had never sought. That look scared me. After all the years we had been together, after all we had discussed, after all we had promised each other, here she was, my death having induced a kind of sudden amnesia. She was searching for signs and portents. Death had made her mad.

And I knew that I could give her what she sought, what

we all, in some secret place, wish could be true, even me. But just because we want something doesn't mean we should get it. We have to live this life as if this life is all that there is. We've *got* to. Good works are worthless if only done in expectation of a reward. Are people doing good work because they themselves are good? Or just because they're fleeing that eternal stick or chasing down that eternal carrot? Once a person believes in God, *all* of her actions are suspect. I had to resist the temptation to reach out to Shelley, to let her know I waited for her in the next life. I had to keep her pure.

"Don't be ridiculous," came a voice at my ear. I turned quickly, but there was no one there.

"Go ahead," continued the voice. "Get on with it. Stop wasting her time. Stop wasting *your* time. You know what you're supposed to do. Reach out to her!"

I spun again, but still could not find a speaker.

"Who's there?" I said.

"You know who's there, Seth," said the voice. "I shouldn't have to tell you. You've denied me all your life, but this time you *know*. You can feel it."

"Are you're telling me that you're...God?"

"Of course, I'm God. Accept it, Seth. You were wrong. It was one thing for you to deny me before. But now? Faced with this? Don't be so stubborn. Reach out to your wife. Wrap up those loose ends of your life. Say the things you wish you'd said before. That's the reason you're still here. Until you take care of those tasks, you won't be able to move on. You think that just because you're dead your work is done on this Earth? It's only just beginning."

I hesitated for a moment, then blurted out the only answer I could possibly give.

"No."

"You'd say no to God?"

"Why should I stop now?"

"It won't be so hard, Seth. All you have to do is exactly what you did in life. Just talk to her. She'll hear you eventually. They always do."

I looked at Shelley, who sat extremely still while glancing nervously around the room, peering into its recesses for... what? I could tell that my actions had brought her no comfort.

"I can't. Don't you get it? Even if she were to hear me, it would be all wrong. So it turns out there's a God after all. So I was wrong my entire life. So what? That doesn't change anything. Those who believe, don't you see, they have to believe on faith. If I were to reach out, and if that caused Shelley to suddenly believe, it would be an ethical disaster, because then it won't be on faith alone."

"I insist. It's not just about her. It's about you as well. There's a journey you have to complete."

"Insist all you want," I said. "My answer will still be no. I love my wife too much to put her in that kind of position."

God sighed. It felt like a light breeze on the back of my neck.

"So don't worry about talking to her just yet," said God. "All you have to do is keep watching her. That alone will change your mind. It always does."

Then God fell silent, and left me to be alone with my wife as she mourned.

And so I watched. What else was there to do with an afterlife?

She stood and set the bible on the kitchen table once more, then took a final drag of her cigarette and snubbed it out.

I followed her as she went off to our bedroom to sleep. Or rather, to try to sleep. She tossed and turned fitfully, always staying on her side of the bed. I wondered how long it would be before where I had slept would no longer be a forbidden zone. Occasionally, she would open her eyes and look to where I should have been, and her eyes would well with tears, not knowing I was still there. I could stop them, I knew, but there were worse things than tears.

I was grateful for those glimpses of her, even in her sadness, even knowing I would do nothing to take that sadness away. But still, studying her while she was unaware made me uncomfortable. It made me feel like a voyeur. It seemed wrong for me to be able to watch her without her knowledge, to share moments she assumed were private. But as the hours went by, I grew in touch with a deeper distress. There was a disturbing cognitive dissonance just to see her at all without seeing me there as well. For one of us to exist without the other…was that even possible? It had to violate some constant law of nature. I had never seen her without me before, not since those first few final lonely moments, when I'd caught sight of her across the length of a living room at a party to which we'd both been independently invited, a party from which we went home together and after which we were apart no more. So it felt unnatural to see her like that, for once attached we were never supposed to be apart again.

When I'd still lived, we'd even fantasized from time to time about how we were going to die. It was always going to be as a team, snuffed out in the same instant in some accident which would claim us both, and neither would thereafter have to be alone. A house fire. A plane crash. Brought down by a lion during an African safari. But not like this. Being separated by death was something we'd never even considered.

Abandoning the bed, Shelley wandered the house. She stumbled from time to time as she walked, not from the darkness, but as if our home had suddenly become an unfamiliar place. In the kitchen, she opened and closed cabinets and the refrigerator door repeatedly, looking for something which could silence her hunger, and finding nothing. Finally, she slid to the floor with her back against one wall and sobbed into her hands.

"You have to eat, Shelley," I whispered, without thinking. She reached for a dish towel and dried her eyes, then rose and returned to the refrigerator, its light showing the weariness in her face. When this time she pulled out a bag of carrots and began to eat, I knew that I'd made a mistake in speaking. I was determined to whisper no more. But could I be strong enough?

In the den, she pulled down one of our many photo albums from a shelf. She sat in the large leather loveseat we used to share—once more staying away from the side which had been mine—and began to slowly turn its pages. I slipped in beside her, watching as her fingers traced my face. We'd had so many good times together over the years and around the world. There we were surrounded by penguins in Antarctica, shadowed by the Great Pyramid in Giza. It should never have ended. She lifted the album and pressed her cheek against mine.

"Now would be the proper time to say something," said God, reappearing to torment me. "There's nothing wrong with that. You can deliver comfort to her, Seth."

Yes, I could. But I wasn't going to speak. Not to my wife. And not even to God. Not in that place. Not when there was a chance that Shelley could overhear it. So I rose from the loveseat and left our home. I'd had enough of this torture at the hands of God. There was no point in staying. Nothing was going to change my mind. I hurried down the street determined never to return to my house or to Shelley, my magnificent Shelley, again.

Unfortunately, that didn't mean that God would not follow.

"You can't walk away from her," said God. "You have to get back there. There are still things you have to say to her."

"You send messages your way," I said, picking up my pace, even though I knew it would do little good. "And I'll send messages mine."

"Where do you think you're going?" said God. "Your story's not over. There's no escape from it. Not yet."

"I didn't listen to you in life and I don't plan on listening to you in death," I cried, dashing into the street, running for the other side even though I knew I could never run fast enough to escape God.

"That's your wife back there," God said softly. "The woman you say you love. Why don't you go ahead and act as if you love her."

"Yes, she's the woman I love," I shouted. I stopped in the middle of the street and waved my fists at the sky, not caring as cars sped through me. "The woman I swore to be with 'until death us do part.' Well, I *am* dead! We've *been* parted! And *you're* the one who parted us."

"It's naïve of you to think—"

"My wife deserves better than magic," I said, interrupting God, and not giving a damn. "Let her believe in what is real. Not omens. Not portents. Not miracles. Let her believe what she's going to believe because *she* wants to believe it, not because of the threat of punishments or rewards. Leave her alone. Leave *us* alone."

"So where are you going?"

"I have no idea," I said, continuing to the other side of the street and hurrying away from my home. "I just know I had to get out of there. It was too painful to see her like that. If I stayed any longer I don't know what I would have done."

"*I* know what you would have done. You would have relented. You would have made the choice to ease her pain. You would have done the things you needed to do so that you could fully leave this world and continue on to the next."

"You're right. Which is why I'm heading the other way. Because I'm not as selfish as you. Which is why all I know about the place I'm heading is that it's in the opposite direction."

"Why do you hate me so?"

"I don't hate you. And I don't hate Santa Claus or the Easter Bunny or the Tooth Fairy either. It's just that I don't find you necessary."

A burst of wind rose up almost strong enough to knock me down, as God snorted.

"That's it!" he said, more loudly than he had spoken before. "I've had enough! Do you really think I'm not necessary? If that's the way you choose your world to be, then that's the way it shall be. Omens? Gone! Miracles? Banished! You want your world to be free of my presence? Then that's the world that's yours. Enjoy."

I stopped walking then, and stared at the heavens. I had no idea why I was looking there, when his voice always came from right beside me. But the habit of thinking of God as *somewhere up there* was that ingrained, even in me.

"No tricks?" I asked.

"I'm no trickster, Seth. You must be thinking of my competition. I promise you. You're on your own now. And your wife is on her own now, too. She'll see no signs that there's another world."

"I don't believe you," I said. "You could never keep your hands off of us. I've read your bible. You love to meddle too much."

The only response was silence. God's words no longer rustled the hairs at the back of my neck.

"God?" I said, first quietly, and then in a shout. "God!"

I laughed, and quickly spun around and started back to my wife.

By the time I returned home, I found Shelley in rooms that were difficult to recognize. It was as if I had been gone for months. We'd always kept a neat home together, no clutter, no mess, having been frightened into tidiness by our family histories, but suddenly our possessions were scattered everywhere. Pages of photos had been torn from our albums and now carpeted the floors. My clothing was draped haphazardly on the furniture. Every closet and cabinet had been opened and the contents mounded on the floor in front of their doors. Shelley paced the rooms, muttering to herself while kicking up whatever was in her path. I ran up behind her and kept pace with her as she roamed, but even though the gap between us was small, I still couldn't decipher what she was saying.

"It will be all right, Shelley," I thought to myself, keeping my lips sealed as I followed her along her ragged path, not trusting that God would keep his word and let me keep my words to myself. "Soon you'll forget me. Soon it won't hurt so much. I promise. I've seen it happen."

She dropped to her knees, her eyes frantic, and pawed through the photos that detailed our history. She whimpered as she found what she'd been looking for, and lifted an image of us side by side on the Galapagos Islands, walking through a crowd of sea lions. She spoke again, and this time I could understand her. This time, I could tell that she was murmuring my name.

She leapt up so quickly that I couldn't get out of the way, and walked through me to the bathroom, the photo tucked under one arm. Once there, she peered down into the sink, filled with the contents of the cabinets she had already opened. Laughing, she sunk her hands into the sea of containers and pulled out a medicine bottle I recognized.

"Oh, no," I whispered, realizing where Shelley's thoughts were straying. "Not that."

She shook the bottle. There were enough pills for what she intended to do. More than enough.

"I'm here, Shelley," I said into her ear as I bent over her. I couldn't let her kill herself. I tried to hug her, making a circle of my arms and willing myself to become solid enough so that she could feel my presence, but my embrace passed through empty air. Tears ran down my face and dripped off my chin only to pass through Shelley as well. "I'm here, Shelley. I'm still here."

As she uncapped the bottle and downed its contents, I pleaded with God, alternating in calling out his name and my wife's. But God did not answer.

"I get it now, you bastard," I shouted. "I have to tell her there's no need to mourn or grieve. I have to tell her that there's still hope that we'll someday be together. So let me do that. Let my voice be heard."

My wife dropped the bottle on the bathroom floor and returned to wandering our house, but her careful steps turned to staggering. My pleading grew beyond words, transformed into a garbled scream of anguish, but there was no answer. God had abandoned me. Or I had evicted God. It no longer mattered which.

Shelley stumbled to the couch and sat, sweeping away the pillows. She called my name repeatedly, and each time she spoke, the words sounded more slurred. I tried to cradle her head in my hands, to get her to her feet, but it was as if I wasn't there. Then she slid sideways, laying down, her eyelids fluttering.

"Where are you now, God?" I asked. "Punish me, but don't punish her."

I knelt beside the couch, sobbing, and could do nothing as her breathing slowed and her eyes closed. For one horrible instant, her breathing stopped completely, but then she opened her eyes.

"Seth?" she said, my name intelligible in her mouth once more, and as I looked down at her, I could see that she could at last see *me*.

"I'm here. Shelley. I've always been here."

She sprung up to hug me in a stranglehold. I was no longer like a mist to her. I could see over one of her shoulders another Shelley still lying there on the couch.

"You killed yourself for me," I said.

"I didn't want to live without you," she said. She stood, pulling free from our hug and gazing at me at arm's length. "I thought it was better to die with you. But I had no idea that death could be like this."

She leaned in close again and smiled.

"So tell me again about there being no afterlife?" she said.

"You shouldn't have done that, Shelley," said God, suddenly reappearing at a moment I couldn't have cared about him less.

"Who's that?" Shelley asked, tilting her head.

I took her hand and led her out of our house, led her out into a world that was once more ours.

"It doesn't matter," I said. "It doesn't matter at all."

IN A STRANGE CITY LYING ALONE

The longer I can remain quiet, the longer I can remain still, the longer it will take for them to find me, and the happier they will be.

Well...happier probably isn't the best word. Are any of us ever going to be happy again?

Maybe not.

But when they find me, they'll feel relief at least, won't they? That's still possible, isn't it? I have to believe relief, that sigh of the soul, for those working at this nightmarish job, those trapped in this terrifying time, those who volunteered to be in this sad, sad place, can be as welcome as joy.

Relief can be hope.

These men and women, their spirits shattered, their city ash and ruins, used to the more human-sized battles of putting out fires or prying accident victims from crushed cars, are struggling to beat back the despair brought on by this unimaginable catastrophe. They need some glimmer of hope in order to go on.

I know I certainly do.

If I can help them grab hold of it, maybe I'll find there's

a little bit of that hope left over for me, too.

And so I don't move. And I wait.

But you know something? As I wait, I don't hear them getting any closer.

Yet I can hear…something. Muffled voices I can't quite make out. But it's not them.

This not moving, it turns out to be easier than I thought it would be. I honestly don't think I could move much anyway, even if I wanted to.

I can't seem to feel my legs anymore.

Not that I'm complaining. That's how I wanted it. That's the way it needed to be. Unless I'm trapped, really truly trapped, unless they can feel they've rescued me, well, where's the hope in that?

Besides, here in the darkness, I feel close to my parents in a way I haven't for years. From time to time I shut my eyes and try to imagine them both. (Though do I really need to shut my eyes? The darkness down here is so complete there's little difference between eyes open and eyes closed.) Mom and Dad were planted down in darkness, too, not so long ago, and not so very far from me.

Only it wasn't by choice.

Once, they were hundreds of feet above me, side by side in that tiny office of theirs, buying and selling, and seemingly never the same thing twice, measuring out their days in margins so thin they had little left over for themselves in either time or money. How they didn't go crazy I'll never know.

They worked together that way for years, held aloft by concrete and steel and the dream of a city they thought would keep thrusting up forever and would never be knocked down. I squint, trying to see them as they were, high above my head, but it's dizzying to try, their past as distant as birds in the sky.

But unlike birds, they fell.

They fell when the city fell.

A city I'd left behind.

I'd loved it once, this city. I loved them, too. When did it change? When did their embrace become less comforting than claustrophobic? I can't remember. All I know is that, as if a switch had been flicked, the city had suddenly become more prison than playground, and I felt as if I was both jailer and jailed. I no longer knew who I was any longer apart from them or it.

So I ran. I got out while I still could, before I became like my parents. But even after I was gone, I could still hear their voices in my head, and hear the sounds of taxis late at night on rain-swept streets as well. You live with a person so long, you live with a thing, and it gets inside you. It's as if I'd taken a piece of them with me. But though they kept haunting me in that way, though the city's tug was inescapable, I never thought I'd return.

But then someone attacked them, attacked it, and I had to come back.

At first, I spent my days climbing through the rubble, as we all did, part of an endless human chain clearing away the debris, and spent my nights collapsed on cots at a nearby hospital. I thought I could find my parents, I really did. But I soon realized, as so many of us were forced to do, that for the most part, that belief was a delusion.

I worked as many hours a day as they would permit and my body would allow. I got a little loopy from exhaustion, I think. From time to time, I thought I could hear them, Dad worrying about me, insisting in that endless annoying loop of his that everything would go wrong, Mom assuring me that all would be right. But though I felt their presence beneath my feet, we never found them. According to the news, from dust they came, and to dust they had returned.

Those few we did find were beyond talking, either dead or so battered in brain and body they were barely alive.

But I never stopped looking.

I wasn't the only one. I was surrounded by seekers. I felt for them, with their crumpled and tear-streaked faces. But strangely, the ones I felt for the most were the rescue dogs. They were the only ones of us who didn't choose to be here. They didn't feel called. They were brought here.

The trainers felt the same way about them that I did. They knew that their animals couldn't handle the endless disappointment and despair. So you know what they did to lift the spirits of the poor things? They had us hide, so we could pretend to be found.

And the dogs, the dogs would be so happy! Their eyes would be bright again, and they'd lick our faces, and...

And I thought...

If I could bring that joy to a dog, even in the midst of this Hell, then why not a person?

Wait. What was that?

Did you hear it?

Have my rescuers figured out what I've done? Are they any closer to finding me? I don't think so, but...there are those voices...

I can hear them now, this time I really think I can, Dad, calling from far off, asking me how I could have been so thoughtless as to do what I did, and my mother, shushing him and telling me not to worry. I smile at their familiar banter. How could I have felt that oppressive? How could I have run from them? I'd give anything to see their faces again.

No...it's not them. What am I thinking? I've just been down here alone for too long. But it's not my rescuers either.

What's keeping them? I want to see their faces when they set me free. I need to see their faces.

That's why it had to seem real, you see. That's why it had to *be* real. People, especially not trained emergency workers, can't be tricked the same way the dogs can.

And so as it grew dark, I slipped away. It wasn't that hard. The acres seem endless here, and even with all those wanting to help, there aren't enough people to be everywhere at once. I wriggled down into the rubble, crawling as if through a maze, hearing the concrete and steel shift around me...

I never expected the girder to slide and pin me where I lay. But they had to have heard it as it happened, right? I was actually a little pleased and proud, because surely, that would make them believe.

And so I waited.

And I wait still.

Oh, I can imagine their faces when they find me, when they lift that final piece of debris and discover both me and the strength to go on.

We could all use the strength to go on.

I don't know that I have the strength to go on.

What's that? I do?

Who said that? I thought I heard somebody say that.

But no one is there.

Am I making sense? I don't think so. I think I've become delirious. I let myself get too hungry and thirsty, and I no longer know how many days I've been down here.

Yes, Father, I know. I'm impulsive, and I keep doing these sorts of things over and over, jumping in before I check how deep the water is. And no, Mother, I won't cry. I know you'll make sure I'm safe. You always do.

No.

Always *did*.

I should have planned better for this. I didn't really have

a plan, not before, when I left this city, and not now, that I've returned.

I feel in my heart a person should choose a place, shouldn't they, and not be chosen by it? If you end up where you started, but you never moved from the spot where you were born, that's not choice, that's inertia. That's why I really went away, I guess. But now I'm back. And I didn't come back. I was *called* back. So after all those years, all that running, it's still not of my choosing either. I still don't *know*. Isn't that silly?

I feel hands on me, and when I open my eyes, even though I'm still covered by the rubble I pulled down upon myself, I can make out the forms of my rescuers. After all this time, my eyes have gotten used to the darkness, I guess, and I can see their outlines better.

It's a man. And a woman. And they lift me up to the surface as if no concrete and steel bars are in the way.

It is only when the sun hits me and I try to make out the change I've made upon their faces, which is what all this was for, that I see my two rescuers were…my mother and my father.

I tilt my head. No one else seems to be paying any attention to us as they go about their business seeking signs of life. And I so much wanted to see the relief on their faces. I want to shout, "Over here! I'm over here!" But when I look back to my parents, there is relief on their faces.

And I imagine that there is relief on mine.

My mother takes my right hand, my father takes my left, and they lift me to my feet. I no longer feel dizzy. I no longer feel thirsty. I no longer feel as if I need to look any further for the place I am meant to be.

No one disturbs us as we leave this place of pain and sorrow, leave to return back to my city.

Back to my city forever.

BECOMING INVISIBLE,

BECOMING SEEN

As Martin stood over Adrianna, her cold body entirely hidden from him by nothing more than a thin sheet which he imagined had previously covered other bodies equally as cold, he pushed away the image of those countless dead strangers and thought—

For years, I've lied to my family. I've lied to my friends. I've lied to Adrianna. And most of all, worst of all, I've lied to myself.

It's time I stopped lying.

Slowly, with trembling hands, he folded back the sheet to reveal her face, and only her face. He had stared at her longingly more times that he could ever count, but not one of those instances had been accompanied by such a sense of freedom. Because for once, he had no fear she would open those beautiful eyes to see him, really see *him*.

He had become invisible.

Hating that it needed to be this way, but surrendered to the fact that this was the way it needed to be, he lowered his face to hers and kissed those blue cheeks, which felt cool, comfortably cool, against his lips.

At last, he thought. *At last I get to find out who I really am.*

MARTIN WAS surprised at how little it bothered him when the rear door of the police car slammed. Even though he'd ended up locked in there by choice, he'd expected his first time in such a vehicle would be anxiety-producing. Instead, it was only the touch of that hand to his scalp, pushing him gently down to ensure he didn't bang his head, that raised his blood pressure. Martin didn't much like being touched unexpectedly, not even when that touch came from an old friend.

"Sorry," said Joe, pulling his hand back after Martin winced under his cupped fingers. "Habit."

Joe walked around the rear of the car and slid behind the wheel. Then, with a nod to Martin and a smile at Randy, his partner, he drove away from the station.

"Wish I could have let you ride up front," said Joe.

"No problem," said Martin. And it wasn't.

The partition sealing him in the back seat didn't disturb him at all. In fact, he believed it would make the night much easier. He could set aside his usual struggle to keep up a front. The unceasing tension between his inner life and the mask he allowed others to see was exhausting. It would be much better for Martin's plan if his friend could only catch glimpses of him in the rearview mirror. At that remove, perhaps Martin could continue passing for normal. *Objects in the mirror are more normal than they appear*, he thought, and suppressed a laugh.

He'd known Joe since they were kids growing up on the same block, but had lost touch. It was Martin's fault, of course. He'd made a conscious decision to keep his distance, to not let others get too close. It was the only survival skill that made sense, once he realized his desires were so different from those of others.

So when Joe's name popped up online as a suggested friend, Martin was prepared to ignore him as he'd ignored all the others. Just as he was about to mouse-click Joe into invisibility, though, he noted that his old friend had become a police officer, something he'd never have predicted, and Martin suddenly saw a way free from the prison he'd constructed around himself. Martin realized that if he tread carefully, Joe could end up being useful.

Not in the way Martin allowed Joe to believe he'd be useful, of course.

The serendipity led to some messaging, a couple of meet-ups for beer—filled with the kind of small talk at which Martin had always been miserable—and now this outing, which he'd been able to make Joe think was his idea, a ride-along so he could see what daily life was like for a cop. (At least, that's what Martin had let on was its intended purpose.)

"Thanks for doing this," said Martin, feeling something had to be said as they drove through the night.

"No problem," said Joe. "It's nice to have some company."

"Hey, what am I?" said his partner.

"Tell me a story I haven't heard a thousand times before, Randy, and then we'll talk." After a few silent moments, Joe tilted his head back toward Martin. "Hope you get what you want out of this. Things have been quiet lately."

Martin shrugged. What other options did he have to capture his goal? And so he tried to remain hopeful, even as Joe's predicted quiet continued. The two men had to stop to take a report from sobbing parents about their runaway.

They shuttled a homeless man to a shelter. (Martin squeezed to the opposite end of the squad car for that, hoping the man wouldn't be insulted, wouldn't think it had anything to do with his homelessness. He'd have done that to avoid contact with any stranger, but didn't know of any way to say that without revealing too much.) They checked on a couple of burglar alarms which had gone off, but there ended up being no signs of break-ins.

The shift was almost over when a call came in that turned out to be the one Martin was hoping for, yet dreading at the same time.

When Joe parked the car at the mouth of an alley, Martin could see on the ground, not so very far inside, a woman. He instinctively reached for the door handle that wasn't there.

"This one you're going to have to stay in the car for," said Joe.

Martin stared as the two men walked deeper down the alley, wishing he could follow. He needed to see more, desperately wanted to be beside them as they stood above what he refused to call the corpse, because that would change everything.

The body.

As they circled her, Martin could glimpse through their legs that when she'd lived, she had been young, perhaps in her early twenties, though at that distance he could not be entirely sure. She was fully clothed, her blouse only slightly torn, her tight jeans undisturbed, which meant he could make out none of her skin other than the one hand flung in his direction and, because her head was twisted toward the depths of the alley, that soft spot on the back of her neck.

From what little he knew of how crimes like these turned out—knowledge gained from TV, sure, but for some reason he trusted TV when it came to such things—this appeared to be a case of violence, not sex. He knew those two often overlapped, but they didn't seem to have done so now, and this relieved Martin, because he didn't want to think of others having had her in that way. And thankfully, there was no blood, for which he was grateful. Martin didn't need blood, never imagined blood when he allowed his fantasies free rein.

He felt strangely cheated that the woman's unknown assailant (who would likely remain forever unknown based on what Joe had let on about the statistics of police work) hadn't allowed his victim to fall facing the street. He wanted to look in her eyes, to see the nothingness there. He wanted to rub the back of a hand across one still and cooling cheek. He wanted to place an ear against her lips and hear…silence. He was surprised by how many things he wanted now that he was at last in the presence of death. Most of all, he wanted to have the things he wanted so they'd be merely wants no more.

His breath, coming more quickly than usual, had frosted the glass of the window, and he had to swipe at it with a sleeve so he could keep her in his sights. It was her fault he had to do that.

No. No, it wasn't her. He knew that. It was him. He had always known that. It was never about them.

As he devoured whatever it was of her he could see, he found himself squirming. Raw reality was having as much of an effect on him as his unsupported imagination previously had. He needed to adjust a sudden erection to make himself more comfortable, surprised he needed to, yet not surprised at all. What he'd feared about himself, what he'd recognized in himself, was true. He may have had doubts, but his body had none. Bodies did not lie.

Joe returned to the squad car and popped open the rear door. It wasn't until the cool air hit Martin that he realized how overheated he'd become. There was now nothing between Martin and the object of his desire save space and time.

"Looks like whatever happened here is long over," said Joe. "So it's probably safe for you to get a little closer if you want your first look at a dead body. Just be careful where you step."

"No," said Martin, a little too quickly perhaps, since his supposed curiosity was the reason he'd given for the ride-along. He'd love to gaze closely upon a dead woman for the first time. But to do so while others watched? That would be far too personal an act. Besides, at that moment, it would also be embarrassing to stand. What would be revealed about Martin's nature would surely revolt Joe. How could he possibly explain it? Martin's reaction just wasn't normal.

But since when had Martin ever been normal? He'd let Adrianna see that part of himself, slowly, and over time, but Joe? Never.

"I'm OK where I am," Martin added. "I don't think I'm ready to see someone like that after all. But thanks, Joe, really. Thanks."

"No problem."

Joe slammed the door, locking Martin away once more with his lies and his desires and his unbearable sense of urgency.

Maybe I should be locked away, he thought, unable to take his eyes away from the dead woman, unable to stop thinking of what he wished he could do to her while she lay in repose. *But maybe…maybe there's another way.*

MARTIN SLID his lips across Adrianna's cheek to press them against hers, which did not press back, did not push away whatever part of himself called to her in this state. He turned his head to listen for the exhalation which, if heard, would tell him…what? That she might speak, tell him to stop, remind him that his desires were disgusting? He was never entirely sure of the nature of what he feared. His needs were beyond reason. He only knew that there was a meaning to be found in silence, and in Adrianna's absence was the only place he could find his own presence.

He pulled the sheet further down her body, revealing her pale form, naked, unmoving. He'd seen her unclothed before, slept beside her naked body, had tried, had failed, to do more than sleep. He'd done that for her, for them both, more than once, but there was something about her, about any woman alive, from which he inevitably recoiled. He couldn't control it. (He didn't know at this stage in his life if he'd choose to control it even if he could.) But seeing her this way, seeing her now…this was different.

When he touched her cold hip, there was no reaction from her. She didn't smile, didn't open her eyes to pin him with her gaze, to possibly judge him. Oh, he knew that consciously judging him was a thing she would never do, she'd told him that endlessly, but inside Martin, beyond and beneath choice, there was always that fear. That fear of being seen. That fear of being recognized. But no one would see what they were doing here together, him moving, her unmoving, in this room. No one could stop what he was driven to do next.

Adrianna was…perfect. And, if he was being honest with himself (which he had moments before promised to be, sworn to be), she always had been. Until today, though, that perfection had been hidden behind a veil (or so he told himself), suspected but never fully seen.

But now...

He didn't take the time to undress, even though when he imagined this, when the scenario he thought would never occur played out in his mind, he'd always seen them both as naked. But here in the actuality, his erection was too insistent, painful even, for him to pause to strip down. He no longer felt quite himself, or maybe he was now finally fully himself, and so he hurriedly unzipped and climbed atop the table. He reached for the lubricant he'd left nearby, because he'd expected Adrianna would be beyond providing any of her own (he'd once read that nails grew after death, but surely *that* response did not continue), and then, almost faster than thought, he was inside her at last.

"Oh, Adrianna," he sighed as he thrust, and thrust again, feeling complete, finally complete, after all his lonely years. All those years of unfulfilled longing. All those years of disappointing himself and others. All those years of feeling broken somehow. They were exorcised from his reality, gone as if they'd never existed. For how could anything that felt so right, so real, so true, ever be wrong?

With Adrianna unmoving in his arms, Martin suddenly became certain that the missteps in his life before then were not the false paths he'd thought they were, that each had a purpose which had steered him straight to this. The things he'd thought were failures which had caused him to change schools, change jobs, change cities, change friends, his frustrating inability with all the other potential partners, all of it had led here, and his perceived mistakes had not been mistakes, but course corrections on the road to his eventual union with Adrianna.

The fullness of emotion brought on by this perception overwhelmed him, and as he continued his rhythmic movements, he did not know how long he could last. And after a lifetime of waiting, he wanted the moment to last forever. He deserved that.

But then—

Adrianna twitched, and the pretense was ended.

Martin tried fruitlessly to ignore her signs of life, but could not, and his desire instantly fled. Instead of swimming toward her, he found himself flailing to get away. He deflated, both physically and metaphorically, and rolled off her, suddenly no longer in the morgue they inhabited together in his mind, but back in his bedroom, the scene of so many previous catastrophes. He began crying, and when she touched him, he shrugged her hand from his shoulder.

"I should have known," he said between sobs, sliding to the floor beside the bed. "I was a fool to think that this would ever work."

"You're no fool," said Adrianna, sitting up and pulling the sheet around her shoulders, still frigid from the ice bath which had cooled her down for the attempted masquerade. "You know me better than that. Would I be with a fool? There's so much more to us than this. Next time we try, we'll get this right. I can do this for you. Let me do this for you."

"No," he said, swiping a sleeve across his face. "It's impossible. No one is that good an actor. Not even you."

"You've been that good an actor," she said. "You've been that good an actor your whole life. But you don't have to act with me. You know that, right?"

He gazed up at Adrianna and smiled weakly.

"You're a good friend," he said.

"I'm much more than that," she said. "Do you know how difficult it is not to react when you touch me? Maybe it would be easier for someone who didn't feel about you the way I do, but...I didn't play along with this just out of friendship."

"I know," he said. "And I...I love you, too. Since that

first day I heard you humming to yourself over the cubicle wall, and joined in, I sensed you were different from the others. When we stood and looked at each other, I knew, I guess, that there could be something more. And then there *was* something more. But…"

"But?" she said, sliding off the bed to settle down beside him.

"But I don't think your love, my love, any love can be enough. If love could have fixed me, I'd have been fixed a long time ago."

"But we can keep trying, can't we? I felt you inside me. That wasn't a lie. We can figure this out. We *can*."

He took her hand, with its fingers that gripped to hold his hand tight, and because he'd come to care for her as he'd cared for no other, made an effort not to pull away. He'd never wanted to hurt her. He never wanted to hurt anyone. So he held her and tried to think of what to say next. But nothing came, and he gently placed her hand into her lap.

"I don't know," he said. "I just don't know."

"You're scared," she said. "I get that. But I'm not going anywhere."

Which was, he realized, exactly what scared him the most.

"I COULD LOSE my job for this," said Joe as he unlocked the door to the morgue. He looked up and down the empty hallway, then waved Martin in. "If the video cameras weren't busted, I wouldn't even think of it."

"I know," said Martin, trying his best to sound sympathetic, but not really caring, even though he knew he should. Because what would be learned that night inside the brightly lit room with its metal tables and niche-lined walls was more important than any job, any friendship. This was the night he'd discover whether he could be made whole, and nothing else mattered. "I appreciate it. I do."

"You really sure you'll be able to sleep in here?" said Joe as he looked around and shook his head. "There's no way I could. The dead don't bother me out there, but in here...I don't know, there's something that feels wrong about it."

"I can only try," said Martin, cradling a duffle bag that contained a blanket and...other things. "We'll know one way or the other by morning."

Yes, thought Martin. *We'll know.*

What he would know, and what Joe thought would be known, were two different things. He'd shared with his friend a traumatic incident from childhood, an incident which had never really happened, but which he'd made sure was rich with the ring of truth.

How he'd been trapped in an elevator with one of his aunts, how that had caused her to have a heart attack, and how he'd been stuck in there with her body for hours.

How he'd had nightmares ever since, and great difficulty in getting a good night's sleep. How that had affected his entire life, and how therapy had availed him nothing. How the serendipity of his finding Joe again after all those years and learning his occupation made it occur to him that if only he could overcome that fear, the whole of his life might change.

Lies. All lies.

But Joe was his friend, or believed he was, at least, and so had accepted them. Or even if he hadn't fully accepted them, had been willing to go along with Martin's suggestion, which he'd done his best to make seem spontaneous.

And now they stood together in a morgue, the future having finally arrived.

"You sure you want to go ahead with this?" said Joe. "You sure your shrink's OK with the whole idea?"

"She's fine with it," said Martin. "Don't worry."

Martin wasn't seeing a psychiatrist, hadn't since he was a kid and his parents insisted he visit one because he'd seemed so withdrawn. What point would there be? He already knew what was wrong with him. Or what would eventually prove to be right.

He leaned on the door, desperate to close it, the nearness of his goal making casual conversation even more difficult. He didn't want to come across as too excited, but was appearing reserved even possible? Hopefully, Joe would think his change in demeanor was only a case of nerves.

"See you tomorrow," he said.

"That's what I'm hoping," said Joe. "I don't want there to be a reason for me to get any phone calls before then, understand?"

"Got it."

And then Martin was alone.

Well, not entirely alone. For behind each of the rectangular metal doors, stacked three high and the length of the room wide, were bodies which had once held souls. They'd lived lives which had sculpted their personalities onto their flesh, etching each moment of their existence onto malleable, ephemeral skin. They were gone, and yet, they were also not, because the evidence remained. Now all Martin had to do was use the signs of what had been left behind to make the right choice. Behind one of those doors was the woman which would either cure him, or prove him irrevocably broken.

He studied the doors with their labels listing names, ages, heights, weights, and causes of death. But that information was too little to delineate a life, and certainly not enough for him to decide. He had to see for himself. He had to judge. The one meant for him, for this moment, couldn't be just anybody. Or, he thought, any *body*. (This time he allowed himself a smile.) But there was no denying that it would have to be someone…special.

Stacy. He'd start with Stacy.

He wrapped trembling fingers around a door handle, wondering if he was truly ready. But even as he hesitated, he knew that whether he was up for this or not didn't matter. There was no other direction in which he could go. It was either this…or end it all. And end up on a slab himself. And that he was really not ready for.

He grimaced, swung open the door, and slid out Stacy's slab. She was a young woman, or had been a young woman anyway. Her dark hair pooled around her shoulders, and she was covered by a sheet pulled up to meet that hair. She'd be naked underneath, they'd all be naked, he knew, but he wasn't going to take advantage of the situation and peek. It didn't seem proper for him to see anything more than what this woman would have chosen to have him see during their first meeting in real life, had they ever met. His interest, however much it might have seemed that way when he'd tried in the past to explain it to others, was not prurient.

What he sought, the missing piece of his puzzle, would only be found above the neck. Only then, once the connection had been made, would he go further.

He studied Stacy's face, which even in repose, told him that she had not been happy. He could read that easily. Had she known that when she'd lived? Seeing her history sculpted there made him pause and wonder—what was his life imprinting on his own face even at that moment? What were others deciphering about his inner life when they looked in his direction?

He shrugged that thought away. This was definitely not the time for self-analysis. All that was important now was that he end up with someone who'd led a mostly happy life. He slid Stacy back where she would remain until her family, or some person who loved her, he hoped, claimed her, and slammed the heavy door shut. It echoed more loudly than he wished.

Next came Brianna, with red hair and a crooked grin which had survived even though she had not. She had died in her early 50s. Though she seemed serene, the writing on the card in her door tagged her as an apparent suicide. Yet there was nothing about her that indicated she had been distraught. Perhaps, thought Martin, that was because she had fully chosen her destiny, as he was attempting to choose his. He should have felt a connection with her, he knew, because he, too, had occasionally contemplated taking that way out. Instead, and to his surprise, he found himself judging her. Hypocritical of him, he knew. But he couldn't deny the emotion, and he wouldn't pretend otherwise. His time for pretense was over.

He looked at four more women, Alyssa, Christiana, Rafaella, Vanessa, rejecting each, surprised he could afford to be so choosy when finally afforded this opportunity, worrying that perhaps the one he needed was still out there, not yet ready to be brought to this place—before he found the one that seemed…perfect.

Was that a smile, a warm genuine smile, he saw on her lips, or was he just imagining it? He had enough self-awareness that he knew it could be either, but in the end, did it really matter? Her eyebrows were full, and even completely relaxed as she was, for no one is so relaxed as in death, one was slightly higher than the other, as if she was considering him with an almost quizzical expression. Her eyes were closed, and he let them remain that way. He'd heard that eyes were the windows to the soul. Whatever. There was no need for either of them to look out or in. He preferred those windows shut. Her earlobes, which he could tell had once held numerous piercings, now were as naked as the rest of her, and that those had been stripped from her made him sad, sadder, strangely, than the far more permanent fact of her death.

He pressed one palm against a cold cheek, and smiled. It fit perfectly, as if they had been designed for each other. She was his and he was hers. There was no point in him searching or delaying any longer. She was the one.

He struggled to squeeze down beside her on the narrow slab, but it wasn't quite wide enough for them both. He had to turn her onto one side so that she faced him, and then slide her over, so that they could both fit together there. She was so heavy, far heavier than she appeared, dead weight for the first time literal rather than merely metaphorical, but then, he'd never touched a dead person before, so he had nothing to compare it to other than the living he'd touched in life melded with his dreams and fantasies.

The rolling slab creaked beneath the two of them, and he worried for a moment that it wouldn't be able to hold them both, but it would have to, wouldn't it? After all, she was a small woman, and he was only slightly larger. Certainly many of the dead who passed through that room were not, and some surely even outweighed them combined. He decided he had to risk it, even as he knew he was long past deciding anything. What was to happen next was beyond choice.

He reached under the sheet to grasp her wrist and used it to fling her arm around his chest. She did not hug him once he placed it there, could not hug him, but though that arm did not move from where he set it, it did not make her embrace less real. It comforted him like a snug blanket. He held her tight, sheet still mostly between them, pressed his cheek against hers, listened to the beating of his own heart.

That he could hear no other beating sped his thrub-dubbing faster than he had ever known.

He whispered her name, learned just moments before from the index card on the door to her compartment, in her ear, filling the syllables with the love of a lifetime. He knew he was saying it for himself, that she could not hear him, but he imagined that she could. And it was far more exciting to imagine that she could than if she actually could.

He pulled the sheet entirely away, let it drop to the floor. He bent one of her knees, forcing it over his hip. It wasn't that easy, as she had stiffened, but then...so had he.

He didn't need to wait any longer. There was no need to postpone the inevitability with foreplay. He unzipped, and slid on a condom, so no evidence would be left behind. As crazed with passion as he was, he still had sense enough for that. The act of doing so, though, almost got him off all by itself, so intense was his excitement.

He forced his way in, apologizing as he did so, and even though he was hard, it hurt. But he didn't mind the pain, which only reinforced to him that this was really happening. He was happy it didn't hurt her, though, glad she was beyond knowing such things.

Once he entered her, it didn't take long. It couldn't. All it took was one thrust, then two, and he exploded. He bit into his forearm to muffle a scream. He tasted blood, his own blood, telling him that he was alive, and then, almost immediately, began to cry. Not, as he'd always thought he might when contemplating his reaction as this finally occurred, out of self-hatred, but out of happiness.

For the first time Martin could remember, he was truly happy.

MARTIN WAS THINKING of Stacy again, the woman who'd completed him in a way he'd never dared dream could happen, not really, when Adrianna startled him by snapping her fingers under his nose, bringing him back to the familiar coffee shop where they were in the middle of one of their lunch breaks. He had to take stock of where he was for a moment, almost as if he'd been woken groggily from a nap, needed to remind himself, *Oh, here I am.*

He'd been drifting away from Adrianna frequently, and not just her, but most everyone he knew, since the events of the weekend, submerging often into a kind of fugue state, drawn there by that impossibly deep connection he'd felt with another human being for the first time. He could tell she believed he was pulling away—not understanding that rather, he was being pulled—and so their time together this week had been strained, as she fought to prevent him from vanishing into himself.

"Sorry," he said. But he wasn't, not really. He'd much rather be lost in those memories at the moment than focussed on having lunch with Adrianna. Not something he would tell her, though. Just because he'd finally found what he'd been looking for didn't make it necessary to hurt her. She'd been good to him in a way no one ever had been before, seen something in him he did not see in himself. And certainly, none before her had either.

"What's going on?" she asked. She leaned across the table and spoke in a whisper. "Are you still thinking about…the other night? About us? We can try again, you know. We *should* try again. I've been practicing. You know. Holding my breath. Remaining still. Not moving a muscle. *Any* muscle. We can get this right. I know we can."

She appeared so vulnerable in her hope that he was touched, and he tried his best not to react. Not yet. There could be no right between them, he was sure of it, not now that his night in the morgue proved beyond a doubt that whatever Adrianna could deliver to him would be just a pallid imitation. He'd have to lie to her, now and forever, had spent a lifetime lying, but knowing the right lie was not an easy thing.

His recent lies were taking him into unfamiliar territory. Like the lies he'd had to tell Joe about what had happened, both in the morgue and after, how he'd felt he was approaching a breakthrough, lies both small and large that were necessary so that his friend would let him return for a repeat performance. (Because he'd have to return. He'd have to.) They were lies he couldn't even begin to share with Adrianna, because on learning them, she'd see how false they were. She knew him for what he was, which meant that upon the mention of a morgue, she'd know exactly what he was doing in that room. His prior openness would make it hard to hide now. He had a momentary regret that he'd opened his soul to her, even though that decision had given him great comfort at the time.

"Well?" she asked.

"No," he said, in a single syllable that trailed off, promising more to come. But he had no idea what that should be, and so sat there looking at her as she looked at him expecting an explanation it was not within his power to give.

"No what?" she said. "We can't stop now. We can figure it out. No one should have to continue living the way you do. You deserve for us to work it out. I know what it's like to need something you can never have. It's not good."

He wanted to tell her that she'd misinterpreted what he'd just said, that his no didn't mean they should stop trying, but rather that they should just...stop. He had found someone else. Some*thing* else. But he didn't want to hurt her by telling her that, especially not considering the unique nature of the person he'd found and the type he would find fulfillment with in the future. He'd dated before, had broken up with women before, but it was never due to a reason like this, and usually, he was broken up *with*, because they'd tire of what he could never fully give them. So he just let his "no" hang there for awhile, took another sip of his coffee, and tried to think of a way to say what needed to be said.

But before he could think of those right words, she reached across the table to touch his hand. He looked into her eyes, and what he saw there made him stop looking for those words. He thought, *I can't hurt this woman*. And so he instead decided to say things he did not believe.

"Sure, we'll try again," he said, and her smile brought him a surprising amount of happiness. "Of course. Just…not immediately. I need to get my head straight first. Let's wait a bit. Let's wait."

But even as he spoke, he was also wondering how quickly Joe would let him return to the morgue to do again what he'd done before.

———

STACY, the woman he'd made love to the previous week in the morgue—and yes, he thought of it as making love, even though he knew how ludicrous that would sound to anyone else—was gone. But then, of course she'd be gone. As he stood in the center of the room once more, scanning the wall of doors and the new names which had taken the place of the ones with which he was already familiar, he knew it was foolish that he'd thought, even briefly, she might have remained, knew that bodies cycled through the morgue quickly on the way to their final destinations, whether buried or scattered or even sent off to medical schools—but still, that twinge of disappointment was there. There would never be a second encounter, a chance for rediscovery, a deeper exploration. She was gone, and he would never see her again.

But there would be another. Many others, in fact, or else…what? He didn't know the alternative for sure. He only knew that having achieved what he'd desired, losing it would be worse than never having had it at all.

Martin had convinced Joe to let him spend a second night at the morgue with yet another fabulation, this time explaining how his first night visit had helped him, the way his nightmares had lessened in both frequency and intensity, the encouragement he'd received from his (non-existent) shrink, who (or so Martin claimed) had been happy with his progress and suggested he continue with the extremely unorthodox treatment. Martin had draped enough believable detail on his story that Joe had been convinced. Joe was a good friend.

At least one of them was.

Thinking of Joe, of their one-sided friendship, Martin flashed on Adrianna, and it occurred to him that though he had been a lousy friend to them both, he'd been especially deficient with her. But then, he always had been. He knew that.

Was this thing of his which had finally become a reality instead of a dream the impediment that had all along prevented any true closeness? Was that why Adrianna and all the women who had come before her were such better friends to him than he could ever find it in himself to be to them?

Maybe. Probably. But in the end, it didn't matter. It just *was*. And this was not the place to spend thinking about such things. He didn't have time to waste.

He was aware he'd been lucky the previous week, knew how much of a risk he'd taken, yet here he was taking another one. The locked door behind him wouldn't have stopped anyone who needed to deliver a new body. He understood that. And he got that if he was caught in the act —an act which he wasn't really sure how to name, because necrophilia sounded so cold, so clinical, so stripped of the love that he felt motivated him—being arrested would be the least of his worries. But he couldn't retreat from his plan now. It would be like willingly returning to a life in a cage. And he'd already had too many years of that life.

He slowly opened the first drawer, inside of which the card promised he'd find a woman named Trinity, and was filled with a combination of hope and dread, one strengthened by the success of his first experience. What if he found no one special this night? What if there was no one meant just for him waiting to be revealed? He needed more than a random compliant form. Whoever he chose had to be exactly that. Chosen. She had to have that certain slant of chin, earlobes with just the right amount of fleshiness, those lashes resilient under his thumbs.

She had to be like…like Adrianna.

Which poor Trinity was definitely not. She appeared starved and beaten, and seemingly went out of this world with a struggle. She made him realize how lucky he'd been the first night that he'd been able find someone not showing signs of a violent end. That wasn't usually how people ended up here. No, it couldn't be this one.

He pushed the first drawer shut, then quickly caught it before it clanged too loudly. His desire was clearly making him careless. He hurriedly move to the next niche.

No, not Alyssa either, with the large bruise on her left cheek. (*Who could do that to a woman?* he thought, knowing all the while that some might ask the same question about him.) Nor Jasmine with a gunshot wound just under one breast. Not even Tiffany, for whom the cause of death wasn't quite so evident, but whose teeth forced her lips into a frown.

He considered and rejected each one with less deliberation than he had the last time. Because, he guessed, having experienced Stacy, he knew there was someone out there waiting for him.

And then…there she was. Mia.

He only had to look at her for an instant to know that. How had she died? He did not care. It did not matter. Seeing her stretched out before him brought back memories of that song his father had sung to his mother about seeing a stranger across a crowded room…though if Martin had seen this stranger across a crowded room when she'd been alive, there would have been none of the magic he felt at this moment.

Tears rolled down his face from the richness of his emotions, and one dropped from his cheek and onto hers. He kissed the spot where it had fallen, then climbed on top of her and gazed down into that calm face, staring lovingly at the lids of those closed eyes which would never open, never cry again. Another tear fell, giving her the appearance of being as happy as he was. He flattened himself upon her, stroking her close-cropped hair, tucking his chin into one side of her neck, whispering something into her unhearing ear which surprised him even as it came.

He didn't remember having said "I love you" before and having meant it. Had he said it to Adrianna? He wasn't sure. (But how could he not be sure? He should be sure.) He thought he had, but the love he shared with Adrianna was a love which could never be fulfilled, never be carried through to completion, not like what he had with Mia. He just wasn't made that way.

He slipped his left hand under her back and used it to balance himself as he moved his right down her side to one hip. His fingers tingled as they slid along her smooth and slightly clammy skin. He couldn't help but laugh as giddiness overtook him. He moved his free hand to his waist, and was about to shift his weight so he could unzip when he felt against his stomach...

What?

There rose a strange kind of (at first) nearly imperceptible vibration, one he'd never known a body to make, which grew into a trembling in her gut, then exploded into a rumbling. How was a body even capable of that? He jerked slightly back at first, but when the movement subsided, he decided to attribute it to nothing more than trapped gasses moving through her recently deceased body, gasses set free by his act of laying upon her.

He'd heard of such things, so when the sounds and movements began again, he assumed this was an inevitable byproduct of the path on which he was now walking. He smiled lovingly and waited for her movements to pass. But this time, they did not.

Then she turned her head toward his cheek so swiftly and urgently that his own head was shoved aside, and he screamed, pulling back from where he'd been nuzzling her. He fell off her and off the slab onto the hard floor and looked up in horror as the woman, seemingly dazed, sat up, her movements jerky. For a moment, Martin, puzzled, uncomprehending, imagined this was one of those cases he'd heard about in which a coroner misdiagnosed as dead a person who was not, and fear spiked in him that she would report what he had been doing, a fear replacing that which he'd been feeling from her abrupt reanimation alone. But then Mia's eyes snapped open, and she looked at him steadily, unblinkingly, and he knew...not knowing how he knew...that she was hungry.

Her jaw began to chatter, clacking open and shut so fast

and with such force that a tooth flew from her mouth to bounce on the linoleum. Her arms then rose and reached out for him, causing her to fall from the slab, collapsing forward in a jumble of clumsy limbs. As Martin skittered backwards across the floor, he could tell to his horror—she wanted him. And not at all in the way in which he'd wanted her.

He got up to his feet far more quickly than her stiffened body allowed. She had trouble rising, and once upright, she staggered back against the slab, which gave him time for a frantic scan of the room. He needed a weapon, but saw none. (Where were all the knives? Where were all the bone saws?) He backed away, bumping into a desk, and swept his hand behind him without taking his eyes off the woman. He grabbed something and threw without thinking…but it was only a stapler, which bounced off her chest. She kept moving forward, mouth impossibly wide, growling loud enough that the sound of it hurt his ears.

Hating to take his eyes from her, but knowing it was his only hope, he turned and ran for the door, which he barely had time to unlock before she caught up with him. Her fingers ripped through his loose shirt and she dragged him across the room. As she climbed his back, he curled away from her, hoping that by bending he'd put his neck out of the reach of those teeth, but there was only so far he could go. She was much too strong for him.

As Martin rocked with all his strength, trying to shake her from his shoulders, he heard the door being flung open, followed by Joe's startled voice.

"Jesus, Martin. What the Hell is going on in here? What are you doing?"

"Help me, Joe!" Martin shouted, hearing her teeth snapping the air behind his ears. "Get her off me!"

"Is she alive?" asked Joe.

"Yes," said Martin. "No. I don't know. Do something!"

Martin could feel Joe peel the woman from his back. He turned to see him push her across the room. Joe then grabbed one of Martin's wrists and yanked him to his feet. Martin watched with horror as Mia slowly climbed to her feet, her eyes still filled with hunger.

"Shoot her!" he screamed.

"Who do you think I am?" said Joe, backing slowly away from the woman. "I don't go around shooting everything I don't understand. Maybe she's just sick."

"It's more than that," said Martin, his voice cracking. "She was dead. And now she isn't."

Mia sprang toward them, and Joe pulled Martin out of her path. If not for that, she'd have landed where Martin had been a moment before.

"Let's get out of here," Joe said, as she began to rise once more.

Joe pushed him out of the room and quickly followed, locking the door just as the woman slammed against it. She hammered at the barrier with a strength that seemed impossible for her size, but though the door bounced on its hinges, she still wasn't strong enough to break through.

"So what was that all about?" said Joe. "I came running as soon as I heard the noise. You're lucky I was still in the building."

Joe put a hand on Martin's shoulder, turning his focus away from the threat.

For a moment—but only for a moment—Martin felt such relief he thought he'd tell Joe everything that had occurred from when his friend had left him in the room, and not just that, but *everything*, back to when it all truly began —or at least when he realized it had—but he immediately realized his behavior would be more horrifying to Joe than anything the woman had done or become. Better to be silent. It had always been better to be silent.

"I have no idea," he said, knowing that he was lying, yet feeling as if he was being truthful at the same time.

But then Martin could hear other sounds, the movement of more of the dead, awakening (or whatever it was) and trying to break free from their cubicles…and he suddenly did have an idea. A very depressing idea. For if the dead were no longer staying dead, what that would mean for him would be…

No. Better not to think about it.

Better not to think at all.

———

MARTIN HAD BEGGED. He'd pleaded. He'd told Joe how close his help had brought him to a breakthrough. But none of Martin's attempts to convince Joe to allow a return to the morgue had been successful. With the dead suddenly and inexplicably coming back to life, and with the lengths of time before each return varying and unpredictable, Joe insisted there was no way he would let Martin try again what he'd tried twice, but only succeeded at once.

And with all eyes—and the newly repaired cameras—in the station now on the morgue, there was no way they could even think of sneaking him in and out. This was no longer a world in which rules could be bent.

And besides, said Joe, as bad as the nightmares were, was a cure really worth risking your life for?

It was. At least a cure for what *really* ailed Martin.

In what had to be the crummiest case of bad timing ever, the world chose to change right after *he* had changed. It was almost as if the universe was laughing at him. In the days after Joe had saved his life, Martin had called in sick from work and did nothing but watch television. He was too morose for much of anything else. And watching the news, which too often interrupted the regular programming that might have distracted him, made him even more morose. All the talking heads agreed—the dead were coming back to life, which made him feel dead himself. Because where did that leave him? After what he'd finally been privileged to feel, he refused to accept what the world seemed to be telling him— that he would be allowed to feel it no longer. Surely there was a space between death and rebirth into which the future would allow him to insert himself.

"I don't know what to tell you," Joe had said during their most recent conversation, when his friend had to disappoint him yet again. "We're all going to have nightmares about the dead now. You're no longer alone there."

But what Martin couldn't tell Joe was that he *was* still alone, because what he was having weren't the nightmares he'd lied about, but fantasies. Fantasies suddenly, miraculously realized. Fantasies that he needed to continue realizing.

And so, the following week (the waiting had been unbearable, but that's how long it took Martin to do what needed to be done) he found himself sitting in his car, listening to a stolen police radio, hoping his salvation hadn't been snatched from him just when he'd finally learned it was even possible. That was the only way he could think of to learn for sure. Eavesdropping in darkness on deserted streets, waiting to hear reports of a murder (and doing more than just waiting, but hoping for it, praying for it), he felt more guilty about his theft of the radio than he did about any of the things he'd done or was about to do.

As he listened anxiously to the disembodied voices, it seemed an unusually quiet night, with much less chatter than the time he'd ridden in the back of Joe's police car. It was disappointing, but it did make sense. Fear was keeping many people home, and he figured he might have to wait awhile before those adventurous enough to wander out ran into not quite the adventure they were looking for.

So he was relieved when a call came in near dawn about a stabbing at a bar, and a woman's body the owner wanted the Hell out of there. Martin raced to the scene before the police could…or likely even wanted to from what Joe had let on. No one except Martin was in any hurry to rush to the side of the dead these days.

When he arrived at the bar, the only one there was the nervous owner, who smoked a cigarette as he paced the street out front. All of the man's (living) customers had fled, and with no one knowing how long it would be before this particular corpse came back, even he wanted to get away as soon as possible. Which was lucky for Martin—it meant the man didn't particularly care that the person who arrived to pick up the body showed no signs of being a police officer. He never even questioned it. And so Martin was easily able to persuade the man to leave him alone there, as long as he promised to lock up as soon as he was done.

"She's right by the television," the man said, handing Martin the keys. "I didn't touch her."

Martin entered, locking the door behind him. It took a moment for his eyes to adjust, but then, there she was, right where the man had said. Apparently, the woman had stood on tiptoe to change the channel on the television, someone hadn't liked it, and it ended with her dead on the floor. He still had trouble understanding why people did such things. But the why of it didn't bother him so much at that moment. He may not have understood. But he was grateful.

He knelt beside the woman, lifting her chin so he could get a better look. Her eyes had remained open, and her gaze, no longer under her control, was focussed through and beyond him.

She was pretty, with high cheekbones and a smile that

had survived her death. Not quite his type, though, but she would have to do. He could no longer afford to be picky. (Could he ever truly have afforded to be picky?) He tried to scoop her up in his arms, the first time he'd ever done anything like that, and failed, falling to the floor beside her, narrowly missing the pool of blood that had spilled from her wound. Seeing no other option, he tucked his hands into her armpits and and dragged her, feeling as he pulled her along that she deserved better. Her shoes peeled off as they staggered awkwardly together to his car, but he left them where they'd separated. She wouldn't need them ever again, and neither would he. Shoes had never played a part in his fantasy.

The streets were still deserted, and no one saw him place her—clumsily but gently, ever so gently—in his trunk. He wished he could have set her beside him in the passenger seat, but thought…no. It wasn't that the blood, which still occasionally dripped, bothered him. Rather, he didn't want to chance her sudden reawakening while his eyes were busy on the road.

At his apartment, after first checking he wouldn't be seen (the streets there were deserted as well, so in that moment at least, his curse was also his blessing), he took her upstairs and laid her out on his bed, the same bed where he and Adrianna had so recently pretended. But this would be no act. He unbuttoned her shirt, dark with blood, and beneath the damp cloth saw for the first time where she had been stabbed. As he washed her wound, he marveled at how so small a cut had such a large effect. People were like balloons, he guessed. Prick them and they explode.

Once her skin was clean, he draped a sheet across her side so he would not have to see the evidence of what had ended her life. He didn't like thinking of her violent end, of anyone's violent end. He preferred to think of her as simply having fallen asleep and not having woken up.

He closed those staring eyes, wiped away her makeup, and sitting beside her, wondered how much time he had. He could have hours. He could have days. He could have no time at all. He knew he was playing Russian Roulette with a dead woman as the bullet, but he didn't care. He only hoped whatever time remained would be enough.

He felt safe behind the locked door of his own apartment, or as safe as anyone could sanely feel beside a dead body that would soon come back to life, so he was comfortable undressing, unlike at the morgue, where he had to be alert for interruptions. He folded his clothes neatly and laid them on the end table beside the hammer and butcher knife he'd previously placed there. He hoped neither would be necessary, that he could get done what he needed to do before the inevitable, but it was best to prepare for all eventualities.

As he lay atop her, he felt himself grow hard immediately, as he expected he would. He wanted to enter her quickly, but he also wanted to make this time last. So even though his body urged *stay, stay, stay*, he rose from the bed and found her bloody clothes. She didn't carry a wallet—her pants had been much too tight for her to do so—but in one pocket he found a credit card and driver's license.

Maxine. Her name had been Maxine. It was a good name. And she deserved a good name, especially now.

Martin returned to the bed and called her by that name, imagining as he did so that she was able to hear it. That its syllables, spoken slowly and repeatedly, comforted her. He massaged her temples, kissed the space between her breasts, stroked her thighs, whispered that name over and over until it lost all meaning, became all meaning.

Then he could bear to wait no longer, and it was time.

Maxine hadn't been dead as long as his first discovered lover, but dead was dead, and a lubricant was still needed, which he retrieved from a drawer. (And how strange, he thought, that he'd felt a need to keep that hidden, while leaving his weapons out in the open.) He shuddered as he entered her, but having entered her, moved no further. He paused, as devoid of movement as his partner, and took several deep breaths to regain his composure. As soon as he was sure of himself, sure he'd hold back until the moment was right, he began to move again. And then, slowly and steadily, he loved her.

What was he looking for here? Why this not that? He'd questioned himself for years, starting as a teenager, as others did of themselves, but he never came up with an answer. As he moved rhythmically above Maxine, Martin knew in reality what he'd always hypothesized—that the question was its own answer. There are some things that exist in a place beyond reason, and as he dotted Maxine's forehead with little kisses, rubbed his cheek against hers, lifted one of her feet so an ankle dug into his back, he knew that he was what he was, and always would be. And he felt no shame in that. He had finally found himself.

Thank you, Maxine. Thank you, Maxine. Thank you. Thank you. Thank you.

He was about to finish, could feel his skin tingling as the moment began to overtake him, when to his horror, her vaginal muscles snapped tight around him, both halting his orgasm and trapping him against her. He was doubly horrified, because not only would that reaction, or any reaction coming from any sexual partner, have repulsed him, but also the movement meant she was alive again.

Martin flailed against her, trying to roll off her as yet only partially reanimated body, but could not. He was painfully engorged, and stuck. He lunged toward the end table, but couldn't get quite close enough, so instead of grabbing either of his prearranged weapons, he ended up sweeping them to the floor.

He was naked, defenseless, and pinned inside a dead woman. Which meant, he knew, that he would soon be dead himself.

Her eyes snapped open, and this time, he saw to his horror that she was no longer looking flatly through him, but directly at him. Her lips peeled back, revealing teeth which soon would be aiming for his throat, and he shrieked. He snatched the pillow from under her head and pushed it over her hungry face. Laying an elbow across the pillow, he struggled to keep those teeth from his flesh, at the same time rocking himself to one side and fumbling at the floor with his other hand. He managed to graze the hilt of the knife with his fingertips, but in doing so only ended up pushing it further away. Maxine, or what had once been Maxine, reached her hands around his back and pulled him closer. As she did so, he could feel through the pillow the dull gnawing of her teeth against his cheek. It was clear that slim protection wouldn't keep him safe for long. She would surely chew through soon and that would be the end of him.

He screamed, and hurled himself to the side, unbalancing their conjoined bodies so that he fell off the bed and pulled her over on top of him. Near hysteria, he quickly rolled once more so that she was under him again—but now she was on top of the weapons, and they were still out of his reach. She kicked wildly, her legs hammering against the floor as she tried to launch herself up at him. The pillow was still wedged between them, was managing to keep her head pinned against the floor, but he knew his strength wouldn't last forever. And meanwhile, his erection, trapped in the vise of her corpse, refused to diminish and release him.

Then came a banging at the door, and the shouting of his name.

Adrianna.

"I don't know what's happening," she said, her voice muffled. "But I'm coming in."

She still had a key, though she hadn't used it in weeks, and he hadn't had the heart to ask for it back. Thank God for that. He heard the thunder of her footsteps behind him, even over the banging of Maxine's limbs, and then—

"Move your head," Adrianna said. "Move it! Now!"

As he craned his neck to the right, Adrianna yanked the pillow away, and before Maxine's teeth could rip into Martin's neck, she brought the base of a lamp down against the dead woman's skull.

Once, and Maxine shuddered and wailed.

Twice, and she quivered and hissed.

Then a third time, and she stopped moving, this time permanently. Her body relaxed once more into death. And Martin was free.

Adrianna helped him rise from the corpse, but they didn't stand long, for together they tumbled to the floor, their backs against the bed, the dead woman at their feet. Adrianna reached behind her to pull the sheet from the bed and drape it around his shoulders.

"Tell me the truth," she asked quietly, and then paused so long he wondered if she'd changed her mind and decided she really didn't want to know. Only after she looked away from him did she say with great precision, "Did you kill her?"

"No," he said loudly, offended she would think he was capable of such a thing, even as they sat before the evidence of exactly what he was capable. "I would never do something like that. I could never. You know that."

"But you'd do something like *that*," she said, tilting her

head behind them toward the bed where Maxine's reanimating had interrupted their lovemaking.

"But...that's different," he said. "That doesn't hurt anyone. I would never hurt anyone. Don't you understand? I thought you understood."

"Oh, I understand," she said. "But you *are* hurting someone. You're hurting yourself. And you're hurting...you're hurting me."

Adrianna leaned her head on his shoulder. He tensed, but she did not lift it, though she had often previously responded to those types of signs. She sighed, then spoke as if to a child. A child that was loved. But still, a child.

"What are we going to do with you, Martin?" she said.

"There's nothing to be done with me." He shifted uneasily, wishing she'd move her head, but knowing no way to tell her to do so, not after she'd saved his life. That she was still there after what she'd seen was remarkable. He didn't know that he'd have had it in him to remain by her side had the situation been reversed. "This is who I am. This is who I'll always be."

"But don't you get that this is not going to work? You can't go on like this. Especially not with what's started happening in the world. What you want, it can't be made real. Not anymore. You and me, that's real. I've been watching your apartment, waiting for you to realize that. If I hadn't, who knows what would have happened."

"I know what would have happened."

"Well, it didn't. And you know what that means. It's a sign. It's the universe telling us something. We've got to keep trying."

He shook his head, pulled the sheet more tightly around his shoulders, wishing he could enclose himself in a cocoon.

"No," he said, trying his best not to sound mean, just totally honest, which is what she deserved. But he knew his best wasn't good enough. It never had been. "We both know it will never work. You do, don't you? If you know me, really know me, then you also know that. There's no way we can fix this."

"There *is* a way," she said. "There's got to be a way."

He felt dead inside. Thinking that, and of those who actually were dead inside, almost made him smile. Almost. But the events of the night showed him he'd have no reason to smile again. He'd been bent one way all his life, and now that he'd finally figured things out, the world was suddenly bent another way, and despair was the only sane reaction. Dead inside felt just about right.

"I love you, Martin," said Adrianna.

"And I love you," he said. "I've told you that. But I also told you that love is not enough. Love was never enough. If it had been, we wouldn't be…"

He gestured at the twice-killed body before them.

"…here."

He leaned away from her, letting her head slide from his shoulder. He closed his eyes, hunching forward. There was no future for them, could be no future for them. He saw that. Why couldn't she?

In a few moments, he could hear Adrianna, without a word, without a touch, getting up. Then he heard the closing of his apartment door.

And then he was alone.

With Maxine. But alone.

And alone, more alone than he had ever been, was, horribly, the way it was going to have to be from then on.

———

IT TOOK Martin longer to dispose of Maxine's body than he'd originally thought it would when he first picked her up what seemed like a lifetime ago. Not because of the difficulty of the mere physical act of loading her back into his car, transporting her, and then abandoning her, but due to the time it took for him to fully commit to the decision that, yes, she had to go.

After Adrianna had left, he seemed to fall into a fugue state that prevented any action, even as he told himself repeatedly to get on with it. When that finally passed, the first thing he was able to rouse himself to do was replace the pillow over Maxine's face so he wouldn't have to see the mangled results of his rescue. The second thing he did was remove the sheet from around his shoulders, the sheet which Adrianna had lovingly wrapped there, fold it neatly, and then place it over Maxine's stomach, hiding that wound, too. The third thing he did was less something he did by choice, and more a thing that occurred beyond his doing of it. It just happened uncontrollably.

He looked down at Maxine, all signs of the violence which had been done to her, first by a stranger, and then by his friend, obscured, and felt his attraction returning. For an infinitesimal sliver of time, he was actually thinking of continuing with his original plan and seeing it all to completion.

Then, before he could turn that impulse into action, the thought disgusted even him, and all the shame and embarrassment over what were his essential drives, a shame and embarrassment which he'd thought had been erased through his recent actions, came flooding back. That he'd considered acting out on his fantasy in that instant, however briefly, sickened him, and he thought, now he knew how the world would regard even the least of what he'd done. He swore to himself he'd never give in to such a thing, as doing so would turn an act that was supposed to be beautiful into something sordid.

And yet.

And yet…

He found he could not, no matter how much he thought he should, immediately part from Maxine. And so he sat beside her all that day, and into the next as well. After his most recent moments of temptation and his rejection of it, she no longer called to him in that way, and when he looked at her, she was not a sexual object, but rather a symbol of his horribly lonely future. That empty future floated before him, filling his mind. She was more than just a dead body. She was physical proof of the void to come, the period at the end of his sentence. And his sentence was life.

It wasn't until she began to decay and her smell grew overpowering that he was finally able to let her go. He clumsily dressed her back in the clothes in which he'd found her, clothes now stiffened by her dried blood, and used a hat and scarf which Adrianna had left behind to hide the head wound. He then hustled her down the stairs and into his car once more. This time he allowed her to sit up front, her head tilting against the glass so that anyone who spotted them would assume she was napping.

He still wasn't entirely clear about what he wanted to do next, and so at first drove aimlessly, wondering where he should take her. Where he should *leave* her. He knew one easy answer was to just return her to the bar where he'd picked her up, even though before everything had gone wrong he'd initially rejected that idea. But it occurred to Martin that, after all, the bar owner probably deserved to end up with the disposal of the body being his problem simply because he hadn't helped that night, hadn't intervened to prevent Maxine's murder. And he certainly should never have let a stranger like Martin walk in and whisk away her body, even with the way the world had changed. Not everyone would have had the same pure intentions.

(Remarkable. Even with the state of Maxine's body, he still believed his intentions were pure.) Martin pushed away those thoughts of making some sort of cosmic point, though. He knew in his heart that she deserved better.

We all deserved better.

He eventually found himself at a nearby hospital, not quite sure how'd he'd gotten there. He gently carried her to a bench which was partially in shadow due to a bulb that had gone out. He forcibly folded her into a seated position, and then placed her hands together in her lap, weaving her fingers together. He sat beside her on the very edge of the bench. But only briefly.

"I'm sorry things had to turn out this way," he said. "You were probably a very nice person."

As Martin drove off, he glanced from the road ahead to her form in the rearview mirror until she shrunk too small to be seen. He made his way back to his apartment, wiping away tears with bloody fingers.

At his building, he took the elevator to his floor and walked slowly down the hall, exhaustion finally having overtaken him. When he got to his door, he pulled out his key, but discovered—the door was already unlocked. He would have sworn he had locked it, it was an ingrained habit with him...and there was only one person he'd ever trusted with a key.

Adrianna.

Even after what he'd done to her with his actions, his words, and his silences, even after all of his crimes of the heart and crimes of the body, she still hadn't left it behind when she walked off that last horrible night. He pushed the door open, but remained outside, uncertain he had the strength to confront the accusations—loving accusations, but accusations nonetheless—he was sure he'd find written on her face.

"Adrianna?" he called from the hallway.

There was no answer. With no other alternative, he entered his apartment, continuing to say her name, continuing to hear nothing in return. Once he reached his darken bedroom, he noticed a sliver of light streaming from under the closed bathroom door. As sure as he was that his front door had been locked, he was even more certain he'd turned off that light.

He crossed the bedroom quickly, but having done so, pushed the door open slowly, whispering her name once more. Inside, he found his answer as to why there'd been no answer.

Adrianna was submerged in the bathtub. Naked. Unmoving. No bubbles breaking the surface of the water. On the bathmat, next to an empty pill bottle, a sheet of paper.

He leapt past them both and yanked her from the water, soaking his clothes, but not giving a damn about it. He kept calling her name as he carried her to the bed. She did not answer. (He knew she would not answer. But that did not stop him from calling her again and again.) He touched two fingers to her throat, pressed an ear to her ribcage, held one of her wrists tenderly, but…nothing.

Adrianna was gone.

He staggered back to the bathroom, where he knelt beside the note, its writing smeared from his failed attempt at rescuing her the way she had rescued him. He could barely read it through his tears.

She loved him, she said. She understood him, she said. And she wanted to be with him forever, she said. But she knew…this was the only way.

Do quickly what you feel called upon to do, what we both want you to do, she wrote. Before what inevitably will happen inevitably happens.

Stunned by what she had done, uncertain at first how he felt, he returned to the bedroom, the writing on the damp page growing blurrier in his hands. He gazed at her, imagined her watching his apartment, waiting for her moment to with her death bring their future to life, and considered this impossibility, this inevitability.

She understood, he thought. *I never truly believed anyone could.*

She was so beautiful lying there, so serene. But for how long? How long would she lie there like that before changing and taking back the gift she had given him?

The amount of time that remained was meaningless. She had given herself to him in a way no one else could. He could not scorn something that precious.

He slowly removed his clothes, savoring the fullness of what was to come. He refused to rush this. He folded each item neatly, stacked them on the table beside the bed, and placed her note, by now no longer legible, atop them. He retrieved a towel from the bathroom, sat beside her on the bed, and tenderly patted her skin dry.

She looked peaceful there, as if she knew where she was and what he had begun to do, and welcomed it. He smiled, and wondered—if she could see him now, would he appear peaceful, too? He thought he would, and he wished she *could* see it, could see what she had done for him, though at the same time realizing that if she could, then she'd paradoxically have nothing to see.

He stretched out beside her, and studied her profile. He'd never been able to see her quite like that before, had never managed to catch her unawares. Oh, they'd playacted at it, but neither of them could fake it well enough to pull it off, not convincingly. She knew that.

So she had made it real.

He kissed her cheek, gently. She did not stir, did not turn

her head to kiss him back, which was as it should be. Which was as it had to be. He lifted one of her hands, fanned out her fingers, and spread them across his chest.

That was all the touch he needed from her to be ready.

He rolled onto her, rolled into her, crying out as he did so, feeling for the first time complete. He'd thought what he'd had with the others had already completed him, but he'd been wrong. The others had been strangers, and whatever communion they'd had was but an imitation of this solemn, this euphoric, this liberating act chosen freely by both parties. He gazed at her, the woman who loved him so greatly that she was willing to lead him to this place, and he never wanted their dance to be over. And yet, it had to be over. Because that had been the point of her gift.

Martin balanced above her, alternating between moving slowly and not at all, pacing himself, waiting for that movement in death which he would never have welcomed in life. And when it came, when she fluttered, when he felt the subtle vibrations that signaled her return...rather than retreat, he thrust forward, dove deep, dove for her soul.

She opened her eyes. She looked at him. She saw him, he thought. There was a hunger there, yes. But there was also love. Wasn't there?

"I love you, Adrianna," he said. He knew it, really knew it, at last. It had been Adrianna. It had been Adrianna all along.

And then her lips peeled back into a smile. At least, Martin allowed it to be a smile. And he smiled back.

She hugged him tight, and under the pressure of her embrace, he could feel the cracking of first one, then another rib. The pain was exquisite, but he no longer cared. She lifted her head, and he bent his, allowing her to bite into his neck, and as she chewed until his blood flowed, he came, letting go of the burdens of a lifetime, releasing all his misery, releasing all his loneliness, releasing all his love.

He knew, as consciousness faded, that he would be back. And he was sure that when he returned, Adrianna would be there.

No. He *knew* she would be there.

She would be there.

She would be there.

She would.

SURVIVAL OF THE FITTEST

As Marc headed toward a landing on Española Island, a wave thrust his rubber raft skyward, almost spilling him into the sea. He tumbled back, and the stretch of beach strewn with boulders momentarily vanished from view. A woman sitting across from him had to drop her camera bag onto the bottom of their zodiac and grab his shoulder to keep him on board.

As she steadied him, he thanked her with words that were only partially coherent. He grasped more tightly at the rope that ringed the lip of their raft, and became aware that his face had suddenly flushed from more than just the Galapagos sun. He hadn't yet gotten used to being touched since Melissa had died, and the sudden contact had surprised him more than his near capsizing.

He looked away from their guide, Rafael, and the other eight tourists with whom he was squeezed in the zodiac, and gazed back at the ship anchored behind them. That would help him avoid having to speak further to the woman, or so he hoped. She seemed pleasant enough, with a welcoming smile and bright eyes that seemed slightly startled, whether or not she was, but it wouldn't do for him to get distracted from his purpose here. He stared up at the frigatebirds who paced them, hoping she'd turn away from him.

Which meant that when their raft touched the shore, it came unexpectedly. Melissa would have been amused. She'd often told him he always seemed to be looking back from where he'd come rather than ahead to where he was going. As the bottom of the raft bumped gently where the water stopped and the beach began, Marc had to wave off another one of the woman's outstretched hands.

He scrambled into shallow water that almost reached his knees and walked several yards up to where the sand was warm and dry. Rafael handed him a towel from a waterproof sack, and as Marc rubbed his legs, he realized that the lumps he'd earlier seen scattered along the beach had not been boulders. They began to move.

The closest sea lions turned lazily to gaze at him, their necks elongating as they sniffed him out. Hundreds of them were dripped along the sand, dotting the shore until it curved away out of sight.

Rafael led their small group along that beach, leaving behind others who were climbing out of the next rafts that followed to make landings after them. He reminded them of how they were supposed to behave, relating the rules they'd all been told at the previous night's welcome dinner. Their group was supposed to stay together, always either landward or seaward of the creatures, as sea lions got nervous if they thought themselves surrounded. No matter how cute they seemed, never attempt to touch them, lest you pass your scent on to a pup and the mother then abandons it. Beware the aggressive beach master, the huge bull who would charge to protect his herd if he sensed they were being threatened.

As they walked along, following exactly where Rafael led to avoid disturbing the nests of turtles and birds, the other tourists discussed these rules, and shared what they knew of the life cycle of sea lions. So many facts filled the air that the guide almost seemed unnecessary, except as a presence to shame them into their best behavior.

Marc had nothing to contribute. He'd arrived among these islands unprepared, and couldn't even recall what little they'd been told during their crash course the night before.

He'd never thought of himself as an ignorant man, but the other passengers made him feel like one. It wasn't their fault, or even his. He was just never meant to be in this place. This trip was not a fulfillment of his dream; it had been Melissa's, always and only Melissa's. But still, he blamed himself for not having tried to understand her dream better before embarking on it for himself. All he understood were his own unwelcome dreams, the ones that had begun not long after her death, and what those dreams represented.

He paused and let the group pull away from him, stopping to watch a particularly huge blob of a sea lion attempt to roll over. It wriggled clumsily, sand crystals sparkling down its length. It truly didn't care that he was there, and that amazed him. Melissa had always told him that the Galapagos Islands were as close as one could get in this life to the Garden of Eden. Maybe it could have been that to him once, if they'd come here together, but now that she had been taken from him, it no longer held out that kind of promise.

"They're beautiful, aren't they?"

Marc turned to see the woman who had righted him on the raft was standing just behind him. He nodded, not knowing quite what to say.

"They may look clumsy now," she continued, "but in the water, it's like they're doing ballet. You'll see."

Marc looked ahead self-consciously to the rest of the group from which they'd become separated, then felt ridiculous at his nervousness. He owed it to Melissa to continue acting as if she hadn't taken his soul with her.

"I'm afraid that once I get into the water," he said, "you'll find I'm just as clumsy as I am now."

"My name is Barbara," she said, her smile returning.

"I'm Marc," he said.

"Nice to meet you, Marc," she said, and held out her hand. He hesitated taking it, but before his indecision could become too obvious, a shout came from where the rest of the group had clustered. Rafael was waving the two of them forward, and pointing to what seemed to be a dark smudge at his feet.

"I guess we should see what that's all about," said Marc, turning away from Barbara with a sense of relief.

When he caught up with the others, he found them ringed around a low, bloody mound about a foot and a half in diameter. Rafael told them it was a placenta, and since it hadn't yet been pecked into invisibility by birds, that meant the mother and her pup were surely close by. He instructed them all to spread out and keep their eyes open.

"Isn't this exciting?" asked Barbara.

Others lifted binoculars to their eyes, or framed the vista with their cameras, and Marc had brought neither. Yet he was the one who spotted the pair first, hidden where they had crawled behind the short grass that lined the beach. He didn't speak up to alert the others, just walked slowly and quietly up to them and watched. The mother lay on her back, exhausted, while the pup wriggled frantically against her in search of a nipple. As with the other sea lions Marc had seen so far, neither cared that he was there. Humans appeared to be like air or water to them.

He knelt in the grass, and stared into the mother's moist eyes from no more than a yard away. Did she know, he wondered, how lucky she was to be alive, how lucky she was that her child had survived? He doubted she had that capacity. Most humans even lacked it, treating a successful birth as a certainty instead of as a gift.

The pup finally found a nipple just as the others caught up with him. They murmured, oohing and aahing while Rafael related the facts of life as they existed in the Galapagos, but Marc barely heard what they had to say, lost as he studied the mother and child, lost as well with the mother and child he himself had lost. He didn't pull away from the spectacle until Barbara rested her hand on his shoulder and gently asked him why he was crying so.

He stood abruptly, shrugging off her touch. He couldn't think of any answer that would make sense, so he walked quickly and silently back to the rafts which were shuttling those who'd had enough for the day back to what would be their home for the next week. He sat on the sand and awaited his rescue, staring off at the tiny ship in the distance, a ship which until the day before he had known only from the brochures Melissa had been showing him for years, brochures to which he had paid too little attention until it was much too late to matter.

———

THAT NIGHT, instead of lingering in his cabin as he had during meals ever since the ship had pulled away from Baltra to begin their visits to the smaller islands, and only eating at the last moment when the dining room was about to close so he could avoid too much contact with the other passengers, he left his cabin just as dinner began and the first crush of people arrived. He spotted Barbara from across the room and approached her before anyone else could.

"May I?" he asked, pointing at the empty seat beside her. She was alone at a table meant for four. She seemed surprised to see him. Or maybe, he reminded himself, that was just her eyes.

"Certainly," she said. Her smile, when it appeared, changed her face, making her look younger.

Marc sat, and decided he needed to speak quickly, just in case others did decide to join them. He owed her an apology, which would be difficult enough without an audience.

"About this morning," he said.

She stopped him with the touch of her hand to his.

"No need to say anything more," she said. "I know what it's like when you've been alone too long. You can sometimes forget what it's like to be with other people."

"How do you know that?" he asked.

"Do you think I'd have empty chairs around me if I didn't know?" she said. "I know. I've had losses of my own. I'm like you, Marc. It was Marc, wasn't it?"

He pulled his hand away, ostensibly to spread the napkin on his lap and straighten the silverware.

"I don't feel as if it's been too long," he said, remembering the most recent dream of the night before, filled with Melissa's disappointed eyes, and her angry words. "I don't know that I'll live long enough for it to ever seem too long."

"I know," she said, but Marc knew by her words, by her concerned yet impossibly casual tone, that she couldn't, not really. She'd led a normal life, and her losses has been normal losses, and the price she had paid had been a normal price.

"And it's possible that it will always feel that way," she continued. "But that doesn't mean that you have to live like a hermit. I didn't know your wife, but whoever she was, I'm sure she wouldn't have wanted you to live that way."

"No," said Marc. "No, she wouldn't have."

What he didn't say, what he couldn't say, was that he knew to a certainty that his wife didn't want him alone, because every night, night after night, Melissa made *sure* he didn't lead the life of a hermit. Because a hermit had no visitors, living or dead, right? Being alone, being truly alone, might have been a better end.

"How did you lose her?" Barbara asked quietly, surprising him with her forthrightness. She was a woman who obviously measured the limited time ahead as carefully as she counted out the wasted time behind.

He was silent longer than was probably polite while he tried to decide whether he should answer her question. He'd never really had much cause to speak to anyone of it before. All their parents were dead, and they'd had no children. At least, none that had lived. What friends they'd had as a couple were mostly brought to the relationship by her, and once the tragedy occurred he'd dodged their phone calls until they simply drifted away. So he had no experience with speaking of the unspeakable. Just in obsessing over it.

And dreaming of it.

Before he could reach a decision, a young couple, garbed in khakis and happy in their ignorance, came up to the table, their hands entwined, and asked whether they could join them, looking from Marc to Barbara and back again. There was no way Marc could speak of what was hidden beneath his surface in front of them. But he couldn't bring himself to say no, not when the happiness being thrust in front of him was so rare. And besides, there was still another week ahead of him on the ship if he truly felt like baring his soul. So Marc gestured them on, and Barbara waved at the empty chairs.

As Marc had expected, the couple—the woman, Kandi, all giggles, and the man, Carl, all coy smirks—were indeed newlyweds, in the Galapagos for their honeymoon. After the introductions, talk turned to their exhausting day spent exploring the island.

"That big round puff ball was the cutest thing, wasn't

he?" said Kandi, once the appetizers had arrived and she had speared her first shrimp and was twirling it in cocktail sauce.

"Which big, round puff ball was that?" asked Barbara. Marc could sense her amusement, but Kandi seemed immune to it.

"They all looked the same to me," said Carl, with a laugh. "A puff ball is a puff ball is a puff ball."

Marc was pleased to discover they knew as little of the history of this place as he did, though their ignorance was born of different reasons. They were here for the snorkeling, and because everything was so cute, and to make love beside portholes that looked out upon a different sky and an unfamiliar sea, while Marc was here because this place had mattered once to someone he loved, and he felt he owed this visit to her, that in coming here, he could... what? Say goodbye? Leave his heart behind so it wouldn't have to break each morning when he woke to an empty bed and a remembered absence? No, he wasn't really sure why he was here, only that it seemed like a thing that was overdue and must be done, with the exact reasons to be filled in later.

Barbara was the only one among them who seemed to have bothered to show up accompanied by the facts.

"Oh, no," she said. "A bird *isn't* a bird isn't a bird. You'll see that as we move on. Each island's species are uniquely different. You've read your Darwin, haven't you?"

Carl shook his head while holding up his hands in surrender, then turned to look sheepishly at Marc.

"Admit it, Marc," he said with a grin. "You haven't either."

"You've got me there," said Marc.

"When it comes to things like that," said Carl, "the wives are always more interested than us, right? Husbands don't have to sweat those kinds of details."

"Husbands?" said Marc, confused. "You think…we're married?"

He looked to Barbara, then turned away quickly when it became clear she was less concerned by the error than by his alarm over it.

"I'm so sorry," said Carl. "I just assumed—"

"So tell me more about this big puff ball of a bird as you call it," Barbara interrupted to ask Kandi. Marc was grateful Barbara had turned the focus elsewhere, and he sensed she knew it.

"It was about as big as a Thanksgiving turkey," said Kandi. "Big and fat and round as a bowling ball. And the amazing thing is that it was stuffed like a turkey, too, so stuffed you could almost hear it slosh. I wish I could remember what the cutie was called, but I'm no good at things like that. I could show you a picture of it if that helps."

Before Kandi could retrieve her digital camera from her lap, Marc and Barbara spoke at the same moment, with the same words, though with vastly different tones.

"It was an albatross," they each said.

"Are you *sure* you two aren't married?" asked Kandi.

Barbara patted Marc's hand before he could respond, and he found he didn't mind her touch quite so much this time.

"That was a baby albatross we saw," continued Barbara. "It spends all of its young life on that one spot, while its parents fly off to sea to hunt and bring back fish to feed it. The one we saw probably had two gallons of fish oil inside it, getting ready for its growth spurt, for the day when it will have an eleven-foot wingspan."

"Wow," said Kandi. "I'm just glad we saw it when it was still cute."

Marc hadn't thought it was cute. All Marc had thought, after Rafael had pointed it out and identified it, was, *so that's an albatross.* Since Melissa had died, Marc had thought of himself as carrying one, but he'd always kept that thought in the realm of metaphor, never believing that he'd ever actually see one, no matter how many times Melissa had probably mentioned them. Maybe that's why he had to come here, to discover that they weren't always so frightening as all that. Sometimes they were just little balls of fat. Maybe someday his could grow wings and fly away…

When the time came for dessert, the newlyweds begged off and vanished. Marc surprised himself by hanging on. He'd only planned on coming down long enough to apologize, and there were implications, after all, to lingering conversations over coffee. But Barbara acted as if there weren't any, and just gestured at the disappearing couple.

"Honestly," she said. "They have no idea, do they?"

"No," said Marc, and he was surprised to find he was the one smiling this time.

"Were we really once so young?" she asked.

"Not me," said Marc. "I can't remember *ever* being young."

"So we're back to the doom and gloom again," she said.

"Where else?" he said. "That's where I live."

"I think," she said, "that there was something you wanted to tell me."

This time, given the opportunity, he didn't hesitate. He began to tell her everything. He didn't think he'd even ever told *himself* everything before. How he'd lived a life of loneliness until he and Melissa had met. How they'd found each other at an office party, and fallen instantly in love. How she'd longed to visit this place, but could never afford it, and how they decided to splurge and go into debt for their tenth anniversary. How they were surprised by an unexpected pregnancy, one that they'd welcomed. And how instead of ending up with a child, Melissa had sickened, and nothing, not surgery, nor drugs, nor radiation, nor prayer had worked.

And then, how he was alone again, and how he'd stayed alone, for the five long years since.

"Our fifteenth anniversary is coming up," Marc said. "It's in just a few days."

"You poor thing," said Barbara. "You sound haunted."

He was stung by her use of that word. It felt like a slap. He'd never thought of the clouds which hung over him and the dreams which came with them in that way. But now that Barbara had mentioned it...

"Can I trust you with a secret?" he asked, realizing then that whenever someone asked that question, they usually knew the answer before the question was even asked.

"Of course," said Barbara, leaning into him. "We only met last night, I know that, but still, I feel as if we've known each other for years."

Marc had no memory of having met Barbara the night before at the welcome party. Until that morning, she'd been lost in a blur of faces he never expected to know better. But he felt he should tell her, should tell *someone* of the dreams and what he was here to do about them.

But then the waiter coughed at his shoulder, and he looked up to see he and Barbara were the last guests in the dining room, and the staff was hoping to close up for the night. It had been years since Marc could remember time having passed so quickly. Usually, it crawled, because he was carrying Melissa on his back. Perhaps in talking about her with someone else, he had managed to put her down for at least a moment.

As the staff put out the table settings for the next morning's breakfast, Marc walked with Barbara into the passageway outside the dining area.

"Now what?" asked Barbara, as they took the stairs up to the deck.

"I was just thinking," Marc said. "Carrying an albatross can be exhausting."

"You can choose to put it down," she said.

"No," he said, as they paused by the railing to look out at the sea. "I don't think I'm capable of making that choice."

"Then you can at least choose to let someone else carry it with you," she said, patting his arm and then leaving it there. "You're not the only one who's been made to live a life alone. And we weren't made to live that way. That much we can choose."

"Yes," said Marc, covering her hand with his own. "Yes, you're right."

They watched the setting sun until it had vanished completely, and it wasn't until much later that he realized he'd only been thinking of Melissa intermittently, rather than constantly. As they continued talking in the darkness, Barbara did not bring up the as yet unspoken secret he had tried to offer, and Marc did not attempt to revisit the matter. Whatever unexplored potential might exist between them, he still had to go through with his plans, and if anyone was going to get in trouble for them, he wanted it to be only him.

BACK IN HIS CABIN, Marc eyed his narrow bunk with suspicion. It had been a pleasant evening, the first such after a long desert of loneliness, and he didn't want the dreams that would surely come to wash it away. He hoped to stay awake as late as he possibly could.

He sensed he could have spent the night with Barbara if he chose. She could have delayed the restless sleep that awaited him. But it wasn't yet time for that. He knew he had to put down one burden before his hands could be free to pick up anything else.

The only distraction he was going to allow himself that night were the guidebooks he'd brought, Melissa's guidebooks, which he'd barely opened up until then. He'd felt that all he needed to know about this place he already knew. Melissa had been a good teacher, even though he had been a lousy student. But it had been an exhausting day, and so he fell asleep sitting in bed with books scattered across his lap, staring at Melissa's scribbled notes in their pages and thinking of how they had once been across her lap.

And then Melissa was there in the cabin.

She did not come to him with scary faces or menacing gestures, none of what he once had thought would accompany a ghost. She was just sitting there, tucked in bed beside him as she once had always been. Her eyes were sad, and at the same time, a little afraid.

"Don't do it," she said, as casually as if she were asking him what he wanted for breakfast.

Her voice brought back such memories as nearly made him weep, but at the same time he felt a spark of guilt, guilt for what he'd earlier been contemplating about Barbara.

"Nothing happened," he said to his dead wife. "Nothing is going to happen. You don't have to warn me."

She shook her head. Did she not believe him? He had never lied to her before.

"Don't do it," she repeated, more urgently this time.

"I won't, Melissa," he said. "Please...I didn't come here for anyone else but you. I waited too long to do it, I know that. I should have come earlier. But I'm here to make amends."

She lunged for him then, grabbing his wrists. An electric

shock coursed through him at her touch that both frightened and exhilarated him.

"Don't do it," she said once more, pulling him toward her for a kiss.

But he woke before their lips could touch.

The bed was empty, the cabin dark. In the quiet of the small room, he felt her absence more than ever.

He looked forward to the end of his journey here, when he would set them both free.

MARC HAD ONLY SEEN a few flamingos in his life before, and those had either been in a cage or on a neighbor's lawn. But the marsh on Floreana Island held hundreds of them that were neither imprisoned nor plastic.

Barbara stood beside him as he marveled at the flock. Through some unspoken agreement, they had ended up on the same raft when the passengers gathered to disembark at their latest island. And when they'd come ashore, they'd continued together walking side by side on the path inland as she shared trivia with him about this bird and that tree. Though he sensed he shouldn't use that word when he thought about it, because from the passionate manner in which she spoke, it was anything but trivia to her. When Eduardo, their guide for that day, complimented Barbara on her knowledge, Marc felt an unexpected pride he knew he shouldn't have allowed himself to feel.

Standing there, looking out at the flock which seemed to stretch as far as he could see, reaching the base of mountains that vanished upward into mist, he recognized he was feeling less oppressed.

"I wonder if albatrosses are jealous of flamingos," he said, surprising himself. Barbara clasped his hand then and gave it a little squeeze. He squeezed back, not letting go, refusing to give credence to the previous night's dream warnings.

What would Kandi and Carl say if they should see them now? Marc was glad those two were off as part of another group, because he didn't want to make his feelings concrete enough to verbalize an answer.

Eduardo next led them to a wooden barrel stuck in the sand. He told them whalers had used it in the eighteenth century to leave messages for each other, and how in modern times, that custom continued, albeit altered. And with a different barrel, of course.

Eduardo stuck his hand into an opening in the barrel and pulled out a handful of postcards. He passed them to those who stood closest to him, and explained they were supposed to take a look at the destination and deliver them personally if possible, that is, if the recipient happened to live close to their home. In that way, they would help carry on and be a part of the whalers' tradition.

Barbara slid a few postcards from her shoulder bag and tossed them into the barrel for someone else to deliver in the future.

"No one you want to write?" she asked him.

"No one left to write," he said. He'd already told her how and why, so he didn't explain again. But being reminded of reality, his buoyant mood was gone.

As the postcards slipped from hand to hand so they each could examine them, Marc reached out for the stack held out to him, not really in the mood to take part in the ritual, expecting to pass them unread quickly on to Barbara to pass on to the next outstretched hand. But something made him glance down just as she was about to take them from him. Written across the top card in large letters were the words "Don't do it." He froze as Barbara grabbed the stack, and wouldn't let go.

The postcard's recipient was unnamed, and the message was unsigned, but the handwriting…

The handwriting was Melissa's.

"What's wrong, Marc?" asked Barbara, giving the stack a little tug.

"It's just the sun," he whispered, turning the card over and over in his hands, a photo of dolphins appearing and disappearing again. But each time, the handwriting remained. "I think I've had a little too much sun. That's all."

Marc casually removed the top card and made a show of fanning himself, giving the rest of the handful to Barbara. When she looked away while passing the stack on to the next in the circle, he slipped the card into a pocket. By the time she looked back at him, he'd made up his mind.

"I think I need to go back to the ship now," he said, turning back toward the path that had brought them there.

"I'll go with you," she said, starting to follow.

"No," he said, stopping her. "Don't let me take you away from this. It's something you've been dreaming of for years. We'll catch up at dinner."

But they didn't catch up at dinner. Back at the ship, Marc told the purser he wasn't feeling well and asked if a sandwich could be sent to his cabin. He leaned the postcard against an ice bucket on the dresser of his small room. He paged through the guidebooks he had been eying the night before, looking at Melissa's scribbles in the margins. There could be no doubt that the notes and the card had been written by the same person. He slid a suitcase out from under his bed, and retrieved a shoebox which he placed on the dresser next to the card. He drummed his fingers on the box's lid, but could not bring himself to open it.

"What is it that you want, Melissa?" he said. "What does 'Don't do it' *mean*? Don't do what I came here to do? Don't do what I never anticipated coming here to do? It was just dinner, Melissa, and a walk along the beach. I'll never be able to replace you. So what are you trying to tell me?"

There was no answer, but then, he didn't think he really expected one, because since her death, she had only spoken to him in dreams.

He was interrupted in his pleading by a knock at the door. It was only the purser with his sandwich. But he couldn't bring himself to eat, and so instead he tucked directly into bed. He hoped that he would dream of Melissa, and that in the dream she would more explicitly tell him what he was to do, but for the first time in half a decade, she did not visit him.

———

MARC WOKE in the middle of the night, disoriented and drenched in sweat. The air in the room had grown stuffy, and his covers had been kicked to the floor. He needed fresh air, and from the ship's rocking as it made its way at speed to the next day's island, he knew there'd be plenty of it up on the deck.

He dressed again and then made his way down narrow passageways, seeing no one. At this time of night, as he circled the deck with a stiff wind in his face, the vessel seemed deserted. Which was just as well, because if he had seen anyone, what would he have said to them?

If he saw Barbara, what would he say to her?

That his dead wife had sent him a postcard warning him against her? Or perhaps, that his dead wife had warned him against doing what he'd come to do on the final day of the trip? How could he possibly say such things? Share what was really going on in his head and the ship's doctor would likely restrict him to quarters.

Better to say nothing. Better to do nothing. Better to

treat the other passengers like the strangers they really were. Better to take a step back from Barbara, go back to treating her the way he'd been treating people ever since Melissa had died—pleasantly, politely, and kept at arms length. There was safety in that, the safety he needed to accomplish his mission.

The moon was only a quarter full, but still cast enough light for him to see the billowing waves as the ship cut through them. The island that waited ahead of them was only visible in the distance as an absence of stars along the horizon. Another time, another life, Marc could have considered such a vista romantic. But no longer. Now the stars and the sea only reminded him of the fact he'd once had someone to share them both with, but did no longer.

As he neared the prow, he noticed a glow coming from the bridge, so he wasn't entirely alone at that hour. Someone, of course, had to be steering the ship smoothly (well, somewhat smoothly, he told himself as he moved along unsteadily) to his destiny. He peered in as his path took him by, but did not pause, hoping to get past without conversation, but then the door slid open, and the captain stuck out his head.

"Couldn't sleep?" the man asked, the glow of the instrument panels providing more light than did the moon.

Marc nodded.

"You're in luck tonight," he continued. "Go up front and take a look down. In a few minutes, you're going to have something special to brag about to the others."

Marc did as the man suggested, interested more in continuing his solitude than in gaining any conversational gambit for the following day, even though he could use something else to speak of besides postcards, and what was to come. He stood at the prow, nothing more ahead of him but the rhythmic breaking of the waves, which were hypnotic in their randomness, and made him realize he was still tired. Sleep no longer brought him rest, and sometimes he thought the more sleep he got the less rested he was. But nothing unusual was occurring, regardless of what the captain had promised, so he thought perhaps he'd better head back to bed to at least try.

But then he could see straight lines raking the chaos of the sea, as if missiles had been fired at the ship from an array of unseen enemies, and soon the area directly beneath him was filled with dolphins. They all faced in the same direction, speeding forward, getting an extra boost from the motion of the ship. It was a game to them, the dolphin version of a roller coaster, he imagined. Marc had seen that behavior before during the day, but these dolphins were different—they glowed as they broke the water, awash in an eerie green light. They seemed happy somehow, and though he knew it was silly to ascribe anthropomorphic feelings to animals, as some of them leapt into the air in front of him, to him their mouths almost seemed curved upward in smiles.

He turned back and looked up at the captain, who waved and then gave him a thumb's up. Marc waved back. He hoped that was enough of a thank you for the gift of what he'd seen. But he'd had enough for one night. For all he knew, the dolphins could go on until dawn like this. It was time to abandon them so his head could hit his pillow once more. He'd need his energy the next day to properly avoid the others.

But then, as he gave one last look below, a dolphin transformed. Melissa was now down in the midst of them, Melissa glowing as she swam along in the waves, Melissa happy instead of lost in the various miserable emotions she showed him in his dreams. He called out her name and leaned as far as he could over the lip of the prow without tumbling into the water himself.

"What do you want?" he shouted, but he doubted she could hear him over the roar of their passage. "Melissa, talk to me! What are you doing here? What are you trying to tell me?"

She gave him no answer, just sped along, seeming to ignore him, and it wasn't until the other dolphins broke away, their playtime over, and headed back to their homes, that Melissa took a brief look up at him, only to dive suddenly below the surface, vanishing, taking the green glow with her.

"Come back, Melissa!" he cried. "Come back!"

But the sea was empty once more, his heart was empty once more, and nothing he could say could change that. As he stumbled past the bridge on the way back to his cabin in a daze, the captain stuck his head out once more.

"Amazing, isn't it?" he said, grinning. "The algae in this area is phosphorescent, and at night, when the dolphins break it with their snouts…well, you saw the result."

"Yes, I saw," said Marc. "Thank you."

He hurried back to his room, where he discovered that the postcard was gone. But the shoebox, and what lay within, still remained. He cried beside the open package until the morning came, then fell asleep sitting at the desk and stayed asleep until he was woken by a knock at the door.

"Marc, are you in there?" came Barbara's muffled voice. "Are you all right?"

He removed his shirt so he'd have an excuse to keep Barbara out of the room, then opened the door a crack and peered out.

"I brought you some food," she said, holding out a covered plate.

"Oh, hello, Barbara," he said, without much energy. He hoped that she'd blame his lack of enthusiasm on his feigned illness, and not take it personally. He didn't want to hurt her, though he knew he probably would, and that when she looked back on this trip, if she thought of him at all, she would probably blame herself, no matter how he handled the uncomfortable situation.

"How are you feeling?" she asked.

"Woozy," he said, opening the door slightly wider so he could take the plate. "I'm not really up to talking."

He peered beneath the plate's covering to find eggs, bacon and a croissant. It was what he had eaten the day before, and he was amazed she had noticed. And a little regretful as well. It meant that her pain would be that much greater.

"Maybe it will help you get your strength back."

"I appreciate it," he said, keeping the door firmly between them. "But I'd better get back to bed."

"Feel better," she said. "We'll be docking at Santa Cruz Island today. You won't want to miss Lonesome George. It's going to be a big day."

"I don't think I'll be able to make it," he said, but when he saw the disappointment play across her face, added softly, "We'll see."

He thanked her again and quietly closed the door before he could be drawn into further conversation. He set the plate on the desk, but didn't get around to eating. There was no way he could eat when he was this excited.

Barbara had been correct. Today *was* going to be a big day.

———

MARC PEERED FURTIVELY OUT through his porthole at the harbor of Santa Cruz Island. Unlike the other islands of the Galapagos, which were mostly uninhabited, a small city had grown up there. It was difficult to believe this was where his journey would end. That soon there'd be no more dreaming.

He watched as zodiac after zodiac headed for the small dock to shuttle passengers ashore to visit the Charles Darwin Research Center and Puerto Ayora, the latter really more village than city. He couldn't identify each tourist as the rafts pulled away, fattened by life preservers and topped by floppy hats to protect them from the sun. Barbara, ever enthusiastic, was surely on one of the first few of them. So once the rush had cleared, he placed the shoebox in his waterproof back-pack and headed for the ladder that would load him into the zodiac. His delay had helped him just as he had planned, because there was no longer much of a line. He ended up among a small group of stragglers he did not recognize, and their raft ended up being only half full. He felt relieved. There'd be no attempts at conversation that day, and they would not be looking to him for companionship once ashore for their self-guided tour.

As he stepped off onto the dock, he knew he should head straight for the cemetery. He felt the tug of it deep in his heart, but after years of delay, after having left this promise unfulfilled for so long, he felt Melissa would understand a wait of another hour.

He boarded a small shuttle bus for the Charles Darwin Research Center, and ignored the beauty of the ride, lost in his own thoughts. The backpack was heavy in his lap, heavier than it should be for what it carried, but he dared not put it down. What if through his inattention it was stolen? What would he do then? There would be no end to Melissa's story, nor to his own. So he closed his eyes and clutched the bag tightly until they arrived at the facility.

However interesting the other displays might have been, he walked past all of them. Only one exhibit held meaning for him now, and so he headed straight for the enclosure that contained Lonesome George. Most of what Melissa had told him and Barbara had repeated had vanished from his mind, but Lonesome George had stayed, just as it had stayed in this place, and stayed and stayed, seemingly immortal. Marc remembered what they had called it, the last of its kind, and perhaps that fact stuck with him because he somehow knew that someday he, too, would be the last of his kind. There was something romantic about it, and something tragic, too, and when Marc thought of himself he didn't know which word best described him.

He leaned over the barrier to look at the large tortoise munching on a cabbage. He couldn't remember the name of the island from which it had been plucked as the last survivor, but he *could* remember it was at least one hundred years old, if not older. It had spent most of its life alone, hopeful for a mate, but never finding one, rejecting the females of other species who were presented to him in the hopes that at least a part of his genetic makeup would live on. It didn't look depressed about its circumstances, but then, with a tortoise, who could tell? Marc knew that if he were faced with such a situation, he would make a choice.

He had a choice to make now. But with no other possible way of ending this, did it really deserve to be called a choice?

He left the station and returned to the town. He passed the restaurants by, even though he had gotten hungry and regretted not at least nibbling at Barbara's offering, and passed the souvenir stands as well, because he wasn't planning to take anything from this place, but instead leave something behind.

The small cemetery was unlike other cemeteries he had been forced to visit in his lifetime. He could almost call it cheerful. The stones and markers had a primitive, personal feel to them, many adorned with mosaics of broken glass and pottery shards. Custom had allowed the mourners to express themselves, unlike the uniformity he was used to back home, where fitting in held the highest priority. As he admired the display with one part of his mind, another part was scouting for the best place to do what he needed to do. Though he'd always realized it would all end here, he'd forgotten that a cemetery, even a small one, was not specific enough a destination. He had to find exactly the right patch of ground, and quickly. His backpack continued to be heavy beyond its weight, and he needed to put it down.

As he wandered the grounds, attempting to sense that perfect spot, he had little company. Whether it was due to the day of the week or just the time of day, there were no mourners here, just an occasional tourist like himself wandering through, no one who might find his own presence curious or interfere with his plans. No one invested enough in the place to bother to stop him.

He took his time, eying each marker in turn, seeking a sign, and instead finding only names he could not easily pronounce, and dates which reminded him that life was short and cruel. Eventually, he spotted a stone engraved with the image of a tortoise crawling along the ground, a dolphin arcing high over its head, and he thought, this is the place. This is where it should happen. The tortoise was who he was, who he had been before he met Melissa, plodding along, and now it was who he was after Melissa, lonely. The dolphin was Melissa herself, always leaping high, as she had the other night, reaching out to him, glowing, giving him, he now realized, a sign.

He had to do it here.

He slipped the shoebox from his backpack and knelt before the marker. He could barely believe this would all be over soon. His fingers shook as he lifted the lid.

When he saw what was revealed inside, he tumbled back.

Resting atop what he had brought with him was the postcard that had been delivered to him on Floreana Island. "Don't do it," the card still said, only this time, scribbled beneath that earlier inscription were the words, "Please, Marc."

And it was signed, "Love, Melissa."

He slumped to the cool earth and wept.

"What do you want from me, Melissa?" he said between sobs. "I'm only trying to finally do what you wanted. I'm sorry it took so long. I'm only trying to do what I promised you I'd do."

When enough tears had passed that he was once more able to function, he lifted the shoebox into his lap and felt the cool and familiar metal inside.

"It can't go on like this," he said. "It just can't."

He turned his head, and found himself eye to eye with the leaping dolphin of the grave marker. It seemed to be smiling, the way Melissa had been when he'd last seen her, swimming through the surf in the night. He traced the curve of its flank with one finger, and smiled himself.

A scuffling in the dirt nearby broke his concentration, and he looked up to see Barbara walking through the cemetery. She hadn't noticed him there yet. He hurriedly put the lid back on the box and stood, brushing the dirt from the seat of his pants. She noticed him as he popped up above the stones.

"There you are, Marc," she said hesitantly. "I was just about to head back for the ship when one of the guides told me you were feeling better. *Are* you feeling better?"

"I think I am," he said.

"Did you manage to see everything you wanted to here?" she asked.

"I think I have," he said, shifting the backpack easily from one shoulder to the other. "Let's go. It's time to get back to the ship."

ONCE ON BOARD, Marc no longer hid in his cabin, but instead joined the others for the rest of the day's meals. After dinner, one during which he did his best to keep all conversation light, he walked the deck with Barbara as the ship started its passage to their next and final island.

He sat beside her in a deck chair, and while they stared off together at the sunset, he found the strength to begin an apology to her for the way he had been acting.

"I'm sorry," he said, but found that he could only follow those two words up with silence, instead of the words he really wanted to say.

"You certainly are," she said sharply, then softened a bit. "What's been bothering you? You started to tell me the other day, but then…"

Her words drifted off, and this time, she was the one who let the silence linger. They sat quietly until the sun was gone, and then without another word, she was gone. He did not blame her. Unless you are with someone who can tell you everything, why bother to stay?

He returned to his room, but did not sleep. He waited until the middle of the night, and then went up to the bridge. This time, instead of trying to speed by, he popped in to sit with the captain for a moment.

"Will they be back again tonight?" he asked.

The captain shook his head.

"Doubtful," the man said. "We won't be passing anywhere near that area. Sorry."

But Marc did not believe him. He *could* not believe him. Tonight it would all be over. He felt as sure of that as he'd ever felt of anything. So he excused himself and went to the prow. He peered over, down into the surf, where he saw nothing beyond the surface of the impenetrable sea.

He waited, barely able to breath.

"I'm going to do it," Marc said. "I'm going to do it whether you tell me I should or not. It all ends right now."

As he reached into his pack, the dolphins came, streaking toward him like arrows aimed at his heart. They frolicked and glowed below, and there in the midst of them…

"Melissa," he whispered. She leapt up, spinning, iridescent, and paused to smile at him before tumbling back into the sea. He removed the shoebox from his pack, and opened it, so that the smooth metal within glowed in what remained of the moonlight.

"Is this what you really want?" he asked.

She leapt again, so high that it almost seemed she would not stop, and as she reached the apex of her arc, Marc unscrewed the urn's lid. He tilted the urn, and what remained of Melissa's body sprinkled down into the surf, and then what remained of her soul plunged into the midst of it. One by one, the dolphins left, until there was only Melissa. She smiled at him, and then slowly vanished beneath the waves.

There was a jerk at his arm, and Marc turned to see that the captain was beside him. He realized then that the man had been shouting, but he'd been unable to hear any of it. The man cupped his hands between his mouth and Marc's ear.

"You're not allowed to do that," the man yelled.

"I know," said Marc, staring down to where the ship broke the waves below. "But I had to do it anyway."

The captain did not stop Marc as he put the urn in his backpack. As Marc swung the bag over his shoulder, he felt something in his shirt pocket, something which hadn't been there earlier. It was the postcard again, only this time, it bore no writing, only the imprint of a pair of lips. Melissa's lips.

Marc pressed them to his own, and as he said goodbye,

the wind ripped the card from his fingers and tossed it high into the air, where it hung for a moment against the moon like a distant albatross passing in the night.

Tomorrow, he would have to tell Barbara all about it.

Tomorrow, he would have to tell Barbara everything.

THAT PERILOUS STUFF

"Are you sure you want to get out here?" the cab driver turned to me and asked as we pulled to a stop alongside my mother's house. I could tell what he was thinking as he took in the front porch overflowing with dented bicycles, rusty tools, and machine parts, the unmown lawn with grass so tall it could swallow a small child, and the trash bags stacked against the garage to form towers that seemed certain to topple, and it wasn't very different from what I'd thought when I'd turned my back on the place years before.

So actually, no, I wasn't all that sure I wanted to get out here, but I had no interest in explaining to a stranger why this sudden trip home to see my mother and brother left me feeling that way.

"I'll be fine," I said, not quite sure of that either. You can never go home again, they say. Well, unfortunately, they're wrong. Which meant I had a challenge ahead. For Mom and Lou collected more than only stuff. They also collected uncertainty and resentment and fear, and other emotions as well that I'd done my best to abandon. So my main goal this visit—other than dealing with Mom's latest difficulties, at which Lou had only hinted—was to make sure neither of my relatives offloaded any of those traits on me.

"Here," he said, passing a card back over his shoulder along with my change. "You might need this. It's not always that easy to get a cab to come all the way out here."

A card with a taxi driver's cell number was a reminder I wasn't home—my chosen home, that is—any longer. I'd grown used to summoning a car with the swipe of my thumb. But now, I was at my first home—my birth home—where such things were still impossible. And looking at the house, obscured by Mom's hoard—though from the disassembled machinery out on the porch, it was undeniably Lou's hoard now as well—I knew there was going to be a whole lot more I'd find impossible here.

The driver—Marco according to his card—pulled my suitcase out of the trunk—a small one, as I hoped not to have to stay long—and I was soon alone on the crowded porch of the house I'd had to run from, until my brother's call had me running back.

I leaned into the doorbell, but it didn't work. Of *course* it didn't work. Thing had always fallen apart here, and Mom was always too busy bringing more stuff into the house to bother fixing whatever stuff she already had. I could have opened the door myself if I'd brought my key, but it had been so long since I'd crossed the country to visit that I no longer knew where it was.

Does that make me a bad daughter? Sometimes I think so. Other times I think—if I'd been a better one I'd have ended up trapped like Lou. And unlike him, I don't think I'd have survived.

I took a deep breath, thought for a moment of immediately phoning Marco and telling him, you were right, and no, I didn't really want to get out here, please take me back to the airport so I can catch the next flight away from this place, OK?…

But then I pushed all that aside and knocked.

I heard Lou stumbling nearer in response to my rapping —I recognized it wasn't Mom because she no longer walked well enough to even get up to stumble—and wasn't sure why he sounded off balance and was continually knocking into things. Until he opened the door and I could see things were far worse than what I'd feared, and a spacious living room was now nothing more than a large storage locker with a narrow pathway running down the middle.

Magazines and newspapers which had obviously once been stacked into piles had long ago slid into dusty mounds. Dozens of lamps, their necks broken, their lightbulbs dangling. Baskets filled with so much clothing it would have taken weeks to launder.

So many possessions it was impossible even to perceive them all. So much chaos it looked as if half a dozen homes had exploded and then been scooped up in a hurry to fill this house. I'd suspected it could be worse…but *this* much worse?

"What happened, Lou?" I said, too stunned to get out more words than those, asking about both my mother and the house at the same time. But Lou knew that. And didn't like it.

"No time to get into that now," he said. "Mom's really gotten worse."

Seeing the worried expression on his face, I wanted to hug him. But he and I had never had that kind of relationship, and I was too angry and distracted by the mess around us to have the ability to break through the barrier of that just then. Maybe later. I reached up to pat his shoulder and left it at that.

"Yes, I know," I said. "You told me as much on the phone. Where is she?"

"Are you sure you're ready?" he said. "You haven't seen her in a long time, so you're going to be shocked, I promise you. Better prepare yourself."

I didn't think anything could have shocked me more than what I'd already seen. The house was claustrophobic enough before I'd left—Mom's hoarding squeezed out the space my younger self had needed to breathe—but I wrestled my suitcase through the door—which did take some wrestling considering how narrow things had gotten—and steeled myself. Lou had to walk sideways down the hall—a hall once decorated with family photos and Dad's darting trophies, but now more a tight path through a moving van—as I followed him to the back of the house.

There, in what used to be the small dining area next to the kitchen, Mom was in a cot, propped up by pillows. So many pillows she almost seemed to vanish in them. A wall of televisions, none functioning, some with cracked screens, others with snapped antennas, filled the room across from her. The sink in the connected kitchen was overflowing with record albums, the stovetop piled with dented birdcages which, thankfully, were empty. And I hated to think what might be in the oven.

"You've got her staying down here?" I said, trying to speak quietly, but too angry to do so. "In the kitchen? And how could you let this happen to the kitchen anyway?"

"She can no longer do the stairs, I told you that," he said, only answering my first question. I doubted it would even be possible to get answers that made sense to my other questions from either of them.

I knelt beside Mom, having to clear a space to do so— were those really empty potato chip bags, just left lying there?—and took her hand. She turned briefly toward me at my touch, not really seeing me, then looked back at the blank screens. I wondered what shows she thought she was watching, or if she even had enough of her old self left to believe she was watching anything.

"Mom, it's me," I said. "It's Jo. I came as soon as I could."

Lou muffled a snort, but just barely. I resisted turning at the sound. He didn't understand what it was like.

"How are you doing?" I whispered.

She tilted her head slightly, first this way, then that, as if to indicate, take a good look at me, how do you think I'm doing? Or perhaps to indicate nothing at all, bobbing in concert to winds of memory she alone felt.

"She's been like this all week," said Lou, hanging behind me less to give me a moment alone with her than because there wasn't space for all three of us in the room at once. "She's stopped talking. She's stopped even knowing I was here."

"Then what's she still doing at home?" I said, no longer bothering to whisper. Mom wouldn't know what we were saying anyway. "Let's get her to a hospital."

"Jo, you know there's nothing physically wrong with her. At least nothing anyone can fix. It's her brain. It's just…it's just what happens when a person gets old. I didn't call you here because I believed you could fix this. I called so we could decide what to do next. Together. As a family. Besides, she has a living will. If she wants to die here, here is where she'll die. This is where she's comfortable."

"She's not dying any time soon," I said, hoping that saying the words would make it so. "And here? Die here? This isn't a house anymore. This is a waste dump. I know you inherited some of her…her sickness. But how could you let this happen?"

"I didn't see you trying to stop it."

"It wasn't either of our jobs to stop it. But it wasn't our

job to make it worse either. It was our job to live. To escape it."

"Well, you managed to do that, didn't you?" he said. "I hope you're happy."

The bitterness in his voice hurt. But it didn't cause as much pain as staying would have. I knew that. And I think he knew that, too. At least a little.

"I wasn't going to do it," he said, looking over my shoulder at Mom. "I wasn't going to be the kind of man who leaves."

"I'm sorry, Lou," I said, apologizing not just for me, but for Dad, and how his leaving had changed everything. "I really am. But I had to, you know that. I…just couldn't. I couldn't. You've always been stronger than me. But still, you…you've lived here too long. It's gotten inside of you. I don't think you're able to see the place as it really is anymore."

"I didn't call you here for interior decorating advice," he said. "I called you here to help figure out what to do with Mom. I thought that was the right thing to do. That's how siblings are supposed to behave."

I got up off my knee, nearly slipping on—oh, great, were those candy wrappers?—and rolled my suitcase closer to Mom. And then I sat on it, because there was nowhere else to sit. I'd have liked to sit in a chair, but there wasn't a cleared surface anywhere in the room. Or, I was guessing, based on the clutter there and in the living room, anywhere else in the house. I took Mom's hand, squeezed it. She didn't squeeze back.

"Living will or no, we've got to get her out of this…this place. She collected, she hoarded, she wouldn't let go of things…but she never intended to die in filth."

"There's no filth here," he said. "We're not hoarders."

Now it was my turn to snort.

"Do you see rotting food here?" he continued. "Dead animals? These are just the things that matter to her."

"The things that matter?" I said, angrily kicking at the wrappers around my feet. "How could all these things matter? And matter to whom? Her? Or you? It couldn't possibly have gotten this bad if you hadn't enabled her. You should have said no every once in awhile. You should have put on the brakes instead of pressing on the gas."

Lou sighed, which he always did when he didn't really want to talk. There had been many sighs in our relationship, more the worse Mom's compulsion got.

"Maybe I shouldn't have called you," he said. "It's just like old times. And old times were never very good."

"Well, they weren't all bad either. And you did call, so let's try to deal with the situation as it is."

Mom's expression was blank, her reaction to the bickering of her children nonexistent. I'd normally have pulled Lou into another room to have a discussion like this, but as far as I could tell, it was almost as if we weren't there at all. Once, any harsh words between us would have terrified her, but now, nothing. That wasn't the Mom I knew. And I wanted the old Mom back, even with all her flaws. If I couldn't do that, I at least had to do right by her.

"Look, there aren't many options," I said. "We've either got to get her out of here, or get all this stuff out of here. It's one or the other. That's it. There are no other choices. Regardless of what you think Mom thinks she wants, this house has become a health hazard, and if anyone from the county were to see inside—"

"No one's going to see inside."

"You're not thinking clearly, Lou. People don't need X-ray vision to know something's very wrong here. The way you've let the porch and front yard go, I'm surprised neighbors haven't already complained."

Lou looked away, which told me...they already had.

"Do you realize the cabdriver almost wouldn't let me get out here? He thought the place was abandoned or belonged to drug dealers or something. Is all this stuff really necessary?"

"Will you lay off about the stuff already, Jo? Dealing with the stuff isn't going to fix anything. This is Alzheimer's we're dealing with. Nothing else but that matters."

"If nothing else matters, then let's start clearing out some of this mess. If she stays—and OK, maybe you're right, maybe she should stay, I'll give you that for now—she'll need nurses, and believe me, no one is going to be willing to work here. They'll walk through the front door—if they even make it to the front door—and turn right back around and leave."

I dropped Mom's hand, and reached for the top few magazines from a stack on top of the bureau that completely blocked off the mirror.

"Not tonight," Lou said quickly. "It's late. Can't we leave this for tomorrow? Please? This is going to be tough enough. Let's leave it until after a night's sleep, OK?"

I had to admit...Lou was right. He might have let himself become trapped in a house of sludge, but he wasn't stupid. And I truly was tired from the long flight. Besides, decades of debris weren't going to be cleared out in one night. Looking at Mom, though, inert, focussed on nothing but her inner self, if her inner self remained, I wasn't sure how many more nights we had left.

I let Lou lead me up the stairs to my old room, following closely in his footsteps so as not to dislodge any of the stuffed animals, paperweights, figurines, and other incongruous objects piled on the steps. I shuddered to think what my room would look like, and regretted not checking into a nearby motel. But...it was my mother, and I felt I owed it to her to try to spend as many more nights under the same roof as I could. Lou had done it for a lifetime of days. I should at least be able to handle a few.

He shouldered open the door and...yes, it was just that bad. It appeared as if all the junk mail that had arrived during my absence was piled in one corner. Shoes and purses exploded out of the open closet, its door no longer able to close, and beneath them I spotted bicycle pumps and empty picture frames. And why were there half a dozen microwaves at the foot of my bed, a bed barely visible under dozens of throw pillows and even more baskets of laundry?

He dragged my suitcase over to the one bit of open floor-space and started removing the piles from the bed and adding them to the other piles that ringed the room, filling in the space at the top until they touched the ceiling. I was sure it would all collapse on me as I slept. Or tried to sleep.

"It's good to see you, sis," he said, once he'd cleared my old mattress.

"It's good to see you, too, Lou," I said.

And it was. I couldn't deny that. But seeing all Mom's stuff...that was never good. We had to get through it, though. We had to.

TRYING to sleep any longer was pointless. I'd given it a good shot, but this wasn't a bedroom anymore. I felt as if I'd crawled into a long-abandoned storage unit. And closing my eyes didn't help. Whether in darkness or in light, I could still feel the pressure of all those possessions. So I sat up and moved to the edge of the bed, having to first carefully choose the side with space left over for my feet.

I looked up at the tower of boxes and trash bags that ringed the room, the tennis rackets and ukuleles, dressmaker dummies and slightly broken umbrellas, the detritus from a thousand yard sales, and wondered what would drive anyone —two anyones—to first gather and then keep it all. But I couldn't think of an answer. Maybe there was no answer. I gave up trying to puzzle one out and flicked on a light.

Where once there were windows visible along the outer wall of my room, now there was just a clumsily constructed wall of useless objects. A wall built of the forgotten. A wall covered with dust. How long had it been since anyone had gone through all these things and asked each item to defend its existence?

It wasn't going to be me. The stuff, as invasive as it was, didn't really matter. Lou was right, though for the wrong reasons. It was Mom that mattered most of all. And if what was keeping her confined to the first floor was her health, that's what had to be cleared up first, not every possession.

Since I couldn't sleep, I headed downstairs. As I passed Lou's room, I could hear him snoring. At least one of us was having no problem sleeping. Obviously, none of this bothered him. Since he'd inherited—or more likely absorbed—the same disease, I guess he found this way of life, these surroundings, normal. Just as well. Better he slept while I did what I had to do. Seeing me move any of their things would only make him anxious, I knew. Luckily, Mom was apparently too far gone for it to make her anxious.

She was awake, too, still watching the dead televisions. Wonder what she saw screening there in her head that was keeping her awake? No way of knowing.

"Can I get you anything, Mom?" I asked. "Do you need something? A glass of water? A snack?"

She didn't answer, didn't even look in my direction.

I obviously wasn't going to get information out of Mom, and was too filled with nervous energy to do nothing, so looked around until I spotted the tall stack of magazines on the bureau, the ones Lou had stopped me from handling. Wouldn't hurt to at least do some small bit of neatening up. If I was going to stay there for a few days, I had to do something to remain sane.

Mom didn't seem to care as I sorted through the sometimes decades-old issues and stacked them in neat piles by the door to the back yard. After an hour of that, I'd managed to create the only clear surface in the room. In the house, perhaps. The mirror, revealed after who knows how long, was covered with dust, and I swiped at it with a palm so it could do what it was meant to do. Which reminded me of how many things there were in the house that no longer did what they were meant to do.

I looked in the glass and saw both myself and Mom reflected back. We looked so much alike, even with what the years had done to each of us, hers spent grasping and never letting go, mine spent running and always letting go.

But if I'm the one who'd been doing the running, why was she the one so far away?

I pulled out some chipped china knickknacks which had been hidden by the magazines in the space between the mirror and the bureau. Cats and dogs and turtles and elephants, covered by dust and cobwebs. To have been treated like that, could any of them have really mattered? They deserved better. They deserved to belong to someone who cared, someone who would put them to use. I gathered in my arms as many as I could, balancing them carefully, or so I thought, but I must have been more tired than I realized, because a penguin slipped, and as soon as I made a grab for it, the others followed. I managed to catch about half of them, but the others dropped to the floor, one of them shattering. A figurine of two dogs broke into many pieces, and their heads rolled. If not for the cups and saucers stacked by the foot of Mother's bed, they would have vanished beneath.

And then I heard Mom's voice for the first time since I'd arrived. It was loud, it was not happy, and it made me feel as if I was twelve again.

"What are you doing, Jo?" she shouted. "You stop that!"

Shocked, I hurried to her side, let the rest of the statues tumble from my arms onto the mattress where they landed safely. I took her hands, looked into her eyes. She was back. If only for a moment, she was back.

"I'm here, Mom," I said, amazed that she had roused enough to speak. I didn't care that her words had been angry ones, as long as she was no longer locked inside her head. "I came back to help."

"You call that helping?" she said, not looking at me, but at the shards of broken dogs scattered across the floor.

"I'm sorry, Mom, I didn't mean to do that," I said. "I was just trying to clear a little space. You know living like this isn't healthy for you, don't you? Let me try to make things better for you. Please let me do that for you."

Mom shook her head, and pursed her lips.

"Your father gave me that," she said. "Your father gave me that and you broke it."

"I'm sorry, Mom, I wish I'd known, but when there's so much, who can—"

And then suddenly, Lou was in the room with us, uncaring of the rubble he had to push aside to enter.

"What's going on?" he asked, his voice even louder than mother's had been.

Mom waggled a hand at the floor.

"I told you not to do this," he said. "You told me you would wait until morning."

"I couldn't sleep," I said. "It had to be done anyway. I didn't think I needed your permission."

"No," said Mom, speaking with less strength she had just a moment before. "No."

"No what, Mom?" I said, feeling her fingers begin to clasp mine less firmly.

"I know you care, Jo," she said. "But…all this…all this must stay right here. And I'm staying right here, too. Staying. Staying. Stay…"

And then she was gone again, her gaze blank, her head turned back to the dead televisions. Whatever had animated her had passed, but still—

"Did you see that?" I said to Lou. "She's not as far gone as we thought. Maybe there's a chance we can have our mother back again."

"Maybe. Or maybe you just startled and pissed her off enough to bring her back momentarily. If you started breaking my stuff, I'd wake up from a coma, too."

"Joke if you'd like, but this was a good thing."

"Nothing good ever comes from breaking something," he said, pushing at fragments of dog with his bare toes. "This stuff matters, Jo. Her whole life is here. And mine, too. And yours as well, if you'd open your eyes and see it."

"The only life that matters to me is the life that's inside your skin. Her skin. Not any of this. This is just a prison. And one you two have built yourselves. I wish you'd open your eyes and see *that*."

"If you really feel that way, then maybe it's best if you spent the night somewhere else. Get a motel room. You know you want to anyway."

"What, you don't trust me now?"

"No, not really," he said. "Not anymore."

He bent and picked up the two dog heads, holding one in each hand.

"You don't remember this, do you?"

"I'm afraid I don't. There's too much here to even consider remembering every object."

"Dad gave this to her one anniversary. I don't remember

which one. But I remember that we were young. And I remember that Mom was smiling."

"We would've been young for Dad to have still been around. Or for Mom to have been pleased about it enough to smile."

"Whatever," he said, trying to fit the chipped heads together along the edges where they'd broken. "But know that this is more than just a thing. This is a memory. This is important."

"Perhaps. But can it *all* be so important? Doesn't the sheer number of things make even the most important ones less important? Some things *have* to go. That's why Dad left, because Mom couldn't see that. That's why I had to leave. That's why you should have left, too, a long, long time ago."

"I'll help you with your bag," Lou said coldly. He turned and headed down the hall and back upstairs. And after another longing look at Mom, lost in whatever thickening fog had engulfed her, her one brief moment of clarity gone, I followed him as best I could, picking my way through the litter of other people's lives.

I DIDN'T GET BACK to the house the following day as early as I would have liked. That's because, as I fell asleep in the relaxingly uncluttered motel room, I realized I wouldn't be able to do what I needed to do alone. And with Lou as tight in the grip of this thing as Mom, he couldn't be the partner I'd need. I needed a different sort of ally. Someone disinterested, but passionate. Someone whose word might be believed a little more than mine. Which is why when I entered the house the following afternoon, I had someone from social services at my side.

Oh, it wasn't official, because it can take months to get

something like that going. But not everyone I'd gone to school with had skipped town the way I had, and I was able to reach out to a friend of a friend. So Greta was at my side that morning. She wouldn't be able to force anything to happen, but I trusted that once she saw what I had seen, she'd back me up.

When we pulled into the driveway—or as far in as the washing machines and lawnmowers, not all of which had been there the previous day, would allow—her reaction was much like that of the concerned cabbie. Only she already knew, because of the history I'd shared—I belonged here.

I introduced Greta to Lou, not bothering to tell him that she wasn't accompanying me in an official capacity. Mom was too far gone to pay attention, but maybe it would put some fear into *him*. He was too polite to throw her right out, as I could tell he wanted to do. Thankfully, he was usually able to hold it together around strangers. Greta moved through the narrow hallway, her face blank, not reacting to what must be hard not to react to—yes, she was good—and went to the dining room to meet my mother, with Lou and me trailing along.

"What is this?" he hissed.

"Something we need," I said. "I told you, but you wouldn't listen. This is beyond us."

I moved up tightly beside Greta, because tightly was all there was room for.

"Hello, Mom," I said. "This is Greta. She's a friend of mine. She wants to meet you."

There was no response, not even the bobbing of her head that she'd evidenced the day before.

"Like I said, she was briefly better last night," I told Greta.

"That's only because you broke something Mom cared about very much," said Lou. "And you're reading too much into it. She wasn't *that* much better. It was a blip. Here and gone."

Greta looked at Lou momentarily, nodded at me, and then turned back to Mom.

"I'd like to have some time alone with her if I may," she said. "She could very well behave differently when you're not around."

We stepped out of the room, me gladly, Lou begrudgingly, and once we were by the front of the house, he let his anger out.

"You had no right to do this," he said. "You walked out on her, just like Dad. You left me here to take care of it, the both of you. So I'm taking care of it. Now why don't you butt out. Run like you did before. Forget I called you. We're doing fine."

"This is not taking care of it," I said, waving my arm around the room, though even with being smaller than Lou, there wasn't that much space for me to wave. "By what stretch of the imagination is this taking care of it?"

"By the stretch that she's alive, she's healthy, and what's going on with her is beyond our control and not my fault."

"But how about this!" I said. "Is *this* in your control!"

I grabbed at the nearest box, pulled back the corrugated lid, and found dozens of jelly glasses. Some I recognized from childhood, but most had been collected in the years since.

"Do you really need these?" I continued, in full rant mode. "You have enough of the stupid things to throw a wedding party, and I doubt you ever have guests here. This place is so embarrassing I'm probably the only one you've allowed in for years. Get rid of these, I beg you. Sell them, give them away, let them be of use to someone else, or even just toss them in the trash, but—"

I made the mistake then of trying to lift the box. It was

far heavier than I'd thought, so instead it slipped from my hands. I made a grab for it, but only succeeded in ripping open a section of the cardboard, which let a few of the glasses tumble out. They hit the floor and exploded, and when the box followed, I could hear a loud jingling of glass as its entire contents shattered.

Lou shouted louder than I'd ever heard him before, but I didn't care. It felt good to finally take action against all these oppressive possessions, even if I was doing it subconsciously, doing what Mom could never bring herself to do, doing what Lou, the good son, would never dare.

I bent so I could try to move the box somewhere out of what little path we had, but when I did so, the bottom collapsed, a shower of shards falling on my shoes. I cursed and threw the now empty box against the—not wall, but a wall of other boxes—and in that instant all my anger, all my pain, all my history with Mom's things, those empty things, came out, and I began to cry at last. I flailed my arms about, knocked down other boxes which hit the floor with either thuds or crackles, hurled figurines of sad clowns, and glass globes that should have been decorating someone's garden somewhere rather than clogging a hallway, and bowls of fake fruit, their wax sagging and discolored by age. I grabbed and flung anything my fingers could clutch.

"Stop it, Jo, you're not accomplishing anything," Lou shouted, while doing nothing to intervene. He'd never seen me let loose like this before and I think I scared him a little. I know I scared me.

I kept shouting and smashing things, he kept shouting and dodging the things I threw, but neither of us would stop our vicious dance until Mother made us both jump by shouting impossibly louder than all the noises we were making put together.

Our mother, who according to Lou hadn't left her bed in

weeks, marched jerkily out of the hallway with only the aid of a cane. Greta, trailing behind her, looked stunned.

"My children shouldn't be fighting," Mom said, her voice strong and clear. There was none of the hesitation or searching for words that I'd heard during phone calls in recent years. "I didn't raise the two of you to act this way. You're embarrassing yourselves."

"You're walking," said Lou.

"You're talking," I said. "Mom, you're talking."

Her few words the night before during that brief moment of clarity had been welcome, but this newfound coherence was astonishing.

"Of course, I'm talking," Mom said. "Why wouldn't I be talking? Why are you both looking at me like that?"

"I don't understand," said Greta. "I couldn't get a word out of her. I couldn't get her to react to anything. She was totally non-responsive, and now this. It makes no sense."

"You just got her mad enough," Lou said to me. "Just like last night. And just like last night, it'll fade."

"Alzheimer's doesn't work that way," said Greta. "If that's what she was suffering from, you wouldn't see her spontaneously come back like this. This is something different. Something else. I don't know what's going on here, but whatever's wrong with your mother isn't what you think is wrong with your mother."

"Who said anything about Alzheimer's?" Mom said. "It gets to be too much sometimes and I just get tired, that's all."

She walked up to me and poked at the rubble with the tip of her cane.

"Did you do this, Jo?" she said, with a tone I knew too well.

I suddenly felt like a kid again, flashed back to similar conversations in a house far less cluttered, but still far too cluttered for me, and couldn't respond with anything more than a nod. A trace of tenderness appeared in her face in answer to that nod.

"You've got to stop this," she said. "That's no way for a grown woman to act, destroying other people's things. What gives you the right?"

"I'm sorry, Momma."

"And you, Louis, why were you shouting at Jo that way? She's your little sister. You mustn't treat her so mean."

My brother dropped his head.

"I'm sorry, too, Mother."

After a round of hugs, which Greta stood aside from, watching Mom with continued confusion, I headed into the kitchen to get some trash bags. Considering the number of stuffed ones around the home, I knew I'd find a box of them somewhere. I started to sift through the debris and load it all into the bags as best I could without slicing my fingers, but as I finished filling each one, Mom would stop me from carrying it outside. She said she wanted me to set them aside once I was done bagging everything, that she wanted to go through every item, every fragment, every shard herself to see whether anything could be saved. I already knew what Mom could never admit—there was nothing I'd damaged that was worth saving. I didn't feel like arguing then, though, not with Lou glaring at me, and with Greta looking on in wonder. I no longer want witnesses for what Mom and I needed to say to each other.

"We'll talk later once I have a chance to think about all this," Greta said once I was done.

"There's nothing to think about, young lady" said Mom. "We don't need your help here. We're doing fine."

"I'll call you," whispered Greta to me as she passed on her way out the front door. "Something must be done here. I don't know what, but something."

After the three of us cleared off the kitchen table—which

means we had to fill in the space around Mom's bed first—we had lunch. Not that we could prepare anything there ourselves, because the kitchen was long past being functional, the appliances not just overwhelmed but inoperative, so I ordered take-out. And we managed to have a conversation with Mom unlike any that we'd had in years. We set aside the tough stuff and talked about the things that didn't matter, in one of those moments that seemed it was really the only thing that mattered.

As we shared about which late-night TV host we liked best and what our favorite recent movies were, something nagged at me, and I could quite figure out what it was. The timing of this talk and Mom's resurgence all seemed far too...coincidental maybe? I wasn't sure.

When we finally wore Mom out with our chatting, we rearranged the puzzle of the house once more so she could return to her bed. She seemed devoid of energy as I tucked her in, fading remarkably quickly for how much spark she'd shown.

As soon as she was settled, I went out to the porch with Lou to talk as we used to do when we were kids and wanted some privacy from our parents, not knowing that Mom and Dad probably heard every word anyway. I would have liked to sit in the porch swing, but we couldn't reach it, of course, our way to it totally blocked. So we sat on the steps, one of the few clear spots, even though they were also being narrowed by...stuff. We sat in silence for awhile, until the silence became too uncomfortable, and had to be broken.

"Well, that was weird," I finally said.

"Weird, but good," said Lou. "It's been a long while since Mom's been anything like that."

"If only she could stay that way."

"I don't think that's really possible, Jo. She's getting old.

This is just what happens to people. We've got to face that. Unless we do, we won't be able to deal with it."

"What if it didn't have to happen?" I said. "What if…"

I was afraid to put out there what was clattering about inside my head. It sounded crazy up there and would sound even crazier coming out of my mouth.

"What if what?" said Lou. "What do you mean? Even that social worker you dragged to see her was baffled. Getting old means losing it. And even though we love her, we're going to have to admit—Mom's lost it."

"Look, I know how these things go," I said. "I know what getting old means. But this seems…different. Surely you noticed what happened each time right before she perked up? Some of her stuff was gone, and—"

"It was more than just gone. You destroyed it."

"Yes, I destroyed it. I admit it. I didn't mean to, but I did it."

"Oh, you meant it. Don't deny that. Be honest with yourself."

"Will you forget about the blame for a moment and listen to me. I know what you said. That she only roused because her anger momentarily empowered her. But it's more than that. It's got to be. Didn't you notice, staying with her over the years, that the more of Mom's things there's been, the less of Mom there's been? Even I could tell that, just over the phone, but I never put two and two together. She's slipping away and…"

I could hardly bring myself to say the words.

"Of course she's slipping away," said Lou. "Someday we'll slip away, too."

"Not like this, we won't," I said. "These possessions, they've become so important to her that she's slipping away *into* them. Her hoarding sickness has been willed into something stranger. Something greater. This stuff…it's absorbing her soul. And once I destroyed them, once they could no longer contain her, she got it back. Pieces of it anyway. But not enough pieces. We can't let this go on. We can't. We've got to free her."

"Oh, come on, Jo. That's woo-woo crazy talk. I'm sorry if saying this sounds like a cliche, but you've spent too much time living in California."

"And you've spent too much time not living anywhere but here. If this has done that to her, who knows what it's done to you?"

"Enough!" said Lou, snapping. He stood up stiffly. "Why don't you just go home, Jo. Check out of your motel, hop a plane, go back to that simple, uncluttered life you've chosen, and leave all of this behind. It's clear you're not ready to deal with our family."

He went back inside, leaving me to sit on the steps alone, staring out in the darkness at grass that should never have been allowed to grow that tall.

But he was wrong.

I was ready to deal with the family.

I was the only one ready.

I PULLED out the card Marco had given me and phoned for him to come take me back to the motel, which he said that after he was through with his fare, he'd do. I didn't really care how long he'd take. I was fine with waiting. I had a lot of thinking to get done. And sitting with the house at my back, both the one from my memory and the one that was real, I came to realize what I was in for. But even though I knew what must be next, knew in my heart, knew in my soul, there was still the part of me that thought—what if I was wrong?

Which is why by the time Marco arrived to pick me up, I'd changed my plan, and instead of having him head back to the motel, I merely had him drive me a couple of blocks away and let me off there. I apologized for the short fare, made sure to tip him well, and explained what I needed from him next. He didn't seem to mind. The desperation was probably spilling off me, and he could probably sense that.

I walked back to the house, keeping to the shadows, and watched from across the street until lights went on upstairs in Lou's room…and then off again. Once I figured he had to be asleep, which his snoring from the night before told me he would do solidly (and a good thing, too), I entered via the back door, which led directly into the kitchen.

Off to the side, I could see Mom back in her cot, asleep this time, or so it seemed, no longer staring off at things unseen. I watched her for awhile, wondering if the part of her that mattered really could have gone where I'd thought it had gone. I looked away, scanning the ephemera around us, enough for multiple lifetimes. Could I possibly be right?

There was only one way to find out.

I started with a box above the refrigerator. As quietly as I could, I unfolded the lid and emptied into a bag sock monkeys, Raggedy Ann dolls, and packages of cookies with long-passed expiration dates (why were those things even together?), then resealed the box so no one could possibly notice anything had been taken. Until I was proven right, everything had to be done surreptitiously. I moved through what once was a kitchen and what once was a dining room, looking for the most easily reachable boxes, ones which I could ransack and still leave appearing undisturbed. I took nothing that was in plain sight, loading bag after bag until I'd reached the limit of how many I thought would fit in the back of the cab, and dragged them through the back yard to a side street. I left them there, knowing they'd be safe—as far as I knew, Mom was the only one who rummaged through trash in this neighborhood—then went back to say goodbye. But also a hopeful hello.

Her eyes were open this time, staring straight ahead, and she didn't turn to notice me. I walked into the path of her gaze, hoping to attract her attention, but though I smiled, though I waved, I couldn't raise a response.

I leaned in and gave her a kiss.

"See you soon," I whispered, and then returned to the hoard I'd made off with, where I called Marco again. This time, I did have him take me back to the motel.

When we got there, I told him to skip the main entrance where he'd left me before and instead circle around the back. I pointed to a large rectangular dumpster in a far corner of the parking lot. He pulled up beside it and looked back, puzzled.

"Now what?" he said.

"Give me a hand," I said, climbing out and pulling one of the bags out with me.

"What's this all about?" he said, popping open the trunk.

"You nailed it when you first dropped me off and asked me whether I wanted to get out," I said. "You were right. I didn't. But I had to. That's how family works. And this, this is just one more thing I have to do whether I want to or not."

Marco helped me line all the bags beside the dumpster, and then gave me a hand as I climbed up a ladder built into its side. I pulled one of the bags with me, reached in, grabbed a whiskey bottle molded in the shape of Elvis, and let it drop. The crackle as it burst was satisfying.

"Are you sure you wouldn't rather sell these things?" he asked. "Maybe donate them to Goodwill? You could bring in a couple of bucks. Maybe even help someone. Just saying."

"There's only person I'm thinking of helping right now," I said.

I dropped a collectible plate bearing the Mona Lisa, followed by a Rubik's Cube from which a corner cube was missing. As I did so, I pictured Mom as she used to be. Younger, yes, but it wasn't just younger I was hoping for. I wanted her to be present, to once more have a life of conscious action, rather than the tropisms which had swallowed her, driving Dad away, driving me away, driving Lou to sacrifice his life for hers.

"Can I help you with that?" said Marco. "You've got a *lot* of stuff here. Doing it one at a time like that is going to take you all night."

"I think I'm going to have to do this by myself," I said, tossing in a handful of well-chewed tennis balls. And we'd never owned a dog. From what gutter had she gathered those? "I don't know how I know that. But I know."

He shrugged and drove off, leaving me alone in the darkness, where I finished offloading the rest of the junk. But I didn't remain in darkness for long. Because I knew the things that would not break needed to be burned. I lit a newspaper I'd set aside and dropped it atop the mountain of things Mom couldn't let go of, watched the flames catch the fringe of a pillow, then leap to a stained polyester blouse, and onto the tape spilling out of a cracked cassette cartridge, eventually bringing the whole pile ablaze. The flames danced and dark smoke rose, and as they did, I hoped that whatever was being released to the skies would release Mom, too.

I stayed by the fire until it was mostly ash with lumps of melted plastic poking through, then went upstairs to pack my bag. Because the next day I'd be flying home.

Or at least pretending to.

LOU WASN'T happy to see me once he opened the door to my knocking, obviously believing that after having turned his back on me the night before on the porch, I'd be gone. I didn't care, though. The only thing that mattered was whether *Mom* would now be capable of being happy to see me.

I pushed past him, leaving him behind me, staring out at Marco's cab (since I'd told him to wait), and on into Mom's room. I *had* to stop thinking of it as that, though. It was *not* Mom's room. It was only the kitchen in which she had become frozen.

She was sitting on the edge of the cot, tapping a pencil against a partially filled crossword puzzle in a yellowed newspaper, and looked up the moment I walked in. She smiled, her eyes bright. I sat beside her and took her hand while Lou hung back in the doorway, glaring at us both.

"How are you doing, Mom?" I asked.

"I'm doing fine," she said, her voice strong and clear. There was no sign of her old self. Only her older self, the one I remembered from before things began to go bad. "How have you been, dear?"

"I'm doing fine, Mom," I said, my voice thickening. "But I'm doing even better today."

"I feel the same way," said Mom. "I managed to get a good start on today's puzzle. I can't remember when that last happened."

I didn't have the heart to tell her that wasn't today's crossword puzzle. It wasn't even that year's puzzle. But it was at least a puzzle. That was good enough for now.

"See?" said Lou. "You're not needed here any longer. It turns out there's nothing wrong with her. I guess she was just under the weather for a bit, but when she woke up this morning, she was better. False alarm and all that. Sorry I bothered you. I'll try not to do it again. But you can go home now."

"Oh, do you have have to go already, dear?" said Mom, tightening her grip even more. "It would be wonderful if you could stay awhile. I don't get to see as much of you as I used to."

"I wish I could, Mom," I said, leaving unsaid, *there's a reason for that.* "But I have to get back to work. And Lou's right. Since you're feeling better, I really should go. But I promise—I'll be back soon. Don't you worry about that."

I gave Mom's hand one final squeeze and looked up at Lou, standing there framed by towers of boxes, some of which, unknown to him, I'd emptied. Emptied so that something else, someone greater, could be filled. I hadn't been dreaming. My plan had worked. But I knew it wouldn't work for long.

Unless…

"Goodbye, Lou," I said, forcing a hug on him I knew he did not want.

"Bye, Jo," he said, reluctantly returning my hug. His voice was slightly softer, but only, I imagined, because he knew I was on my way. "Don't worry about us. I've got everything under control."

No, I thought. *You only think you do. I'm the one who's got everything under control.*

I walked back through the narrow passageway Mom and Lou had conspired to create, imagining the hoard melting away, remembering how free and open it had been when I was young and could barely stretch my arms to reach both walls at once. I looked into the living room and saw it not how it was, but how it had been, with stuffed couches which used to beckon me. Out on the porch, I turned toward where the swing had been made invisible by lawn mowers and a tangle of rakes. It would have been nice to take one final swing. But that wasn't possible.

I got in the cab, slammed the door, and looked at the house in daylight for what I knew would be the last time.

"Let's get out of here," I told Marco, even as I knew…I wasn't going anywhere.

———

I LET him drive me to the airport not because I intended to fly out that day, but because I needed him, needed everyone, to think I was leaving town. When I'd arrived, I hadn't thought I'd need an alibi, or suspected, when Marco had first leaned back and handed me his card, that he'd be part of it. But I guess the universe knew better than me what I needed all along.

I went inside the terminal and paused by the plate glass window instead of checking in, making a show of puttering with my luggage until I saw him pull away. I'd get a different flight later, after I did what needed to be done. I took the escalator down to the arrivals area, went back outside, and hailed a different cab.

I returned to my old neighborhood again, thinking how odd it was to cruise those streets more in a few days than I had in the past decade. I had this driver drop me in front of a house where I knew no one would be home, took a few slow steps toward the front door, and watched him drive off. Then I walked the few blocks to my own street and waited for it to be night. Once it was dark, both outside and in, I crept to the back porch that led to the kitchen, and peered through at my mother.

She was awake, leaning back against a pillow, and staring up, but whether she was gazing at the ceiling or something much further away, I couldn't tell. The way her eyes were unfocussed, though, she probably wasn't seeing anything at all. From my angle, the tower of clutter tilted against the far wall looked like a wave about to come crashing down on her.

She deserved better than this. She was going to get better than this. She was living in a firetrap, her soul leached away, and the only way to free her from that constant drain was to make the firetrap achieve its potential.

I opened the door slowly and tiptoed inside, twisting to get around a stack of boxes. What a waste. How long had it been since the kitchen has been usable anyway, thanks to an oven filled with outdated encyclopedias and a range that was now topped with bicycle tires? Let it go, Mom. Let it all go. She would be lost until everything was lost.

I started dropping lit books of matches on the mess near the bottom of the staircase first, so that Lou would be woken by smoke and then wake Mom and get her out. I then moved through the rest of the main floor, lighting ancient newspapers, landscape paintings which would have embarrassed a cheap motel, old clothing worn to rags, craft supplies for projects promised but never done, whatever was flammable enough to get this going. It all caught more easily than I would have thought. I guess even the things themselves knew it was time to let go.

Outside on the back porch, I set the corners of boxes on fire, then I moved around to the front porch and did the same. I looked for a moment at the machines, but there was no point in attacking them. The house itself would take care of those when it all came tumbling down. The bags mounded against the garage caught quickly, their plastic skins melting into flaming goo that set the contents ablaze.

Take it all away, I thought. *Take it all away and bring my mother back.*

I retreated from the house and hid behind a bush across the street, watching as the flames outside grew higher and the flames inside illuminated the windows more brightly, imagining Mom's soul returning to her body with every object that burned or melted or burst. Any moment now, Lou would come running out of the house with our mother in his arms, and I could rush back to the airport for the last plane out.

I wondered how much of her I would get back how quickly, how much of her absence would become once more a presence. And as I waited, and waited, and waited still more, I grew nervous, because…no one was coming. Did Lou sleep that deeply? Or had I done too much too soon, and the fire had spread too quickly?

Whatever the reason, I was sure *something* had gone wrong, and could wait no more. I raced across the lawn, through tall blades of grass close to the house already black-ening, and leapt up the porch steps and through the front door. I was instantly pushed back by the heat and the light and the smoke, and had to fight against them all to move forward. As I pressed through the blaze into the crowded hallway, shoving my nose into an elbow, I cried, my tears drying instantly, and thought *no*, screamed *no*. They can't die, I didn't mean for it to end this way.

I alternated between gasping and coughing, pulling in more smoke with each futile breath, and as my lungs were overcome, my knees began to buckle and my head grew as smoky as the air around me. Then I felt a hand wrap beneath my arm and tug. I tried to rise as it pulled at me, but instead fell away into darkness.

———

AND CAME to flat on my back out on the front lawn, looking up at my mother, her face lit by the dancing flames.

"Are you all right, Jo?" she asked. She placed a hand to my forehead as she used to do so long ago.

I tried to answer, but coughed instead. I tried to sit up, but fell back again, too dizzy to move. Attempting to kill what had been killing Mom had almost killed me. But had the risk proven worthwhile?

"I'll be all right," I answered, my throat raw, my voice raspy. "What's more important is…how are you?"

"Much better, dear." She smiled, and by the flickering of the light, I could almost see her younger self, and I smiled, too. "But the house. What could have happened?"

Flat on my back, I shrugged as best as I could. She put her arms around my shoulders in a way that felt familiar, and helped me up, so I could see what she had no idea I had done, and would never admit to anyone but myself. The house was engulfed, the outer walls blackening, the roof beginning to sag. No firemen had yet arrived to put out the blaze. I couldn't even hear the sound of approaching sirens.

Good.

"I don't think we'll ever know," I said. "But the place was a firetrap, Mom. It was going to happen eventually. If you think about it, I'll bet even you knew that."

"I'm not sure I did," she said, wide-eyed, struggling to remember what she hadn't been present enough to experience in the first place to even imprint a memory. But now new memories would come. That I was sure of.

"How did I get out of there?" I asked. "I can't quite remember. And Lou! Where's Lou?"

"Why, I pulled you out, Jo," Mom said. "I led your brother out, too. That's what mothers do."

It was only then that I noticed my brother hopping at the side of the house, shoulders hunched, approaching and retreating from the remains of what had both nurtured and trapped him, reaching out as if he wanted to pluck possessions from within, but realizing he dared not get too close. Eventually, empty-handed, shoulders hunched, he slowly came to stand beside us.

"We've lost everything," he said, seeing, but not seeing.

"No," I said, pulling him close so that we were both hugging our mother tight. *Our mother.* "No...we haven't."

ONE OF THE LUCKY ONES

If the twins hadn't been clamoring for ice cream, and if his parents hadn't still been so far away, Marc would probably never have remembered his Uncle Neil. But with all the miles behind them and all the miles yet ahead, Marc turned to Kate, and Kate nodded at Marc, speaking silently to each other in that shorthand way some married people can, and they agreed without a word that Jennifer and Stephanie had every right to be hungry. And that was that.

So Marc studied the road ahead for a likely place to stop at which they could stun the kids into a stupor with sugar. His mother (for she's the one who tended to watch the clock) would just have to wait a little longer.

The winding road eventually straightened, revealing a stoplight on the horizon. As the speed limit dropped and Marc moved closer to the intersection, he could make out the signs identifying the four corner buildings that marked the center of the small town—an ice cream parlor, a barbershop, a gun store, and a used bookstore. Marc parked the car and watched with pleasure as his little girls skipped ahead toward the shop and his big girl walked quickly to keep up with them. Life was good, he thought. He was one of the lucky ones.

Jennifer demanded a strawberry cone, and Stephanie begged for butter brickle, while Marc and Kate split a cone, as had become their habit. This time it was pistachio. By the time they were done, the twins seemed to be wearing as much ice cream on the outside as they'd gotten to the inside. Marc smiled as they played patty cake and laughed at each sticky sound their hands made.

"Better wash up before we get in the car, girls," Marc said. As he moved forward to scoop them up, Kate touched the back of his hand.

"I'll take care of it," she said, smiling. "You go do what you have to do. Oh, don't deny it. I saw you looking. But only for a few minutes now."

She wagged her finger at him, though he could tell she didn't mean it, and even as she tried to keep a stern look on her face, she failed, her frown collapsing uncontrollably. She grabbed the girls' hands, not caring what that did to her own, and tugged them lightly along like small balloons.

Marc glanced over at the bookstore across the street, studying it for what he thought was the first time. He hadn't realized he'd been that obvious. But of course he'd noticed it as soon as they stopped. Strange he'd never noticed it as they drove through that intersection during other visits to his parents.

How well she knew him. Old magazines were *his* ice cream. He'd never really cared much for old books, they reminded him too much of school, but when he looked at old magazines, he felt a part of something greater than himself, could imagine the people who'd read them and were no longer with us. He glanced back once at his family, crossed the street, which was so deserted that he didn't need to wait for the light to change, and walked into the bookstore.

He knew he wouldn't have much time to browse—his mother might tolerate an ice cream's worth of delay, but not the time a used bookstore deserved—and so rather than wandering on his own, he had the clerk direct him to where the magazines were stored. There really didn't seem to be more there than he had seen before elsewhere, nor did he expect more. A stack of old *Reader's Digests*. Some *National Geographics* and *Life* magazines. He might as well have been in a doctor's waiting room.

But then, as he moved the boxes around, enjoying the smell of old paper, he came across a stack of *New Yorkers*, and got a tingling sensation. They took him back. Most of them were newer issues, of no value either monetarily or for nostalgia purposes, but as he went through the stack, he came across a few he recognized as ones he would have read as a kid, their covers showing familiar images of an apartment building covered in snow, a large tree in a yard, its autumn leaves about to fall, and other nondescript seasonal images. He picked one at random and opened it, and memories began to flood back.

He was on his stomach in the apartment building in which he'd lived when he was a kid. He was going through magazines much like this one, only they were fresh and new. Maybe it even was this one. The vision was so strong he could feel the carpeting under his bare knees, smell his mother cooking franks and beans in the next room. A *New Yorker* was open in front of him, and he was laughing at a Gahan Wilson cartoon. Back then, that's all he thought *The New Yorker* was, a collection of cartoons, and he enjoyed flipping past each page of text to get to the next drawing.

But...he was only a kid. How did he get his hands on a copy of *The New Yorker*? That's certainly not the kind of thing he would have bought on his own. He would have been spending his allowance on comic books. And as for his parents, he knew that they read the newsweeklies, but he could never have imagined them reading the *New Yorker* either. So where had it come from?

And that's when Marc saw his face, looking down at him as if from a great height. Uncle Neil. He was the one who'd brought these over, on one of his frequent, almost weekly visits, and as Marc read, he watched.

So that's why he was so interested in old magazines. They represented his childhood as much as a cupcake. And yet Marc hadn't thought of him in years. Strange. He'd have to buy that issue, take it to his mother, ask her whatever had happened to Uncle Neil, and why they never talked about him.

That's when his family tumbled into the shop, Kate giving him the *I love you but are you done yet* smirk, the girls giggling and holding out their hands for inspection. Jennifer and Stephanie took Marc's hands in theirs and pulled him back to the car so they could continue on their way.

Marc never saw that magazine again.

───────────

It wasn't until after dessert, while his mother was clearing the dishes and his father was grabbing a beer, that he remembered there was something he wanted to talk to his parents about. Only he couldn't remember what that something was.

"Ma," he began, as she scraped leftovers into the trash. She looked at her son, but whatever it was that he'd been about to say was gone.

There should be a word for that, he thought, the way there was for *déjà vu*, that moment of remembering that you remembered something, trying to remember it again, and failing to remember anything except that you'd once remembered something.

His mother went upstairs with the kids to run them a bath, and Marc retraced his day, the packing, the loading of the car, the drive, the ice cream, the bookstore…and he realized that there had been something about the bookstore, only whatever it had been was gone.

He looked at his father, shrugged, then grabbed a beer himself and went out to the porch swing. He could hear the splashing of the bathwater upstairs, the giggles of the girls mixed with his mother's mock stern warnings.

In a moment, Kate joined him, took a swig of his beer, and kicked back to set them swinging.

"Where are you?" she asked him.

"I'm right here," he said.

But he really wasn't. He wasn't there, under the stars, with the woman he loved, all right with the world. He was back in that bookstore, a bookstore he could only vaguely remember, having realized…what?

He'd have to go back.

His mother was always looking for bonding experiences with the girls, and his father was always up for whatever his mother wanted, so they had no problems with watching their grandchildren while Marc took off with Kate on a road trip. Kate tried to keep things light, but he could tell she could tell he was nervous.

"So what is it you think happened there yesterday?" she asked.

"That's the thing, Kate," he said, unable to turn his head to look at her. "I don't know."

At the bookshop, the clerk looked surprised to see him.

Marc figured it was because after he'd been dragged off the day before by the girls, he'd thought he'd never see him again, that he'd lost a sale. But when Marc headed to the back aisles once more, figuring that going through the motion of poring over the magazines, the feel of them in his hands, would spark his memory, he learned differently.

Where there had been magazines were now only empty boxes.

"What happened to all those magazines I was looking at?" he asked, not even sure what magazines he'd been looking at, only that they'd been magazines.

"Funny thing," he said. "No more than five minutes after you left, a man came in and bought all three boxes. Surprised me, especially after I'd seen you looking at them. If someone goes through them more than once a month, that's a lot."

"Did he give you any idea why he wanted them?"

"He wouldn't say. He wasn't very talkative."

At his words, Marc suddenly remembered a man watching him as he read magazines, and not saying much. He felt dizzy, and had to grab the counter.

"This man," he asked. "What did he look like?"

"Hard to say. Nothing really special about him. Glasses. Mustache. He had a strange, crooked smile, though, almost but not quite a smirk, kind of as if he knew something I didn't, and was happy about it. Say, do you think he put something over on me, that there was something valuable in those boxes?"

Uncle Neil, Marc thought.

Seeing the odd look on Marc's face, the man took a step back.

"Sorry I couldn't help you more," he said, and moved away to rearrange his stock, or pretend to anyway.

"What was that about?" asked Kate.

"Uncle Neil, Uncle Neil, Uncle Neil," Marc said, hoping that if he repeated it enough, it would stick.

"Who's Uncle Neil?" she asked.

"That's what I need to find out," he said.

———

"I NEVER HAD A BROTHER," Marc's father told him with a quizzical expression in answer to his question after the girls had been put to bed that night. "Why are you so interested all of a sudden?"

"What about Mom?" Marc asked a little too anxiously. "Didn't Mom have a brother?"

"Your mother only had sisters. But you already know both your aunts. No, no brothers on either side of the family. What's this about? You were never much interested in your relatives before."

"But what about Uncle…"

Marc paused, unable to remember what came next.

"Who?" his father finally added. "Uncle who?"

"Uncle…"

Marc tried and failed to remember a name he was sure he'd been repeating earlier.

"I don't know," he said. "I don't know."

He only knew that he felt an incomparable sense of loss, even though he had no idea what he had lost.

———

MARC SPOKE with Kate in the dark that night as she fell asleep and he only tried. He tried to remember the past and it was gone. He tried to remember the events of the day before, and the current day as well, and even they were fuzzy.

"But you were there, weren't you, Kate?" he asked, as he

looked at the ceiling and she snuggled next to him. "We were together in the—what kind of store was it? And I remember muttering something over and over again so I could remember it. What was it? A name? An address? Do you remember?"

Kate mumbled at him, but he could not make out her words. She fell asleep easily, always had, and would be no good until morning. He could tell that his own sleep was far away. So he lay there, staring at the ceiling, not even bothering to try. As he studied the guest room ceiling of the home his parents had moved to after he'd moved out, his mind wandered to other bedrooms, other ceilings.

He was in bed, a stack of old science fiction digest magazines to one side, only they weren't so old then, and a torn bag of Oreo cookies on the other side, its contents exploded across his comforter. He turned pages with one hand and shoved in the cookies with the other.

"Don't let yourself get trapped by either of those," said a voice. It was a man, but it wasn't his father because his father was gone, off drinking because of—

Wait. What?

His father gone?

His father had never been gone.

It was a man's voice coming to him as he fell asleep, and had begun to remember. But whose voice?

Marc could almost recognize it, but not quite, as if it was but murmuring from a room next door, and the walls were much too thick for the speaker to be recognized. Though he was nearly out, he knew this was no dream. The speaker was real. The speaker had been real. Marc had once been in a room very much like this one, and someone who'd loved him very much tried to warn him.

But who was it? And warn him against what?

Kate rolled toward him in her sleep, and snuggled up,

and with her warm breath blowing rhythmically against his chest, he became certain what he'd have to do.

His mind made up, he let himself drift away.

HE WAS unable to act on his impulse immediately. He'd already taken one outing without his parents and the kids to try to figure out what was happening, and one absence was all either of them should have to suffer during what was supposed to be their vacation, regardless of the constant itch he felt. So he was both there and not there as they chased fireflies, watched old home movies (movies which seemed familiar, and comforting, and yet also nagged at him, as if they seemed to be missing something), made pancakes, and did all the other things that a long weekend entailed.

As they drove home, Marc slowed the car as they neared the intersection with the bookstore, but because the girls were exhausted and sacked out in the back rather than clamoring for ice cream, he just kept rolling on. There was no need. Whatever clue had been there was already gone. He looked over at Kate, expecting her to comment on the odd expedition they'd made there, but she said nothing, just let her arm dangle out the car window, playing with the wind as they drove, which may have been the oddest thing of all.

Vacation over, he threw himself into work fitfully, and at times forgot what it was he was supposed to be remembering, but often he was reminded of it the way a tongue will inevitably seek out the place where a filling used to be, unable to stay away from what was lost. Somehow he got through those moments, though he spent more time shuffling papers than making sense of them.

Once he'd been back from the long weekend a few days and felt he could get away with it, he called in sick. He said nothing to Kate or the kids, just climbed into the car as he normally would each morning, and instead of heading to the office, drove to his childhood home. He parked in the driveway where his father had first let him get behind the wheel, walked past the forsythia he'd thrown up into after arriving home drunk from Prom, and rang a doorbell he'd never needed to ring before, since it was his home.

He could hear the Big Ben chimes echoing inside, and it took him back, back to visitors, to springing up because someone he was waiting for had arrived. But it only took him back so far. Who was it who'd been coming? Who was it whom he knew would never visit empty-handed? He could not remember. But he knew that the answer was inside.

He rang the doorbell once more and stood on tiptoe to peer through the glass panes at the top of the door. No one responded. No one was home. He circled the house, peering in each of the windows, until he reached his own.

It wasn't being used as a bedroom any longer. A large sewing machine by the window blocked much of his view of the rest of the room. But though he could only make out piles of fabrics and quilts hanging on the walls, in his mind he could see through to the room it had once been. His room.

He went back to the front door and found the rock under which his parents had once hidden the key. Though it was still there, it no longer fit the lock. The rock itself would have to do. He circled to the window of his room and slammed the rock against the glass. He reached in and unlocked the window, cutting himself on a shard. Climbing in, he knocked the sewing machine on its side, then tumbled over it.

He lay there on the carpeting, catching his breath. He knew he should get up, instead of lying there, bleeding on a stranger's carpeting. But he felt closer there to what he had been seeking than at any time that week. He wriggled along the floor as if doing the backstroke, and pulled himself into the position of where the bed used to be.

The ceiling seemed so much farther away than he remembered, but then, so did the past. He scanned the room, replacing what was there with what had once been there. The quilts were gone, and in their place, his posters, his toys, his magazines, all the clutter of childhood. And in the doorway…

Uncle Neil.

He held out a shopping bag, the handles worn from so many visits, so many gifts. Marc needed them, with his father so rarely around.

"I brought you something more to read," he'd said.

"Thanks, Uncle Neil," Marc had said.

He'd grabbed the bag and spread its contents on the bed. There was *Life* and *Look* and strange little UFO magazines and copies of *Scientific American* and even a couple of comics books he was missing. Marc remembered them making him giddy.

"I know you love these," he'd said. "But you should get outside more."

Marc said nothing. He wasn't much for advice, especially from adults.

"Don't get yourself trapped in this," Uncle Neil had said. "Don't end up like—"

Marc looked up at the sudden silence.

"Well…just don't."

As soon as Uncle Neil left the room, Marc dove into the magazines, forgetting that his uncle had even been there, or had gone.

Oh, he'd heard what he'd said, but didn't think about it, not until years later, when it came time to choose his path (at least he thought he had), and then he'd forgotten again. Until now.

But *now* Marc noticed that he was gone.

Uncle Neil. This time Marc would hold onto him long enough to figure out what had happened to him.

A light flashed in his eyes, and he suddenly realized two men were looking down at him.

"Mind telling us what you're doing here, sir?" one of them said, and Marc could feel the past slip away again.

HE DECIDED to pretend to be drunk. That's what his father would have done, except for the pretend part. (Why was he thinking that about his father again? His father *never* drank.) And Marc must have sold it well, because the cops stood down from full alert, took their hands off their holsters. He was no longer some crazy stalker guy who had broken into a stranger's home. He had become the sloppy drunk who'd gotten overly nostalgic after having one too many, and no longer had to be considered a threat.

That didn't stop them from arresting him, though. They handcuffed him, fingerprinted him, and placed him in the sort of crowded room he'd previously only seen on television. He figured the safest thing to there do was keep playing drunk. People tend to keep their distance if they think you're going to puke on them. And it worked. He sat alone in a corner while everyone else who'd been arrested that morning swirled around him. He closed his eyes, and thought of his father, remembered the times that he had come home drunk. (No, not that again. Where was that coming from? But follow it, follow it.)

So…his father…a drunk? If so, what was it that kept

setting him off and driving him to drink? What had happened that made him want to hide from life?

Something, something, it had to be something. And that something was…

His brother.

Uncle Neil.

Dad would go off to check on his brother his calm and sober self, and always return plastered. Marc never knew exactly why, what had been so wrong about visiting Uncle Neil. He'd get hints as his father rambled before collapsing, how sad his choices were, how a big brother was supposed to protect a little brother, how no one should live that way, but what that way was never slipped his lips before he'd collapse. And Marc had been too young to visit Uncle Neil on his own.

But his Dad *had* a brother. That had been real. He hadn't realized it until he'd sat in this place, pretending to be what his Dad really was. Why?

Someone sat down next to Marc, so he lifted his hand to his mouth as if about to throw up, hoping to drive them away. It didn't work.

"How's my favorite nephew?" he heard someone say. He opened his eyes.

It was Uncle Neil, looking decades older than Marc had last seen him, but since he hadn't seen him in twenty years, not even in memory, that made sense. And it all came flooding back then. The visits he'd make. The way those visits—both Uncle Neil to their family and his father to Uncle Neil—had driven a wedge between his parents. The presents he'd bring. The advice he'd give, advice Marc never much listened to.

"If I'm your favorite nephew, why did you go?" asked Marc.

"Because I couldn't save myself," said Uncle Neil. "But I

knew I could save you."

"Save me from what?" said Marc, both astonished and relieved to be having this conversation.

"No one should have to live the way I did," continued Uncle Neil. "A loner. A hoarder. Lost in things instead of people. Someone who never got his life together. Your father knew that, and it ate at him. You don't remember, but the mess I'd made turned him into a drunk, turned his wife into a single mother. And you, you were being destroyed, heading down that path to where I already was. I could see it. So I had to go."

"What are you talking about? People can't just go like that."

"But I did it, didn't I? If a person reads enough of those magazines, he'll figure out a way. If you want it badly enough, you can do it. The how of it, the why of it, it's all in there, just below the surface. But for some people, those words can be a trap. You were going to be trapped. Which is why I stepped into the universe next door. You were supposed to forget about me."

"I did forget you," Marc said, unsure of how that was possible to the extent it occurred. He stared at his uncle, wondering if he was going crazy, while at the same time, realizing that staring was also a way of telling himself that he *hadn't* been going crazy. The things he had started remembering that day at the bookstore, it wasn't insanity, or a form of amnesia, or some repressed traumatic event. Which mean it was...what?

Marc didn't know what to think, and he barely knew what to say.

"There's a universe next door?" was all he could bring himself to utter.

"Yes," said Uncle Neil. "It's not that far away. But far enough. It was the only answer. I'm sorry, Marc, but you see, my life was no life at all. Your father knew that. Your mother knew that. I guess I knew it, too, but it took a long time before I was willing to admit it. But you, you were just a kid. You didn't see it. You couldn't. You worshipped me. Am I allowed to say that about myself? I'm not sure. But I'll say it anyway. I could accept what I had become, I could even accept what my becoming what I'd become had done to your parents, but I couldn't accept the effect I was having on you. So I had to go, to slip sideways, to get out of your way. And it worked. You forgot, and went your own way, instead of mine. You became who you were supposed to become."

"I remember it now," said Marc, seeing his father, and the bottles, and the constant arguing, and his mother's tears. "I remember it all. Thank you for what you did. Thank you for letting me remember. But why did you have to leave in order to fix things? Why did I have to forget you?"

"It was all or nothing, Marc. To set you on a different path, I had to relinquish my place in this world. I had to go to that universe next door, just as if I'd never been, and take those memories away with me. And though it hurt me at times, you never missed them. Until you happened to see that magazine and got an itch. And wouldn't stop scratching it. But now it's time for you to stop. No good can come of this."

"But I love you, Uncle Neil."

"And you show that every day," his uncle said, smiling warmly. "By living a good life. By loving your wife and taking care of your kids. By being a good son to your parents. And you know? That's enough. So it's time to let go. To let me live what life I have left in the next world. I'm okay with it. It's what I chose. It's the only thing I did right. Knowing that you're here in this world, knowing who you've become, is enough for me."

"Let me save you," said Marc. "You saved me. Why can't

I do the same for you?"

"Because you can't. You just can't. You'd lose it all. Kate and Jennifer and Stephanie. They'd be gone. They'd never have been. Let me go."

"I can't," he said.

"Yes," said his uncle. "Yes, you can."

Uncle Neil reached out and patted Marc's head. Marc suddenly remembered how his uncle used to do it all the time when he'd say goodbye. Only this time, though the man's fingers seemed solid for a moment when the first touched his scalp, they then passed through him, tingling as they moved through his head, and then through his heart, and then—

Marc opened his eyes. His neck was stiff from sleeping against the wall at an odd angle. But all that with Uncle Neil was real. Hadn't it been real?

Which meant he had to do something about his uncle. Something more than forget.

When an officer came to tell Marc that his wife had bailed him out, he looked at the man curiously, as if unsure of any reason to be bailed out. He looked around, expecting to continue a conversation with...whom? But then he stood and followed the man to where he was given back his possessions, after which he was handed over to Kate as if he himself was a possession.

She drove off from the station silently, and as they were doing so, his head back, his eyes closed, even as he tried to remember things which were becoming misty, he could remember that silence was unusual. That wasn't the sort of behavior they engaged in. Their relationship was such that they talked things out, even the angry things. Something was off. He knew they had to settle this before they got home. Didn't they always?

He opened his eyes and was about to speak when he recognized the streets along which they drove. He'd thought they were heading home. They weren't.

"What's going on, Kate?" Marc asked.

"Someone had to take care of Jenn and Steph while I picked you up."

Of course. Why hadn't he thought of that? After that stupid thing he did (why had he done it anyway?), Kate would of course come to pick him up alone. No one should have to see their father in jail.

It hit Marc hard when he thought that. But why? Had he once seen his father in jail? He didn't think so, but something about the idea seemed familiar, so perhaps he had a dream about it once.

He tried to remember that dream and other dreams like it all the way to his parents' place, but after several hours, when their car pulled into the driveway, and the twins came bouncing toward him, his mother behind them and his father behind her, he smiled, and stopped trying.

"Daddy, what happened?" they said as he stepped from the car, and he answered, "I don't know."

And he didn't.

He ran at his kids and scooped them up in his arms, or tried to anyway, and they laughed as he struggled to lift them. He tumbled back into a pile of tickles, and though he could see his parents and his wife looking at each other quizzically, wondering at his abrupt shift from what he'd been acting like to what he was acting like now, he didn't care.

"Let's go home," he said, buried under his daughters.

"Are you sure you're okay to drive?" asked Kate.

"I'm okay," he said. "Really. I'm okay."

He hugged his parents, and seeing them side by side like that, the template for what he'd built with Kate, was unexpectedly poignant. How had he ever thought they could have…whatever it was he'd been thinking. He shook his head. He was no longer sure. He hugged them again and felt no absence there.

As they drove home, he spotted a stoplight in the distance, and remembered the familiar intersection, and the stores at the corners of it. What were they again? Ah, that's right, he could see them now—an ice cream parlor, a barbershop, a gun store, and a…

That's odd. An empty storefront. Had it been like that last time?

"Who's up for ice cream?" he called out.

"It's getting near dinnertime, honey," said Kate. "We really shouldn't spoil the girls' appetites."

But then the girls started shouting "ice cream, ice cream" in harmony, and Marc gave Kate a look, and she gave him a look back, a look that said, *oh, why not,* two different but similar looks that certain couples have learned, if they work it right, that is. And so he pulled the car into a spot.

As they crossed the street toward the ice cream shop, Marc glanced momentarily at the storefront with the FOR SALE sign in the window and wondered…had he ever been in there? The layout seemed awfully familiar, which made him feel as if he'd surely once walked through the door. But then his girls grabbed his hands, and he forgot about what might or might not have happened in the past.

"Should we split a pistachio cone again?" he asked his wife.

"Pistachio it is," said Kate, smiling.

And as he pulled open the door to the shop, he once more thought, life is good.

Yes, he thought. He was one of the lucky ones.

A JUDGMENT CALL FOR JUDGMENT DAY

The last words I spoke before I died were about how relieved I was that wherever I died, it would be someplace other than *here*. The Armistice had been signed, the war was finally over, I had survived it, and thankfully we'd all soon be going home. After too many months of blood and sweat and terror, I at last had nothing more to fear from Berlin's rubble-strewn streets.

Our platoon had fanned out wide as we'd picked our way slowly along the strasse, intent on the only task that had meaning for us now that the mission of winning the war had been completed—making sure we left no man behind. As I passed a damaged storefront, peering in through the remains of a broken brick wall to check out the interior before calling the area clear, I knew I was lucky to be alive. So I'd said as much to Manz, the pal who'd been watching my back ever since we met in basic training. For the first time since I'd enlisted, I let myself say out loud how much I looked forward to returning home.

And then the wall beside me exploded.

I was flung up in the air, my weapon ripped from my

hands, and blinded, I had just enough time to think that, damn, I had jinxed myself by speaking too soon. Everyone knows you're not supposed to talk about going home until you have your discharge papers in hand, and maybe not even then.

I didn't remember coming back down.

When I regained consciousness, the fog of the explosion had faded. I knew I was flat on my back, because all I could see was blue sky. I could hear nothing, though. Did I still have eardrums? It didn't matter. I still had my life. This time, though I thought I was lucky, I knew better than to say it. A near-death experience can get your attention. So instead of wallowing in the relief of the moment, instead of whispering a prayer of gratitude, I just tried to figure out what the hell had gone wrong.

Had we been attacked by someone who hadn't heard the war was over? Had the wall I'd been walking by been so battered by months of shelling it just finally surrendered, setting off a stash of munitions as it fell? Or had an unexploded bomb, buried at the base of the wall, chosen just that moment to go off?

It didn't really matter. All that mattered was that I had suddenly become one of the wounded we'd been hunting for. I tried to sit up, to start looking for the rest of the guys, but couldn't seem to get my body to listen to my brain. I couldn't move. All I could do was hope Manz would bail me out just one more time.

The ringing in my ears had started to fade, and I began to make out voices. They sounded at first as if they were underwater, but I could still tell that at least they were speaking English instead of that damned German. I cried out for help—or tried to anyway. No words came, and barely even sounds.

I couldn't feel my right arm at all, but I could at least

sense that my left arm was pinned. I looked down and saw that I'd been hit by a ton of bricks—literally. After I'd been tossed aside by the explosion, the remains of the wall had come down on top of me. I wriggled my fingers enough to free my left hand so I could feel for my lips, to see why no sounds had come out. That's when I discovered my jaw had been blown away. I thought of Emily, beautiful Emily, and of how we would never kiss again. But then I thought of Manz, and of Jackson, and all the others, and how they'd better find me quick. The blood leaking across my face told me I didn't have much time.

The voices had grown clearer, the speakers closer and seemingly no longer submerged. I could make out more than just their language. I could make out their words. But I didn't recognize any voice as belonging to a member of my platoon. Where could they be? Could they all have ended up buried like me?

"This one belongs to you, I think," I heard one say in a tenor voice.

"Yes, I do believe you're right," said the other, more deeply.

From the way those two talked, it was a good thing I hadn't made myself heard earlier. I could expect no help from them. They were scavengers. There'd always been rumors that some Americans were doing that, following behind the soldiers to plunder the dead, but I never believed it. This was the first time I'd seen evidence of profiteering myself.

I could hear the tearing of cloth, the jangling of dog tags, pockets being rifled, and I grew angry, but was powerless to stop them.

"There's nothing golden on this one," the second one continued. "Nonetheless, he's still just as valuable to me. But that's life."

"Actually…not really."

"Don't worry, your turn will come."

"Yes, it will," said the tenor. "I only wish it could come more frequently. It's a shame."

"They can't all be boy scouts, you know. You expect too much of them. But we'll find you a few today, I'm sure."

Their conversation made no sense. I couldn't understand how they were deciding to divvy up their spoils, how they chose which of them got to pilfer each body. I was outraged at the thought that at that very moment, they could be rooting through the remains of my friends. I tried to pull bricks from my chest, but I didn't have the strength.

"Soon this won't be frequent at all," said the one who'd won the first share. "Soon we'll be heading home."

"That will be a blessing."

"For you, maybe. That's the difference between us. Me, I don't know whether I'll be able to fit in back home any more. It's been much too exciting here. Home is so…"

"Peaceful?"

"Boring."

I could hear their steps as they moved through the rubble. There was more jangling, this time not as far off in the distance.

"Ah, at last, this one is mine," said the tenor.

"See, I told you there'd be one for you eventually."

How could they talk so calmly as they stole from the soldiers who died to save their country, men who could no longer help themselves? Had they no souls? They were stealing more from the dead than their possessions—they were stealing their dignity. I felt impotent, because if I couldn't get free, I would surely soon be stripped of both of those things myself. The two would make no distinction between the dead and the merely helpless, as I was…and I might soon lapse from one category to the other. My rage alternated with a fatigue I was afraid preceded death. And these two would surely do nothing to prevent my transition.

"You know," said the one who'd finally found his treasure. "I don't think the only reason you like it here is because you find it boring back home. It's more than just a fear of not fitting in."

"Let's not get into this again."

"It has to be said."

"That's what you told me the last hundred times you brought it up."

"Still. It deserves bringing up again. I don't think you want to stay here because you actually like it here. Could anyone really like it here? I think you want to stay here because you don't like it *there*."

"Enough."

"What I think is that there's someone back home whom you're afraid of."

"Enough!"

"I'm just saying. That's where we're *really* different, you and me. The ones like me, we love the place we're going back to so much only the job could keep us away. While your kind—"

"Forget about my kind. What about his kind?"

Another ripping of cloth and jangling of dog tags. I'd been so lulled by their inane banter I hadn't realized they'd moved even closer.

"Yours again, of course. Most of them are."

"Does it ever bother you? That I get so many more of them than you do?"

"Only because I know how much it will bother *them* in the long run. Not because I'm competing."

"Because it's just not in your nature, is it? I think you're acting just a wee bit too angelic. I never liked that in you."

"You don't have to get bitter. Don't worry—even if we

have to leave, we'll be needed back here soon enough. We always are…"

"Now you're just trying to cheer me up."

The sounds of their boots suddenly sprang from right beside my head. I tried to curse them, but no words came out.

"What have we here?"

Two faces blocked the sky. I couldn't make out their features very well through the glare from the blinding sun. I could only tell one was dark-haired and the other a blond. He could have passed for German. Neither wore a helmet, which was just plain crazy, Armistice or no Armistice.

"Leave me alone," I growled at them. Or tried to.

"Oh, I'm afraid we can't do that," said the blond.

"No, we're not allowed."

I was stunned to realize they'd heard me speak, even though I had nothing left with which to speak. And that, even though their lips hadn't moved, I'd heard them speak as well.

"Who are you?" I said, so thrilled I could talk that I even said it again.

"The important question today is," said the darker of the two, "Who are you?"

One of the pair unbuttoned what was left of my shredded collar, while the other palmed my dog tags. I felt so helpless I didn't care who did which.

"I'm just another G.I. who wants to go home."

"Then you're in luck. We're here to help you get home."

"But the question is—which home will it be? His or mine?"

"Actually, no, that's the answer."

"No, it really is the question."

I never expected that as I lay dying I would be tortured by a pair of comedians.

"We're not comedians," said the blond. "It's just very important that whatever we do, we get it right."

I was weary, too weary to be astonished by the fact they'd read my mind, too weary to argue any longer.

"Stop toying with me," I said, "and just go ahead and do whatever it is that you're going to do. I have nothing to offer you, no valuables to steal. All I've got is forty-three cents and half a pack of cigarettes. And I don't even think I have the matches to light them with."

"You have something more valuable than that," said the blond.

"Yes, you all do," said the brunette.

I squinted to see the kind of men who would toy with me like that, but the glare of the sun kept their faces from me.

"You don't believe us, do you?" said the blond. "I'm not surprised. But just watch. Then you'll understand."

Together, they put their palms on my chest, and the sun grew even brighter, as bright as an atomic bomb, taking away their silhouettes, the bricks that covered most of my body, the street of Berlin. I was nowhere, and I was everywhere. I was all of my yesterdays and none of my tomorrows.

I was a child, throwing rocks at a dog, stopping the playground bully from picking on the small kid, peering over at a classmate's paper to get the answers from a math test, walking back to school to return a pen I had stolen from the teacher, pissing in a milk carton, kicking a dog I swore was going to attack first.

I was a teenager, shoplifting a bottle of beer by slipping it down my pants in the back of the general store, going on a date with the ugliest girl in the school on a dare, playing spin the bottle with the prettiest girl in the school and kissing her in the closet even though she told me not to, stealing money from my mother's purse to be able to get into the movies with that same girl.

I was an adult, ready to go into the army, really still just a teenager, but an adult, trying to screw the prettiest girl I knew with the story that I'd soon be fighting in a war and might be killed and only taking no for an answer after she stabbed me with her umbrella, screwing the ugliest girl because she'd let me, but never calling her again, beating the crap out of my dad the day before reporting for duty because he threatened to beat the crap out of my mother, shooting my first German and being thrilled and sick at the same time, shooting my second German and being only thrilled.

And then the kaleidoscope of my life ended, and I was flat on my back again, pinned beneath a pile of bricks.

"Who are you guys?"

"You're one tough nut," growled one.

"By now, I'd think we wouldn't have to tell you," sang the other.

And they didn't. I could see exactly who they were.

"So…is he yours or mine?" asked what I suddenly saw was an angel. "With this one, it could go either way."

"Yes, it could," answered the demon. "But I sense some-thing…odd…about this one. I've been smelling it all day."

"But…I'm not dead."

They both laughed, mixing together the most beautiful sound I'd ever heard with the most disgusting.

The demon knelt beside me, pressing his face into my own, and I could see it all; the horns, the red skin, the boils, the pustules scarring his cheeks. His nostrils flared, and I knew he was sniffing my soul. I spit into the thing's face and the saliva boiled away. It smiled.

"I see it now," said the demon, sounding astonished. "I know him. He's a relative."

"I'm nothing like you," I said.

It turned to the angel.

"Don't you see the resemblance?" it said.

"You had children?" said the angel. "You never said anything about it before. Why?"

"I don't like to talk about...you know...the old days. But yes, I did. This is my great-great-great-great-great-great-"

I must have passed out from loss of blood. In any case, I lost track of the number of "greats." When I woke, he was still in the midst of them.

" -great-great-great-great grandson."

"I never had children, you know," said the angel. "That may explain how I ended up where I did. It isn't an easy thing to make a child without doing at least one supremely terrible thing in your life."

"I want you to take mine."

"It doesn't work that way. You know that."

"But you said that it could go either way."

"Yes, but only after careful weighing and measuring. You know we don't fling souls to either the fire or the clouds just because one of us happens to be related."

"Stop talking about me as if I'm not even here," I said. "Don't I get a say in this?"

"Actually," said the angel, "No."

"Then just do it for me," said the demon. "Do it out of respect for our thousands of years together."

"Why...you've never asked me anything like that before."

"There was never anyone who mattered before. What you said earlier. I didn't want to admit it then. But you were right, you know. Where I'm heading when this is done can be pretty unpleasant. I don't want him to end up where I'll be ending up. Not if he has any chance of ending up in...the other place."

Now it was the angel's turn to kneel beside me. I'd never seen anything more beautiful. He could be modeling shirts for Arrow. Up close, his blonde hair looked more like feathers.

"I just want to live," I said. "I want to go back to my wife. I want to have kids someday. I want to die an old man, at home, in bed, surrounded by my family. I don't want to die in Berlin."

"It's too late for that," it said. "But you could have something better. I promise you that."

It studied me, looking into my soul. I'd never seen eyes actually twinkle before. There was none of the foul sniffing as with the demon, and I did not feel invaded.

"This one is on the cusp," it said. "But I'm afraid that he's leaning more toward the darkness than the light. He hasn't had an easy life. I don't think that I'll be able to collect him."

"You said leaning," said the demon, kneeling again. "But leaning isn't enough to lose a soul. We've always been able to make judgment calls. We have leeway."

"A judgment call for Judgment Day."

"Don't use that tone with me. You're always so serious. Some days you sound like *Him*. It wouldn't turn the universe upside down if you were to do this as a favor to me. When have I ever asked you for anything?"

"Well, since you bring it up, there was the time—"

"Never mind! Let's just stick to the matter at hand. You said that he was on the cusp."

They looked at each other then, instead of at me, and they became conspirators, suddenly more alike than opposites.

"All right," the angel said. "I'll take him. But don't think I'm doing it for you. I'm doing it for *him*. Anyone who can be allowed in, should be allowed in. You're going home. Going to your real home."

It reached for my hands, and somehow, even through the brick, was able to take them. The real world started fading. As I felt my soul start to get sucked away, that world was suddenly in flames.

When the flames cleared, the demon was cowering, the angel was but a smoking pile of burning feathers, and I was once more what I had once been—the Devil, on Earth to check up on the collecting of souls that were destined for my dominion. But I was also just a man, a real man, who suddenly realized the devil had been hidden inside me, using me as a Trojan horse. I never knew I'd had it in me. And then I could feel that duality fading, feel the spark that had kept me hanging between life and death fading as well.

"Master, I didn't know!" the demon said.

"Nor did he, or else you would never have acted as you did," said the Devil. "You needed to see only a soul meant for me, so that I could see whether what I had suspected was true. You've been surrendering souls meant for me to the other side."

"Never, your majesty. It's just that I thought this one was my own blood. I was tricked—"

"Enough!"

"Yes, master."

"You have been allowing the angels to walk off with too many of the dead. Did you really think I wouldn't sense an imbalance in the cosmic scales? You were sent here to fight for my souls, not surrender them. I can no longer trust you to be a harvester of men. You're coming home with me."

"Please, master. Let me have another chance. This war is over, but there will soon be another, and then another, a string of conflicts until the end of time. I promise never to fail you again."

The Devil paused. I could sense, perhaps because of our recent attachment, that he was considering the demon's pleading. While he'd been hiding within my soul, perhaps some of me had rubbed off on him.

"I can't deny that you have shown a certain talent for war," said the Devil. "You have been useful to me before. Perhaps you could be so again. If I can trust you not to weaken."

"I won't, master."

"Finish your rounds up here," it said. "There are more souls still waiting, and you have delayed long enough. And never let it be said that I cannot be merciful!"

"Yes, master. But…what about this one?"

"What about him?" asked the Devil. "You know what you're supposed to do."

"But…is he really my blood? Or was that just an illusion, too?"

"That's something you'll never be allowed to know. Let that be your punishment."

And then the Devil was gone, and I was left alone with a demon studying me, and no angel to take my side.

"What now?" I whispered.

"I think," said the demon, "I think you suddenly don't look that bad to me after all."

"Are you talking about my soul?"

"No, we'll leave your soul for another day. Look at your body. Look at yourself."

I was suddenly up on my feet, whole again, a jaw where none should rightfully be. And the brick wall I stood beside was whole again, too.

"But…why?"

"Just in case you really are my blood. I figure if I got another chance—why shouldn't you?"

"But what about…"

"Oh, the Devil won't mind waiting, as long as he thinks you can be his eventually. He's really not as bad as he looks.

But don't count on me tipping the scales for you next time. You'd better live well. I'll see you in the next war."

And then he was gone.

"Wait," I called out. "How can you be so sure there'll *be* a next war?"

As I stood in the midst of the rubble of Berlin, my rifle back in my hands, a whisper tickled my ears.

"Oh, there'll be another war…There always is."

I took the demon at its word. It was up to me to be ready for my future. And to hope that an angel would be ready for *me*. I pocketed a still-smoking feather in the hopes that it would help me remember what had been taken from me, what had been given to me. I could hear the voices of Manz and Jackson ahead, and I rushed forward to meet them.

As it turned out, when I died, it *was* going to be someplace other than here.

HERE CHOOSE I

As Lila and I rolled from the couch to the carpeting, not daring to let go of each other, and as we got up to stagger down the hallway, scraping photos from the walls as we passed, and yet again as we tripped over each other and fell laughing onto the bed, I kept thinking, *is this the one, maybe this could be the one, please let this be the one*, repeating the plea in my mind with only minor variations.

We kicked the blankets away, and I kissed her, and with those kisses tried to push those desperate prayers away.

Which was when Lila screamed.

"What is it?" I asked, feigning surprise, while at the same time cursing inwardly. I knew too well what "it" was, but also knew I had to act as if I had no idea.

I'd hoped this seduction would somehow be different. Obviously, it wasn't going to be. I rolled to the far side of the bed and propped myself up on an elbow.

"Someone's watching us," she whispered.

"Who could be watching us?" I said, believing for the moment that if I denied the reason for the interruption strenuously enough, my denial would become true, yet also knowing that words alone would never be enough to free me. "We're on the sixth floor, remember?"

"I don't care," she said, as she buttoned her blouse. She grabbed a pillow and hugged it tightly, when she should have been hugging me. "I can feel it. Someone must be out there."

I walked to the window, and made a show of pushing the curtains aside. The streets below were empty, as I knew they would be, and there was no ledge to support a watcher.

"There's no one…" I began to say, but then couldn't say anything more. The pretense I'd been making that evening that all was well with the world had grown too exhausting to maintain, so the only thing I could bring myself to do further was sigh. No matter how well the night had begun, as my long-simmering flirtation with Lila finally came to a boil, passion had yet again soured into paranoia, pushed there by events completely out of my control. The universe had been sending me a message lately, and I was doing my best to ignore it. But it wouldn't let itself be ignored.

"Don't look at me that way," said Lila. "I'm not crazy."

"There's no one out there," I said, struggling to keep a flatness to my voice.

"I can still feel it, though," she said. "Someone's *watching* us."

Her eyes widened.

"Someone's in *here*."

"Where, Lila?" I shouted, more loudly than I'd meant to. I had no idea how I was going to be able to face her at the agency the next day. "Where is this peeping tom?"

I circled the bedroom, flinging open and then slamming shut drawers, regretting the heated way in which I was behaving while at the same time not being able to stop myself. My fury had broken free.

"Is he in here," I asked, "hiding in the sock drawer? Or

maybe over here, peeking out from under my shorts? Or maybe he's taking notes from under my dirty clothes?"

I kicked the wicker laundry basket across the room, instantly regretting it. Lila didn't deserve this. It wasn't about *her*. It wasn't about any of them. It was only about me.

"Stop making fun of me," she said. "I'm not making this up."

And though I knew she wasn't, just as Barb and Jenny and all of the other women before her hadn't been fantasizing either, I couldn't stop myself from raging on at whatever kept spoiling the mood time after time.

"So maybe there's someone hanging in the closet," I said. I yanked open the louvered doors, and slid the hangers roughly back and forth along the closet rod. "Do you see him there, Lila, hanging with my shirts? Because I don't see anyth—"

I froze, my hand tightening on the bar. Out of the corner of my eye, deep in the darkness, it seemed as if there was suddenly something there after all. A form, crouched with its back against the wall. When I turned to look straight at it, the apparition vanished as if it had never been, but for just a moment, I had been sure that there had been *something*, and that was a first. What Lila had seen was a repeat as far as my recent dates had been concerned, but for me, this proof was new. I had never shared in these hallucinations before, only suffered because of them. But this time...

My skin prickled at the thought of that once-familiar face, and even though it faded into a crumpled, fallen jacket when seen head on, I now suspected who was calling out to me, and if I hadn't been holding onto the closet rod as my legs trembled, I would have fallen atop a mound of running shoes.

"What do you see?" she asked.

"Nothing," I said, for how could I tell her what I didn't want to tell myself? "Nothing at all."

Nothing but the fact that no matter how often I had been hoping for it earlier, this visitation meant maybe she wasn't *the one* after all.

I sat on the far side of the bed from Lila, and kept my back to her.

"I think you should leave," I said, for—yes, universe, I got the message—what more was left for us? I waited for her to speak, but instead of her hitting me with words, a pillow struck me hard in the back of my head.

"You're a jerk, you know," she said.

I knew. Which is why I didn't turn to say anything more. There was nothing to explain. I just sat silently and listened to the squeak of the mattress, the creak of the floor, the slamming of the front door.

I returned to the closet to stare again at the fallen jacket, seeking in its folds a way to reconnect with that fleeting face. Was it really what I'd thought it was? But it would not return to me, and now that I had done what it so obviously wanted and chased off Lila, I doubted it would come again.

At least, not until the next time I brought a woman home.

I HADN'T THOUGHT of Jewel in years, not since I'd last looked through my old address book in search of a quick fix to get through a lonely night. I'd once made it my business to fill that book with names, for how else could I survive? I was so successful the book eventually bulged with overflowing slips of paper—scribbled numbers on cocktail napkins, restaurant receipts, torn scraps of newspapers—as I looked for someone who seemed hard to find. Though I guess that means I hadn't been successful at all.

It wasn't that I was a user. At least, I refused to think of myself as one, even though that's just what I must have seemed like to each and every one of them. But to me, well…it's just that I've always had a problem committing, all the way back to Becky, my first, who I'd abandoned as surely as I had my parents.

I always knew this was my own damned fault, and not theirs. It was all pretty obvious to me. The reason I had such a long string of women behind me—and had always anticipated an even longer one ahead of me—was because I couldn't make up my mind. I'd seen what a crappy life my mom and dad had given each other, suffered every day as a kid through those heart-racing screaming matches that alternated with smothering, sullen silences.

It had been at least fifteen years since I'd last let myself be subjected to that, and as far as I was concerned, Dad had long ago drunk himself into an early grave. Based on his history of alcohol abuse, he was likely long dead, and based on Mom's history of victimhood, she had surely taken up with yet another drunk shortly thereafter.

I'd managed to let go of them both, but I always knew in my heart that I'd never let go of their lesson. It had been instilled too deeply. If I chose wrong, I was sure I'd end up like them, and so as far as women were concerned, I'd found that I couldn't choose at all.

I got that. That's who they'd made me. That's who I'd become. But for the last few months, this inability to maintain a stable relationship suddenly started to have nothing to do with my history. These latest women were not being passively abandoned by me. Instead, they were being actively driven off before any sort of relationship could begin. But by what? And by whom?

I had almost caught a glimpse of what each woman had been seeing thanks to Lila, but that fleeting image wasn't enough to let me admit to myself what I thought I had seen. I wasn't yet ready.

I needed to catch a glimpse of it—whatever it was —again.

And Jewel, unpredictable Jewel, seemed to be the easiest way. She was spontaneous, and that night, spontaneity was what I needed. This time, I *would* have to use her. Maybe afterward, I'd be able to make her understand why.

Turned out she was still waitressing at Traces, a club at which I used to hang out. I hadn't been there since our spectacular breakup. When I lost her, I'd lost a set of friends as well.

I got there early the next night, making sure I arrived before the place could become too packed, so I'd be able to steal more of her time. As I entered, I checked my expression in the long mirrored wall to make sure I appeared appropriately repentant. I was a lousy actor, but it would have to do. I was sorry, all right, but less for what I had done than for what I was about to do.

I sat at a table in what I knew was her zone and waited for her combined curiosity and sense of responsibility to bring her over. I could tell by her own expression that she didn't know what to make of my sudden reappearance.

"The usual," I said. I smiled, trying to make sure that smile was sheepish.

She turned and left without speaking, leaving me to wonder whether she'd bother to return with my beer. But she soon came back to slap down a napkin and center a bottle of beer on it.

"Other bars have beer," she said.

"But other bars don't have you," I said.

She turned away to consider another table of customers,

even though no one had called for her.

"Why are you really here?" she asked.

"I've been thinking—"

"Uh-oh," she said. "We both know what that means. Here comes trouble."

I didn't mind the interruption. At least it came with a smile.

"I'm here to apologize, Jewel," I said. "I was a jerk. Can we try this again?"

"Apology?" she said. "From you? How much have you had to drink tonight already?"

She scrunched up her face in suspicion, and I remembered how cute she always was when she did that.

I held out my hands, palms up, and shook my head in denial. She leaned in close, trying to smell my breath. She didn't immediately pull away. I kissed her, and she lingered long enough to let me taste her brand of cigarette. It brought back everything that had gone wrong before, and promised everything that would go wrong again.

"I get off at midnight," she said.

She went back to work and I drank my beer. I hoped the alcohol would give me an idea on how to get through this without hurting her badly all over again. But only that hurt would bring on what I needed to see.

After a few more beers, I stood up to walk outside, circle the block and clear my head. I left Jewel a big tip. At least when this was all over, she would still have that.

WE NEVER MADE it back to my apartment, or hers. We never even made it out of the bar.

Hell, we didn't even make it to midnight.

When Jewel came over to clear away my second set of

bottles, she took one look at me sitting there nodding and cross-eyed, and said, "Oh, what the hell."

She looked around nervously, then quickly grabbed my hand and tugged me to my feet. She led me behind the bar, then out a door into the alleyway, where the previous day's snow had turned to slush. She kissed me, and the taste of her cigarettes pushed away any thoughts of my wet socks.

A little dizzy from too many beers, I had trouble standing, and so I pressed Jewel against the wall, propping myself up with palms flat against the cold brick. She fumbled at my belt while I dropped one hand to pop the snaps at her hips. Pants around my ankles, I forgot about why I had really come there, until her nails bit into me. And not in a good way.

"What the Hell," she said, her lips close to my ear.

She pushed me away, and turned toward the mouth of the alley.

"Hey, pervert!" she shouted. "Where did you go?"

"What is it?" I asked. I again forced myself to play that game. Maybe it would end up hurting her less.

"Someone's watching us."

I couldn't make out anyone in the darkness.

"Where are you hiding?" she said, not bothering to cover herself up. "Come on out and take a good look!"

I tried to spot it, him, whatever it was, amid the trashcans and dumpsters that lined the alleyway. That, there—was it what I was looking for, or just a pile of black plastic bags which in my drunkenness formed the outlines of a man? There was only one way to find out. I took a step forward, but almost fell because my pants were wrapped around my feet. Jewel reached out to steady me.

"Enough of this," she said, buttoning herself up. "Let's go inside."

"Wait," I said.

"I'm not going to put on a show," she said. "I may be into a lot of things, but I'm not into that."

She moved to the bar's back door, but I held up a hand.

"Please, Jewel," I said. "Stay."

What I couldn't say was that it wasn't so much that I wanted her to stay, but rather that I knew if she left, whatever had come to watch us would leave with her.

I bent over to pick up my pants, contorting so that I wouldn't take my eyes off what I thought I had seen. I moved closer, and this time, the form did not dissolve back into the mundane. I could make out a man, perched atop trash bags as if sitting on a beanbag chair. He didn't get up as I approached, as if he'd been the one who'd had too many beers. His coat, which came down to his knees, was worn, with its cuffs frayed. Bits of food were stuck in his salt-and-pepper beard. He could have just been a hardcore drunk, lost to life, only he shimmered, and I could both see him and see through him. And his eyes, pinning me, told me he still had a purpose.

The closer I got, the more familiar those eyes became.

"Dad?" I said. The vision did not answer. But I knew.

"Is there someone there?" called Jewel.

I knelt beside my father.

"What are you doing here?" I asked. "What do you want from me?"

He raised an arm as if it took him a great effort. He pointed at Jewel, then at me, then back again.

"Come inside," called Jewel.

"Do you see him?" I said.

"I can barely see you," she said. "This is just too weird, even for me. This was a mistake."

I heard the creak of the emergency exit, and then a slam. The instant the door closed, Dad disappeared. I pitched forward, but there were only trash bags to catch my fall.

In my drunkenness, the idea that my father had returned from the dead to haunt me seemed plausible. But what had he come back to tell me?

All of a sudden, the beer caught up with me. I didn't think I could stand anymore, and didn't bother to try. I fell asleep right there in the alley, shivering both from the cold and from what was to come.

I PHONED MY MOTHER, without the slightest idea of what I was going to say.

"Hi, Mom, you screwed my head up something bad, and I know I haven't tried to call you in at least ten years, and I'm sorry about that, but, um, forgetting about all that for a moment, did Dad say anything before he died that would explain why he's suddenly haunting me and driving away all my girlfriends?"

Somehow, that didn't seem like the best approach if I expected to get what I needed.

But I needn't have worried, because when I punched out her number, I learned the line had been disconnected. I shouldn't have been surprised. After a lifetime with Dad, the only calls likely to come in were from collection agencies looking for the money Dad had pissed away on booze, husbands with threats about what they would do to him if he didn't stay away from their wives, and drinking buddies looking for a partner in crime to pick up their bar tabs. Mom had been forced to suffer such calls when Dad was alive, but it made no sense for her to let the torture continue once he was gone.

So I called information, but Mom no longer had a listed number. Maybe she'd even sold the house and moved on—I would have, because memories themselves can haunt as well as any ghost—but for her, I doubted it. She'd grown up there, and no matter how Dad had spoiled those last years in the place, she wasn't going anywhere.

Which meant it seemed like the right time for a road trip.

I tossed some clothes in a bag, looking deep into the darkness of my closet as I stripped my hangers. But I saw nothing out of the ordinary. That just wasn't how it worked.

I drove out of the city, the map of the way home so strong in me I didn't have to pay much attention to the route. City streets turned to highways turned to mountain roads without me having to think about it, and then I was parked there, in front of the house, watching my mom through the kitchen window as she washed the dishes from dinner. I watched her for a long time.

I wasn't surprised to find out, even after having driven so far, that I was suddenly hesitating. Would you want to come face to face with the woman who failed to protect you from her drunk husband your entire childhood? But I also knew that I had to go in, because if I wanted to be free of him, there was no other way.

I pressed the bell at the front door, and waited long enough I started to think this was a mistake, but then pressed it again anyway. And waited some more. I wondered for a moment if she'd seen me come up the walk and decided not to answer. But then I remembered the buzzer had broken years earlier, and they've never had it fixed—why make it easier for the bill collectors?—and so I finally knocked.

I could hear Mom drop a pot, mutter, then shut the water at the sink. Then I could sense her eyes on me through the peephole. Or were they Dad's eyes, watching me from… where? I looked off into the bushes, seeking out his face, like in one of those magic posters in which the image only appears if you cross your eyes long enough. When I looked back, the front door had already opened, and Mom was standing there, eyes wide, jaw dropped, her hands trembling as they worried at the hem of her apron. I stepped forward and took those hands to make her shaking stop.

"How are you, Mom?" I said, and tried my best to sound as if I still cared.

She took a sudden step back, pulling me inside with her, even though I wasn't entirely sure that's what she'd intended. She may have simply wanted to get away from me, but I didn't let go until we were in the center of the living room, standing on a faded carpet I knew too well. I'd found my father passed out on it far too many times.

"You're looking good, Mom," I lied, a lie which she accepted. She had been accepting of lies—from Dad, from me, from herself—for as long as I could remember.

"What brings you back, son?" she asked. She didn't wait for an answer, but instead turned on me and went back to the kitchen. She continued with her chores as if my visit was an everyday occurrence. I came up behind her as she hunched over the sink and plunged her arms into soapy water.

"Dad," I said. "I need to ask you about Dad."

Her hands stopped churning for a moment so brief that someone else might not have noticed the slight pause, then hurriedly continued on as she tried to pretend my question had no effect.

"What is it you need to know?" she asked, in a tone that clearly said, *do we need to do this, son?* "I thought we were done talking about your father."

"Do you remember Dad ever talking about me, right before, you know…"

I didn't know how to say it, and so stepped to her side, willing her to look back at me. But no matter how much I wished it, she would not turn in my direction.

"Your Dad was never a talkative one," she said, trying to sound light, but failing miserably, and only coming off strained. "And it's not for a lack of me trying, believe me. Many's the time I went on longer than I should have trying to pull something out of him, and paid the price. He didn't talk about you much, but it wasn't anything personal. He didn't talk about anything. So, no, I don't remember anything in particular."

A dead end. But maybe there was another way.

"Would it be all right if I went through his things?" I asked. "That is, if you didn't already throw them all out?"

"Go through your dad's things?" she said, her voice suddenly hard. She turned to me, wiping her hands on a dish towel. "That wouldn't be wise, son. Your father is a very private man, and I'm sure he wouldn't react well."

Her words were clear, but I found I couldn't understand them. Had Mom been drinking? Was it her turn to be lost to sensibility?

"What are you talking about?" I asked.

"Just that if there's anything you want out of your father," she said, "you'd better ask him yourself when he gets home. Though I have no idea when that will be, or whether he'll be coherent when he gets here. Will you be staying the night? I'm afraid your old room is being used for storage these days, but you can sleep on the couch if you'd like."

I was too stunned to digest everything she said, so it wasn't until later that I realized how much pain that offer of a place to sleep brought her, and how much she wished I'd go instead.

"Dad's...alive?

"Of course your father's alive," she said, studying me as if I was the one whose brain had become pickled, rather than her husband. "What made you think any different?"

I didn't know what else to say. I backed away from her,

and suddenly found myself outside, with no memory of having made the transition. The last I saw of my mother was through the doorway, and her small face bore an expression of relief. I quickly got back into my car and prepared to return to the city, and to the ghost that seemed to bear my father's face, but which was obviously nothing more than a stranger.

———

I DIDN'T MAKE it far.

As I turned off the street on which I had experienced some of the worst moments of my life, I saw a tree under which I had experienced some of my best. I remembered walking home from dates, and never wanting to actually get there, because of all the drama that waited for me. I remembered sitting and talking under that tree for hours, trying to hold onto something that could ease the pain.

I remembered Becky.

I stopped the car and thought of rock concerts and heavy petting, the occasional beer I boosted from my parents' fridge and the random joint she stole from her older brother, the long conversations in the rain. That tree was a second home for each of us.

Another teen couple might have carved their names on that tree, but I didn't think either of us wanted anything that permanent. Well…I certainly didn't, which is why we finally broke up. She wanted to run with me, to build a better life far away from our abusive families. I wanted to run, too, but I knew that if we did it together, we'd *become* one of those abusive families. Back then, I couldn't picture any other future for us.

And now? My history with women shows I haven't changed my mind.

I hadn't thought of Becky in years. I wondered if she'd gotten out, the way I had. Though the way I had gotten out meant that maybe I'd never really gotten out at all.

I drove to Becky's house. In the darkness, I could pretend nothing had changed. Maybe nothing had. I parked on the street, and tried to see in the windows, but I couldn't tell whether anyone was there. As I took the short walk to her front door, I remembered all the other times I had done it, usually to the sound of raised voices within. It was silent this time, so at least that much had changed.

I rang the bell, and before I could question the wisdom of what I'd just done, the door was flung open and there was Becky, unchanged from memory.

I took a step back.

"Becky," I whispered, almost to myself, ready to bolt. I'd had too much of ghosts.

She looked at me as if I were a stranger. She seemed not so very different than when I had seen her last, only this time, her expression, rather than being what it had been during our final conversation—disappointment? disgust? defeat?—was blank.

"Becky?" I repeated, this time loud enough that she could hear.

"Mom?" she called out, frowning, and not looking away. "There's some weird guy here who I think wants to see you."

Then the real Becky stepped up behind the girl, and I felt like an idiot, because how could I explain to her the reason why I was so willing to accept the idea that she'd never aged?

"Go to your room," she said to the girl, obviously her daughter, and then, once we were alone, to me: "I never thought I'd see you again."

"I guess I always figured I'd see you again," I said. "Only I had no idea how or when."

We stood there looking at each other. I didn't know what

to say or do next. I could tell that she had no idea either. We'd both thought about this moment—I knew I had, and often—but it seemed that neither one of us had rehearsed for it. Finally, she stepped back.

"Do you want to come in?" she asked.

I did, but until she asked me, I didn't really know just how much.

Unlike back at my parents, the interior of her house was very different than the last time I'd seen it. Gone was the flowery couch with its plastic slipcovers. Gone was the wall with photos of dead relatives, a family tree of inherited abuse. The soul-deadening beiges and pastels had been replaced throughout by bright primary colors. If Becky's presence alone had not been enough to clue me in, these changes by themselves, and all the other differences that accompanied them, would have telegraphed that both her parents were dead. She'd been the lucky one, I guess.

She noticed me taking it all in and read my mind. She'd always been good at that.

"Mom and Dad left me not so long after you did," she said. "Only they won't be coming back. They died in a car accident. The way I always imagined it, they were having such a big argument that they didn't even notice when it happened. The way I imagine it, wherever they are, they're probably arguing still."

"I'm sorry," I said.

"You don't have to be, you know," she said. "You don't know what a relief it was when I didn't have to pretend anymore that all those bruises came from falling off my bicycle."

I sat on the couch, suddenly unable to look at her. I was the one who was supposed to have taken her away from that. Everything that happened to her after the day I left might just as well have been my fault. If death hadn't stepped in to free her from her parents, they'd probably be abusing her still.

"So why are you here?" she asked.

"My dad," I said. "I thought…I thought he was dead. I needed to talk to Mom about it."

She sat down beside me. If it had been anyone but me, she probably would have taken my hand.

"Why would you think that your dad was dead?" she said. "He's the same as he ever was, still closing down Kelly's each night and falling asleep on neighbors' front yards. I think he'll be doing that long after we're both dead and buried."

I didn't hesitate. I told her all of it then. I don't think I could have told anyone else. That's why it was a good thing I'd gone back there, whether Dad had actually died or not. There was no one else I could have opened myself up to like that. I'd always told her everything, and even with the time we'd lost, I felt that I could do it still. And when I was done, she didn't even think I was crazy, which is more than I could say for myself.

"So what do you think, Becky?" I asked. "If what I keep seeing wasn't my dad, then what was it? And what did it want?"

"Based on what you told me, there's only one way we're going to find out," she said. "It's getting a little late for you to start heading back to the city. I think you need to spend the night here."

I'd never even thought of using her that way. I guess the fact it had never occurred to me said something about us, about how I still felt about her. But was she right?

"What about your daughter?" I asked. "What will she think?"

"Don't worry about her," she said. "Once I explain everything, she'll understand."

"Becky, is she—"

"Tomorrow," she said. "There'll be plenty of time to talk about that tomorrow."

We stood, and I helped her unfold the couch into a bed. Even as we did it, I had a sense it was all for show. We moved to the kitchen, where we shared a glass of wine, and caught up on the intervening years. At that point, we stayed away from anything serious, so to some extent it was like chatting with someone I'd just met on a cross-country flight. But even so, it was pleasant, and relaxed, and if I hadn't known her already I'd have tried to get her name and number. Eventually, she yawned one time too many.

"We'd better get some sleep," she said. "I have a feeling tomorrow is going to be a big day."

She took my hand, and we walked out of the kitchen, and past the living room and its waiting foldout couch, and on into her bedroom. It had been her parents' bedroom, and I didn't know how she could sleep there. She had to have ghosts of her own. But then she leaned in to kiss me, and I tried to stop thinking of ghosts. But I couldn't, not entirely. No matter how she tasted, no matter how right it seemed, I kept one eye open in search of the thing that would tell me that, no, I was wrong.

As with all of the other recent women, Becky sensed the visitor before I did, only instead of pushing me away, she hugged me even more tightly.

"Something's here," she said.

"What is it?" I asked.

"Turn around," she said.

An old man stood in the corner, lips moving, hands gesticulating, an old man with sad, familiar eyes. But I heard nothing he said, understood nothing he meant.

"I don't get it," I said. "That's my father's ghost, isn't it?

What else could it be? But it can't be, because my father's still alive."

"Look closer," she said. "That's not your father. Don't you see? That's your face. Those are *your* eyes. It's *you*."

I looked beyond the beard, beyond the years, beyond the tattered clothes and the filth, tried to focus on the eyes. The light had gone out of them, but still…

"It *is* me," I said. "But what happened? Is that how I'm going to end up?"

"Why not just ask him?" said Becky. "That's why you're here, isn't it?

No, I wanted to say, I was there for more than just that. I didn't want to let go of her, but she pushed me forward, until I stood face to face with myself. I looked sad. I looked pathetic. Was that what I was going to be like at the moment of my death? I seemed like the sort of person who, if I saw him on a street corner, I'd hurry past, trying my best not to make eye contact. But now there was no escape. I had to look in those eyes.

I had to look in my eyes.

"Why are you here?" I asked myself. "What do you want?"

The other me answered, or tried to anyway, but I still could not understand. He pointed from me to Becky and back again, got angry and began to shout, but I could hear nothing. Frustrated by his inability to communicate, he began to cry. I recognized those tears. I had cried them many times before, and by his presence was being told I would cry them again in the many years I still had stretched out before me. But why? I reached out in my own frustration to grab him by his lapels, and instead slipped through him, slamming into the wall behind. I fell, and as I looked back up at myself, in pain both mental and physical, all I could think was—How could this have happened? How could I have ended up like my father?

And then I knew.

"It's a warning," I said.

"What kind of warning?" she said.

"I've got to go," I said.

I ran down the hallway, past Becky's daughter peeking out nervously from her bedroom, and leapt into my car. Becky followed me out.

"Tell me!" she said. "What are you trying to tell yourself?"

"We're not supposed to be together," I said, slamming the car door.

You're not the one, I thought, as I headed off into the night, and looked at her shrinking in the rearview mirror. *And maybe there won't be a one.*

I FLED my hometown for the second time, realizing that no matter how hard I fought against it, everything I'd always feared would come true, *would* come true. I had become— would become—what'd I been rejecting. My fate was clear. Any choice I made would be the wrong choice, and I'd then be bound together with whomever I chose in a living Hell. After years of running from relationships, I'd grown weary of one-night stands and brief hook-ups, and I'd been starting to consider commitment. That was what would eventually kill me, and that was why I had returned.

Ghosts knew nothing of life and death. Why should they know of time? Why shouldn't they be able to haunt their own pasts? Once I realized that I had been my own ghost, I was suddenly sure of the message.

Stay away, I'd come to tell myself. Stick to the decision

you made so long ago. There's no one out there for you, no one who will bring you anything but misery. Marry and you'll end up like your parents. Better to be alone. Fleeing Becky years ago was the right idea. Flee her again. Flee them all. I broke that vow, and married, and look what it did to me. Run and just keep running.

I got the point.

As I sped through the night, leaving my first love behind, heading back to where there would be no love, I thought of the life of loneliness ahead. I wasn't looking forward to it, but it had to be better than the hellish life my future self had lived. Now that I'd rededicated myself to remaining alone, maybe my ghost would leave me alone.

Maybe this decision could save both of us.

A car came up close behind me. Its headlights flashed. When I slowed to let it pass, it slowed as well, shortening the distance between us. As I cursed the blinding light and looked into the rearview mirror, I saw with a glance not just a slice of my own face, but a second self overlaying me, a self with ancient eyes and wrinkled skin, as if my doppelganger was also driving the car.

The car behind began to honk, and my ghostly self seized the wheel. I had to struggle against it to stay on the winding roads. As we fishtailed around the curves, I screamed, but got no answer.

"What more do you want?" I shouted, looking into the mirror for an answer. "I did what you wanted. I ran. Why are you still haunting me?"

I looked ahead to see a telephone pole I could not avoid. I feared it would be the only answer I would ever get.

I WAS STILL ALIVE, and surprised to find myself so. I could

tell that I was in a hospital from the beeps indicating my vital signs, and by the poking at my chest and the prodding along my arms and legs.

I tried to open my eyes, but couldn't. Still, I saw the room above me as if I could, as well as the doctor leaning in to study me. Only the face the doctor wore was my own, that of my future destroyed self. A wreck of a man, who had just wrecked me.

"Why wouldn't you let me go?" I tried to say, and even though a tube was down my throat, I could hear my voice in my ears. "What is it you wanted?"

"You've been a haunted man long before I started haunting you," I answered, in an older, ruined voice I was hearing for the first time. In that drugged place between consciousness and dream, I was finally able to reach out to myself. "Thanks to our parents, you were made afraid to make up your mind, and never did, and so we died alone. It was that lack of choice that killed us, not any commitment you made. You had no one to take care of, and no one to take care of you. And so…"

He gestured at his hollow cheeks and unkempt hair as if no further explanation was needed.

"You misread me," I continued. "I didn't come back to split you up with anyone. I wish you could have heard me clearly, but it's so hard to break through from the dead to the living, from the future to the past. I came to tell you to stay together. Pick. Choose. Make up your damned mind before you damn us both. Save me. Save yourself. Don't let our parents do this to us. Break the cycle. This is not the only way."

"I don't know that I can," I said. "I don't know that I'm strong enough. It won't be easy."

"You think this was easy," I answered, opening my rag of a coat to reveal my emaciated body within.

The beeping suddenly sped up, and as I felt more hands upon me, my other self began to fade away. I found I could open my eyes, but before I could take in my surroundings, before I could compare this solid hospital room to the ghostly one I had just left, I felt a weight across my chest, and heard Becky murmuring "I'm sorry" over and over again.

"It's OK, Becky," I said. "I'm alive."

"I was following you," Becky said. "I wanted to tell you that you didn't have to go, not this time, that we could work it out, I was sure of that now, but I must have distracted you, and driven you off the road. This was all my fault."

"No, it wasn't," I said. "It was mine. All of it, all of it mine."

It took all I had, but I managed to bend one elbow, and run my fingers through her hair.

"It doesn't matter whose fault it is," I said. "What matters is that we're here, together, now. There'll be no more running."

"How can you be sure?" she asked.

"Look," I said.

Standing in the doorway to the room was an old man who could have been in his nineties. His suit was pressed, his hair was short, his cheeks had been shaved, and his face was split by a smile.

Standing in the doorway was me.

I nodded, and vanished, gone back to God knows where.

"I don't think there'll be any more hauntings," I said.

Becky leaned in and kissed me.

"Are you ready to meet your daughter?" she said. "Are you ready to meet your family?"

"Yes," I said. "I think I finally am."

THE SCARIEST STORY I KNOW

My son runs in, his face lit by flashes of lightning from the storm that had woken us both. He crawls on top of my covers and, smiling slyly, asks me to tell him a story. By now, we both know he won't be able to get back to sleep without it.

But unfortunately for Stevie, it's his mother who's the storyteller in the family; if I don't have a copy of something like *Green Eggs and Ham* in my hands, it's likely that whatever tale he gets will be incomprehensible. Laura was always able to improvise grand adventures in which Stevie vanquished pirates and traveled to the stars; me, I'm lucky if I can cobble together a story stolen from the plots of the last few movies I've seen. I've never been the one in the relationship able to wing it.

So as I look down at my son, with the storm making his face first light, then dark, then light again, I worry—will I be able to give him what he needs?

I don't think so, not after everything that's happened.

"What kind of story do you want?" I ask warily.

"A scary one, Dad," says Stevie. "I need a scary one tonight."

It's been a long time since he's asked me for something scary, and that last time, he grew impatient with my procrastinating, my delays as I struggled to come up with a story, any story, and he wandered off in search of his mother. He couldn't find her, and came back in tears. The story I told him then—or *tried* to tell him then, I should say, because that is all I ever do, just try, and never succeed, for no matter how long the words keep coming, they never achieve story—was one of my worst. We *both* ended up in tears. I don't want that to happen again. Another encounter like that, and where would that leave us? So, as he looks at me hopefully, I keep thinking, and as I grow angrier with fate and with my role in it, a story comes to me. It's not a pretty story, but then, I'm no longer in a pretty mood.

"I'm going to tell you the scariest story I know," I say, the two of us squeezed into the left-hand side of a king-size bed. My gut tells me it's long past time that I share the truth with him, though even as I decide to do so, I wonder if I'm just being selfish. "I'll tell you what it's like to be alive."

He looks at me expectantly, and I am amazed he can muster any hope that anything coherent will come out of my mouth. My one and only hope is that it will make some small sense to him.

"First, you're born. Actually, first your parents are born, and live through enough of their lives to finally meet, but you're not around to experience that part, even though it could very well be the most important part. If you're lucky, like I was, like you were, you're delivered into the hands of two people who love each other very much, and who will love you very much."

"Dad, I thought you said this was going to be a scary story."

"Don't worry, it will be."

He snuggles more deeply into my arm, I give him a squeeze, and we both stare up at the ceiling. It's a ceiling we know by heart. We've had far too many nights lately where I've had to stand in for his mother in the storytelling department, many nights during which I'd tried and failed to take her place. This time, I don't know why—the fury of the storm, the crushing number of times I'd fumbled in the past instead of giving my son what he needed, the feeling of his head on my shoulder this particular night—I think it should be different.

"See, when you start out, you have every need taken care of. It's like magic, like a fairy tale, like going to the carnival and being given every trinket you see. Your parents are there to fulfill your every want.

"You already know about that part. You've already lived through it yourself, but here's what comes next, the part you haven't had a chance to live through. You must go find your own way in the world, with no one to watch your back. You'll have to find a job, and if you're lucky, it will be a job you love—but not everyone is so lucky. You'll find friends, friends who aren't your friends just because you live on the same street, friends who you aren't just stuck with, and then you'll find some friends who aren't really friends at all, and who will betray you. If you're lucky, though, a few of them will be true, and the false will fall away."

"So far this still doesn't sound very scary, Dad."

"Here's comes the scary part," I say, but I know I'm just ranting, that the only one who's scared is me. "If you're lucky, very lucky, you'll find someone you love as much as your parents loved each other. You'll think, this is my life, this is why I bother to breathe. You will think, this is my purpose. This…this is my other self.

"And you will be so much in love you will have a child of

your own. And because you are so happy, because you are blinded by this happiness, you'll think, we have done it, have done what we were meant to do, together we will now see this child become a man.

"And life will seem perfect. Oh, I know that there's really no such thing as perfect, but it's as close as the universe allows. And then"—and here, I'm afraid, my voice breaks up —"the person you love is ripped from you by that bastard death in one of its many forms, and you're left forever alone. Unable to touch them, unable to talk to them, unable to love them. You're bewildered, and unable to figure out how it all went wrong. And that's what scares the hell out of me."

I notice that I'm trembling, and force myself to take a deep breath.

"That's the scariest story I know," I say.

The lightning has long since died, and we're left in darkness together. I regret my words. I'd let myself rage against God, forgetting I was talking to my son, and it's a mistake to let anyone hear what we say to God under the cover of night.

"That's not what being a grownup is like on TV," says Stevie. "That's not what it's like in books. There must be more to it than that. It doesn't always end that way."

"I know. But books lie. Television lies. This is the way it all really turns out."

He looks at me, his lower lip quivering a bit, but what more is there to say? I owe him the truth.

"But I'm not scared, Dad. I wanted to be scared. I'm just sad."

"I didn't mean to make you sad," I say. "But I'm not very good at stories, remember? Mommy's the one who knows how to tell stories. I'm sorry, Stevie."

"I wish Mommy could tell me more stories."

"So do I, Stevie. So do I."

And then he slides off the bed to pad back to his own

room, the one it hurts me to look at, because there isn't a piece of furniture or decoration there that Laura didn't choose.

"Good night, Daddy," he says, as he pauses in the doorway. "I love you."

"Good night, son," I say. "I love you, too."

I lie back in the vastness of my great big bed, listening to the rumble of the storm, which is by now miles distant.

And then I turn to look over at my wife, who has heard none of this. Stevie and I are ourselves like the storm to her, blown along by the whim of the heavens. We're still on her horizon, but almost gone. There is more than just a king-size bed separating us, for she still remains behind in the other world. She is still in the thick of it, still struggling…but she is doing it alone.

At least I have Stevie here with me, day after day, night after night, as we linger. He begs me to entertain him while we wait to depart for whatever place is meant to come next. But Laura has no company to make her burden lighter. All she has is the memory of the accident that took us away from her forever.

I wonder if she still dreams of us sometimes. I wonder if in those dreams, she finds herself telling Stevie the stories that in life she will never get to tell him. I sometimes pray I could peer inside of her to listen to those stories and bring them back for Stevie.

He wants her stories, and so do I, but they are beyond us. I hope that tomorrow night, and the night after that, when Stevie once more comes to me in search of what I can't give, of what I could never give, that he no longer asks me for scary stories, because looking down at Laura, so incredibly close, so incomprehensibly far, I realize that I now only know of one.

LAURA SLEEPS on the right-hand side of a king-size bed, and as she sleeps, she dreams, and as she dreams, she dreams her son rushes in, attempting to outrun a storm. His face is flickering as if fireflies were caressing his cheeks. He crawls into bed, a bed she is horrified to realize she now thinks of as *her* bed, no longer a marriage bed, and asks that she tell him a story.

In her dream—a dream which she knows to be a dream, because waking life now withholds such a basic reward as this—she feels as if she hasn't told Stevie a story in a long time, and yet that surely cannot be, because within that dream, she knows she tells him one every night. There is a sense of heaviness within her that is extreme, a fullness that must be relieved, similar to what she felt while she was nursing him, and so as he cuddles up against her, she reaches into memory and tries to tell him his favorite story, which is, of course, really *all* stories, because it contains in its telling his favorite pieces of every other story she has ever told, back to that first story, when she looked into his wide, uncomprehending eyes and knew she was only telling the tale to herself, yet went ahead and told it anyway.

It is a story with ingredients that should not taste good together, that should clash instead of blend, so mixed up are they in a confusion of genre and style, and yet somehow, for Stevie, the parts cohere into a greater whole. The story contains spacemen and deserts and rushing steam engines, airplanes and oceans and monkeys as big as mountains. But most of all it contains Stevie, the star of the tale, the star of his life, and of hers. She doesn't stop speaking until she runs out of words, but luckily, she does not begin to run out of words until his eyes begin to close.

But once his lids and lashes do drop, she finds she is no

longer herself, she has become someone else. She is a man. She is her husband. At first, in the logic of her dream, it does not bother her; it seems apt. It is only as she closes off the tale and leans in to kiss her son's cheek that things suddenly seem awry.

She could not be her husband. Her husband does not tell stories, cannot tell stories, and never could, and so she can't be him, she can't. And as she tries to make sense of this sense of confusion, she feels the dream slipping away, she feels her son slipping away. The cheek she had kissed is vanishing, and she wakes. She hears herself cry out her son's name.

She looks to the ceiling, a ceiling she once did not have to look at alone, a ceiling that once belonged to three. Awake, the shout of her son's name still echoing, she is barely alive, and she is almost too drained to even know it. Circumstances have left her more like a ghost. She can feel herself haunting her own life, at the same time there and not there.

There are moments when Laura is ashamed. Those are the moments when she is forced to admit to herself that, yes, she believes it is far better off that her husband and son *both* died. For if one or the other of them had remained alive, she feels that the task that was still before her, to walk through the rest of her life, to go on in the face of the inner voice that told her there was little point to, would be even more insurmountable. If Stevie had alone died, she and her husband would probably have ended up getting divorced, not that they'd had any problems previously, but she'd seen it happen to other living couples who fell apart in such a situation, as if the glue which bound them together was suddenly gone, and she doubted that even they could have been strong enough to beat the odds; but if instead it had been her husband who had alone died, that would have perhaps been even more unbearable, for it would have been as if Stevie had been taken anyway—for how could she ever have found the strength to tell her son a story again? And those were the moments she cherished the most, that was when she felt the most alive. It was the only time when she could just be, and not have to think of being.

She looks to the left-hand side of the bed, where, by habit, her husband used to lie, and she can almost see him there. The mattress still holds the impression that he made over so many years, still responds to the weight of his life, and she tells herself that if she reached out, she could feel him there still making that impression, but when she fans her hand across the bed, her promise becomes a lie, for her fingers touch only air.

A storm begins to gather in the distance, and as the rumbling begins, growing nearer and louder, she looks to the bedroom door, expecting Stevie to come into the room, as he always did at such times, seeking reassurance, seeking story, but the space in her universe that should contain him is empty.

———

You run toward them both, seeing them both, even though they both can't see you. To one parent you are but a dream, to the other but a ghost. You climb in the center of the bed and lie between them, your posture favoring neither, your heart loving them both. Each of them reaches out to pat you, one a cheek, the other an arm. As they touch you, they are careful to touch only you, ignoring each other. At least that is what it seems like to you, ignorance, willful ignorance, because you are not yet old enough to understand the fact that it could be blindness.

They each start to tell you a story, and they blend into a strange sort of stereo. It is as if you are parked between television sets tuned to different stations. As their voices overlap, one pulls at you with the past, while the other tugs at you with a future which will never come to pass.

Squirming over on your back, you look up at the ceiling and see the stains there, see the maps those stains made, the islands, shores, and continents. You hold up a hand to each of your parents, pressing your fingers against theirs, though neither knows of the other. Their hands are so large, their fingers extending further than you can imagine yours ever will. You play that game that each liked to play with you, only each now thinks you are playing it alone—pushing until your mother's hand gives way, then letting your own give way when your mother pushes back; pressing against your father's palm until it impossibly moves back, letting him push at your hand until you surrender. It is a dance you have done with them individually many times before, and so as you listen to their stories, your hands oscillate back and forth, first closer to them, then closer to you, their hands reaching toward each other without them realizing it, without them knowing how close they are.

You do not know whether you are bringing them together or keeping them apart, and you do not like not knowing which it is you are doing.

And so, the next time each pushes back against you, you slip your hands out from between them. For an instant, their fingers seem to touch, to pause, but then they continue on to pass through each other as if diving into mist. And yet…they must have noticed something different, for they pull back their hands as if shocked.

Then each retreats as far as possible to the opposite sides of their bed.

HER DREAM IS OVER; the real and final dream, and not just

the dream within the dream. She feels silly now for not having known it earlier. It came to her suddenly, she could not explain how or from where, a spark that ran through her and changed her forever. She'd thought that she'd been waiting to join her son and husband on the other side, thought she'd have to endure a lifetime of that waiting, but instead it turns out that they are not on the other side, and never have been. They are the ones still back there, waiting. There is no Stevie here with her to tell stories to, no husband with whom to share her life…no life.

The king-size bed in which she had tried to find comfort since the horrible accident was gone, the bedroom which had contained it was gone, the house into which her husband had years before carried her through the front door was gone.

She had stayed behind with the people and things of her former life through force of will, existing in a kind of fugue state until she met something greater than that will.

And now, instead of merely existing in life and waiting to join them, she has to merely exist in death and wait for them to join her. She has to wait not her lifetime—she has to wait *theirs*.

Once she had prayed for herself to die, not knowing she was already dead; now, to be joined with the rest of her family, she has to pray for *them* to die, and she cannot bring herself to do that, it would be wrong somehow, to hope that for those you love, no matter that there was a second life beyond; she was not a selfish person before, and she is determined not to be selfish now. She will wait.

She looks down from a great height, and sees her husband waking from a great slumber.

As I WAKE, I flail an arm to my right, and I am surprised that I have allowed myself to do so. For so long, that side of the bed has been forbidden territory, separated by an invisible line I dared not cross…and now, it is only the other side of the bed. I peer into the darkness, attempting to make out…I am not sure what…whatever woke me, I guess. But then a flash of lightning comes, and I know it was only a storm.

But what I see is not familiar to me.

It's my bedroom, but—

The floor is littered with empty pizza boxes and soda bottles, hamburger wrappers and beer cans. It hadn't been that way when I'd gone to sleep last night, I would have sworn it. Laura would never have let me leave it that way.

Laura…

A burst of lightning flashed and illuminated the rest of the bed that I had groped upon waking.

Laura was…alive? Wasn't she?

No. No, she was not. *I* was alive. I had not as I had thought remained behind to haunt her. I had remained behind to do what I was not doing, which was to live. And I could not bear to see it. Until now.

I touched her. Somehow I had touched her. Not long enough, never long enough, but enough to know that she was the one dead and I was the one alive, enough to know that she wanted me to go on.

But how could we have touched?

And then I know.

Then, the answer comes to me.

My son runs in, his face lit by flashes of lightning from the storm that had woken us both.

IT'S ONLY A STORY

Three puppets scattered across a dollhouse by a careless child. That's what their twisted bodies looked like. But no, they were but children themselves, with limbs bent and angled as only those of young boys lost in play can be.

As is also the way with young boys, though the three were friends, bound together by a love of scary stories in every possible form, each was in a different corner of the room, each was looking away from the others, and each was intent on his own personal passion.

On his back in the corner nearest the bedroom door was Ron, butt wedged into the spot where two walls met the floor, his long legs—which had only started stretching during the past year—rising up so far his feet threatened to dislodge a pixelated poster of robots fighting dinosaurs that his friend Biff, whose room it was, had pinned there. He held a comic book, one with a cover showing a vampire sucking the blood from its victim, at arm's length over his head. As he riffled quickly through the pages, the comic, which blocked the lone ceiling light, cast a flickering shadow across his face.

In the center of the room sat Johnny, chin in hands, facing a small flatscreen TV on which a giant reptile tossed scuba divers into its maw. Squirming on the floor, he hugged his crossed knees against his chest, and if a scene turned too violent, would dip his head down behind them. Whenever he thought his two friends weren't paying attention, he'd chew his fingernails. Otherwise, he'd keep his hands hidden as best as he could.

Biff, on the other side of his room, his back to his friends, rocked jerkily on a wheeled chair as he killed the zombies that swarmed his computer screen. He kept one foot on the top of his desk and the other in an open drawer, and as he swiveled seemed in constant danger of tipping and pulling the desk over with him. He'd shout with glee each time his on-screen hammer hit a head and made it explode, but his outbursts slowly changed from triumph to disgust, until he groaned and threw his controller toward the floor… where it would have had a chance of landing had he not been surrounded by a pile of the previous day's clothes.

He kept promising his mom he'd clean up, and he'd get to it, really, he would. But not today.

Not when there were friends to play with (well, play next to), and not when there were movies to be watched, comics to be read, and games to be beaten.

And friends with whom to complain about them all.

"This is boring," he said. "Killing these guys, it's gotten too easy. I mean, I've smashed them with a hammer, like, a million times already."

Ron tilted his head back and looked at his upside down friend. His eyeglasses slid to his forehead and his friend grew fuzzy.

"Yeah, and I've read this one too many times already," he

said, pushing the lenses back up to his nose. "If it wasn't so late, we could make a run to the comics shop—but it's already closed."

Johnny cut off the sound on his horror movie, and let the monsters fight on in silence. He smiled in the flashing light of the screen.

"And I already know who's going to win when Reptilicus finally gets around to fighting Apetoctopus," he said.

They sat without speaking for a few uncomfortable moments, until Biff, always the first one for action, piped up.

"So what are we going to do about it?"

No one answered. But then…Johnny smiled.

"I have an idea," he said. "Why don't we try to all come up with our *own* horror stories?"

Biff looked at Ron, Ron looked at Biff, and then they both looked back at Johnny.

"Great idea," said Biff. "You first."

"No, that's not what I—"

"Hey, it was *your* idea," added Ron, glad it looked like he wouldn't have to be the one to start. He dropped his comic —it wasn't one of the valuable ones, those never left his own bedroom—and turned to place his back against the wall.

Johnny looked nervously around the room, with no idea how to begin. He forced his hands deep into his pockets, so he wouldn't feel compelled to chew his fingernails again. His mind was a blank as he gazed about until his eyes fell on the controller Biff had tossed aside. Then slowly, haltingly, he began to speak.

"There was this factory, see, where this company made computer games," he said. "And, um, the bosses were horrible. Almost as bad as the big boss monsters in the games! They wouldn't let the workers take any breaks. Not to eat. Not to go to the bathroom. And not even to sleep."

"Not even to sleep?" repeated Biff, uncertain whether he was interrupting because the story made no sense or because it made too much sense. He'd read the articles, too.

"Well...they had to sleep in the factory, and were allowed just enough sleep to be be able to keep working," continued Johnny. "But barely that. And so some, um, died from exhaustion. Some got so lonely and depressed because they couldn't see their families, they went up to the factory roof and jumped off and killed themselves. And though the bosses took the bodies away, the souls of the workers, they stayed behind. And because they hated the people who bought the games, who they felt—because they wouldn't have to make them if no one bought the games they made, right?—were the real bosses behind the bosses who'd killed them, their spirits went into the games. And every once in a while, those spirits can get out, um, reach out, and, like, take over who's playing."

Ron glanced over at Biff, who was the best gamer of the three, expecting him to break into the story again, but his friend's intense expression told him...no.

"So one day, this kid is playing, and there's a spark, see, a short circuit, I guess, and suddenly, the kid is inside the game! And he loves it! And he goes around killing zombies, many zombies, endless zombies, and then he killed the big boss, too, the, um, zombie king over all the other zombies, and so he, see, he wins the game. And then right when the game's over, it all fades away, the world within the game, and he suddenly sees he was never in a game at all. He was always in the real world. Our world. It was a lie. So he hadn't been killing zombies after all! He, um, killed his friends. *All* of his friends. And so he gets locked up, and his parents throw the kid's console away, and you think that would be the end of it, but then some other kid finds it in the trash, or maybe at a yard sale, and what happened to the first kid happens to him, too, and—"

"Is this story going anywhere?" asked Ron.

"No, wait, let me think, I'll figure out an ending. Just give me a second."

"That wasn't scary," said Biff. "Not scary at all."

"Oh, you think you could do better?" said Johnny.

Biff looked away.

"How about you, Ron?"

"Hey, why don't we check on that new family who moved in a couple of blocks away?" Ron blurted out. "I heard my parents talking about them. They've got a kid."

"Yeah, let's go," said Biff, jumping up and leaving the room before either of the others could say anything more. Ron hurried after him.

"You guys better have some good stories tomorrow!" Johnny shouted, and rushed after.

Outside Biff's house, they climbed on their bikes and pedaled through the darkness. When they arrived at the end of the cul de sac, they circled slowly several times before stopping side by side across from the new neighbors. The curtains were open, and light spilled from the windows, painting the lawn with long rectangles which seemed to reach toward them through the night.

"Can you see anything?" asked Ron.

"Nah, not from here," said Johnny. "I can't even tell if anyone's home."

"Then let's get closer," Biff said, letting his bike drop.

Hunched over, he crossed the cul de sac, and peered through the front window into the living room. Ron and Johnny crept up to bracket him. Past the living room, they could see a family was sitting around the dining room table. A mother, a father, and...

"Is that...a girl?" asked Johnny.

"I think so," said Ron. "I mean, if it is, her hair is pretty short."

"Oh, well, this was a waste," said Biff. "Might as well head home."

They backed away from the window and returned to their bikes, but just as they were about to hop on and pedal off, the front door of the house blew open, and a large man rushed out, one with more muscles than they'd ever seen without the aid of special effects.

"What are you kids doing?" he called to them, more a rumble of thunder than a shout.

"Run!" screamed Johnny. "It's the dad!"

They leapt on their bikes and rode faster than they ever had before. As the father chased them, they didn't dare look back until his voice vanished away. But even then, they refused to slow down until they were back at Biff's house. They let the bikes fall away and collapsed on the lawn.

"That guy was scary," said Johnny, gasping. "I hope we don't have to see him again."

"Well, we don't," said Biff. "Luckily, we won't ever be going back there."

"Yeah," said Ron. "It's only a girl."

AFTER SCHOOL THE NEXT DAY, they all met up at Ron's house, where he pulled *all* his comic books out of the closet, not just the reading copies, but even the ones he normally wouldn't let Biff and Johnny touch. Usually, all they could do was stare as he dangled them just out of reach in their plastic bags.

"Nuh-uh," said Biff, pulling his eyes away from the neat row of comics on the bed. "I see what you're trying to do. And it's not going to work."

"What, me? No, I—"

"You're hoping we'll forget," said Johnny. "You're hoping you won't have to tell us a scary story. Well, I did it, and now you have to."

He stepped back from the bed and plopped down on the floor.

"Come on, guys—"

"Enough," said Biff. "Stop trying to distract us."

Ron carefully picked up his comics, and moving as slowly as possible, returned them to his closet. Then he sat on a corner of his bed and looked nervously around.

"There's nobody here but us," said Biff. "Get on with it."

"Yeah," said Johnny. "Get on with it."

Ron leaned forward, and whispered in a voice so low that if the other two had been further back they wouldn't have been able to hear him.

"You know that gym teacher who's always trying to kill us?" he said.

"Which one?" asked Biff.

"You really have to ask? The one who makes us climb those ropes until we touch the ceiling. The one who never notices what's really going on during dodgeball. The one who puts a foot on our backs when he doesn't like our pushups. *Mr. Smokes.*"

Johnny nodded. Biff only frowned.

"You know why he makes us do those things? You know why he pushes us until we need help, and then never helps us when we do? Because he's a vampire!"

"What does that have to do with anything?" said Biff.

"Yeah, being a jerk doesn't make you a vampire," said Johnny.

"Listen," continued Ron. "And you know why he wants to hurt us? Because he wants to make us bleed. And then after we do, he drinks our blood. The more we bleed, the more he gets to drink."

Both of his friends made gagging sounds, but that didn't stop him.

"Why do you think he's always so careful about cleaning up the blood? Why do you think he takes away all the evidence we ever got hurt? He says it's to stop other kids from getting infected, but that's a lie. He takes away whatever blood we spill and he—"

"He what?" said Biff. "Eats the bandages?"

"Yes!"

"Yuck!" said Johnny. "That's not scary, that's gross."

"Good enough for me! If I can't be scary, then you know me—I'm gonna be gross!"

He'd read that somewhere. He couldn't remember where, but he hoped repeating it to his friends would work.

"That's not what this is supposed to be about." said Johnny. "The idea was scary stories, remember? *Scary.* Mine was scary."

"Oh, really?" said Ron. "Are you sure?"

"Hey!" shouted Johnny, looking at Biff, for confirmation. But Biff only shrugged.

"So anyway, Mr Smokes is not the only one. He and the principal are in on this together. And it even gets worse— whenever we're told a kid has moved away, he really hasn't. The two of them—"

The ring of a doorbell interrupted him. Ron frowned and scooted over to peer down out his bedroom window.

"Who is it?" asked Johnny.

"This is weird," he said. "Most definitely weird. It's that girl."

"What's she doing here?" asked Biff.

"I don't know."

For a moment, the three boys were frozen, but after a beat they simultaneously barreled down stairs not wide enough to accommodate them side by side. As they pulled and pushed each other, first one was in the lead, then another. They reached the front door in a clump and tumbled against it with a bang. Ron turned the knob and let her in.

"What do *you* want?" he asked.

"Well, *you're* not being very friendly," she said. Now that she was right in front of them instead of being spied on at night, there was no longer any doubt. Yes, short hair or no, this was a girl. Her dark eyes glistened. And she looked younger than they were, but somehow older, too. "My name's Mary. I saw you all out there last night. I'm new in the neighborhood, so I figured I'd come over and check you guys out. I could use some friends here."

The three friends looked at each other, and because they'd known each other for so long—almost two whole grades—each could tell what the others were thinking.

About the father chasing them. His angry face, his loud voice, and the size of his fists. How their hearts pounded as they raced away on their bikes, and how relieved they were he hadn't caught them.

They hoped the new girl wasn't as perceptive to what was going through their minds as they had become. But she surprised them. Because she was.

"Oh, don't mind him," she said. "He's…harmless. So… what were you guys doing?"

"Nothing," said Ron quickly, because he knew—that story he was telling—it wasn't the kind of thing you talked about in front of a girl.

"Actually," said Biff. "Ron here was telling us a scary story. Or trying to anyway. I don't think he understands the game."

"Oh," said Mary, softly. "Can I play? I know a scary story."

"Sure," said Biff, as quickly as Ron had, but for a different reason.

"Oh, no," said Johnny, seeing right through him. "You're not getting off that easy. It's *your* turn, Biff, not hers. No cheating. I did it. Ron did it. Now you have to do it."

Biff looked at his friends beside him, and at the girl who looked at him expectantly from the front porch. He would have sighed had he been the kind of kid who sighed.

"OK," he said, and looking at Mary, tilted his head inside toward the kitchen.

The four of them sat around a small table, and as Ron pulled out milk and cookies, Biff cleared his throat and began to tell his tale.

"There once were three friends who decided to tell each other stories. Because they loved horror. Horror books. Horror games. Horror comics. Horror movies. But that wasn't enough. So they decided to tell their own horror stories."

"Wait, that's not even a story," said Johnny. "That's us. You're not supposed to just talk about *us*. You're supposed to tell a *story*."

"This is a story," said Biff firmly. "But you should be very careful about the horror stories you tell. *Very* careful. Because these three friends soon learned that the horror stories they told…would come true."

"That makes no sense," said Ron. "Come on! Admit it. You don't even *have* a story."

"Are you telling this story, or am I? Anyway, one of these friends told a story about a game that turned its player into a killer…and lo and behold, it did."

Biff didn't really know what "lo and behold" meant, but

it seemed like the kind of thing one said when telling a story, so he said it.

"I don't like this story," said Johnny.

"Shut up!" snapped Biff. "And the friend started to believe that everyone around him was a zombie, and he rose up and killed them all. And then the other friend he told a story about a teacher being a vampire, and—"

"Wait," said Mary. "If the first friend killed all his friends, who was left to tell another story?"

"Obviously, he must not have killed everyone."

"I don't think you know what you're doing," said Ron.

The friends argued, and before Biff could continue with his story, there came a hammering at the door. They all jumped. All save Mary.

"Who's that?" said Johnny, chewing a nail.

"Mary!" came a loud voice from the other side of the door. "Mary, I know you're in there! Don't try to hide from me!"

"It's my father," she said.

"He's going to kill us!" whimpered Ron.

"You guys just stay here," she said, grimacing. "I'll deal with this."

They let her, staying on the opposite side of the kitchen table as she moved toward the front door. Biff eyed the knife block on the counter as she neared the banging.

Then the door opened and then a hand reached in and then she was yanked out. They didn't see the whole of the man until they ran to a window—they didn't dare head to the door, for fear he would grab them, too—and watched as Mary's father pulled her down the street.

Once the two were far enough down the road that the man couldn't immediately turn on them, the three boys tumbled from the house and followed from a distance.

"Is he hurting her?" said Ron. "The way he's pulling, it looks like he's hurting her."

"Should we do something?" said Biff. "We should do something."

"What could we do?" said Johnny. "We're just kids."

By the time the three friends arrived at the cul de sac, Mary and her father were inside their house. They could see her up in her room, and see the father, too, pacing downstairs, an angry expression on his face. Mary looked down at them, and offered a small wave.

"Do you think she'll be OK?" said Ron.

Ron and Johnny both looked at Biff. He would know such things. He usually did.

"Well, do you?" asked Johnny, softly.

"I don't know," said Biff. "If this were a game, or a movie, or a comic, I think she would be. She'd have to be, right? But...I don't know."

———

BIFF AND RON watched the next afternoon as Johnny spread so many DVDs and VHS tapes across his bed the bed itself was barely visible. Werewolves and zombies looked up at them, scaled serpents and one-eyed giants threatened, and interspersed with those were the bloody, frightened faces of normal people, people who could have been someone they knew. Could have been them. Those were the scariest ones of all.

"So which one do you want to watch?" asked Johnny.

"I don't know why you even have these things," Biff said. "You should be downloading movies online like a normal person."

"Yeah, what are you, my grandfather?" asked Ron.

"These were my Dad's," said Johnny.

The others had no answer to that. In the silence that followed, Johnny reached out and snatched one off the bed.

"How about this one, guys?"

As he held it out toward them for inspection, a sudden knock at the front door made him jerk and drop the tape back onto the pile.

"Uh-oh!" he said, shoving his hands into his pockets. "You think that's…him?"

Then there came a second knock, a gentler one.

"No," said Biff. "It's not."

They went downstairs, all of them suspecting who it would be, in a more orderly fashion than their first time. Johnny opened the door, still somewhat nervous as to what he would find, and there was Mary. Only it wasn't the Mary they'd met before. This time, there was a bruise under an eye, and a bandage wrapped around one wrist.

"Wow, what happened?" asked Ron.

"Nothing," she answered, in a way that said any further questions would be pointless. She kept looking down rather than at them. "Nothing happened."

Biff stepped outside and stood beside her, looking down the street in the direction from which she'd have come.

"Is *he* here?" he asked. "Did he do that?"

"It's not something I can—" she began, and then stopped, and lowered her head even further, and then sighed. And then stood up a little straighter, and looked slowly from one boy to the other. "It's my turn now."

"Turn?" asked Johnny. "Turn for what?"

"To tell a story."

"But you're—" Ron started to say.

"But I'm what?" said Mary, louder than they'd ever heard her speak before.

"Come in," said Biff.

Johnny got out cans of soda and a bag of jerky, and they

sat around a kitchen table again. Though it was a different kitchen table than last one they'd sat at with Mary, it brought back for him too many memories of how that day had ended, and stirred fears it might end that way again. He shivered at the thought of her father and hoped the others wouldn't notice.

"There once was an ogre," she began, after they'd all settled in. "It was long ago, yet still close enough to now that people had already forgotten ogres even existed. But, see, the thing is, ogres hadn't forgotten about people.

"Especially *this* ogre.

"Most ogres were content to live their ogre lives, and you know, ogres really aren't so bad when they're only around other ogres. But when they're around people, there's trouble. They don't understand the ways of humans, so they mostly stay away, but when they try to deal with us, or even worse, when they try to pretend they're one of us, it never works, and they grow frustrated, and angry, and instead of giving up and going back to live with the other ogres, things happen. Bad things.

"This one ogre, he would watch us...watch *them*, I mean...from his hiding place, and for some reason wanted to be like us—like them, sorry—even though he didn't know why. Even though he didn't know how. And this ogre...this was one of the ones that felt a need to pretend to be human. Because he was jealous of what we had but he could never have. Which means, unfortunately, he needed to force others to pretend, too.

"So one day, he snuck into a village and stole a woman, and took her back to his cave, and forced her to act as if she was his wife—ogres don't have wives, you see, but this one wanted to pass like one of us, wanted to know what it was like to be more than a creature, a thing it could never know—so it kept her out of contact with everyone she knew, and made her act like one of them until she began to believe she was, too, and forgot all about her old life. But that was not enough for this ogre, because it knew that to be truly human meant being part of a family. Which meant he needed to steal…a child."

Mary's voice, which had been dropping in volume throughout her story, causing them all to lean forward, was now little more than a whisper. They forgot all about the soda and jerky as they ate up her words.

"And that's exactly what he did, too," she continued. "It snuck into a home, took a baby from its crib and brought it back to its cave to live with the pretend wife. But though the child went along with pretending she was an ogre, she never believed it. She could not eat rocks. She longed for the sunlight she was never allowed. Her voice could not make the sounds that ogres did, whose speech could sound like thunder.

"She knew the truth the ogre denied her, and her stolen human mother had forgotten, but she needed to pretend she didn't in order to survive. So she never let him know as they moved from cave to cave, further and further from the village where she had been born. But it didn't last. Because one day the ogre looked at her, and her lie did not hold. He saw the truth of the child, and realized at last that to pass as human was impossible. And she saw that it saw, and thought that perhaps *now* he will take me home, *now* I will be free…"

The boys were silent, not moving, barely breathing. Mary leaned closer to them, and shouted.

"And then the ogre bit her head off and ate her up!"

They jumped back. Johnny banged into the table, knocking over his can of soda, creating a spill which headed toward the pile of jerky. Ron scooped up the wizened strips before it could reach them. But Biff stayed still, able to do nothing more but continue staring at her.

"Sorry about that," said Johnny, by way of apology. "But that was some story."

"Yeah," said Ron. "I know what you mean. It really spooked me."

"No," said Biff, looking at her strangely. "That was no story."

"It was," said Mary, the voice which had been so measured and controlled while telling her tale now quivering. She cleared her throat. "Really, I promise, it's only story. Nothing more. Now I'd better go, before—"

"Before what?" said Biff.

"Before…nothing."

And then Mary was gone.

"That was creepy." Said Johnny. "But it *was* only a story, Biff. Wasn't it?

"No way," Biff answered. "No way that was only a story. Did you see that bruise? Did you see that bandage? She was trying to tell us something. Tell us that he's been hurting her. Or worse. We have to do something."

They sat in silence for a moment, until Ron finally nodded.

"Maybe you're right," said Ron. "But…"

His voice trailed off.

"Yeah," said Johnny. "This is really life, not a video game. What can we do?"

Biff smiled. It was the kind of smile they'd only seen before when he was hunched over, staring into a screen, and watching zombies die.

———

LATER THAT NIGHT, long after their parents slept and in

dreams thought them sleeping, too, the three boys snuck out of their homes. As they biked over to Mary's cul de sac, what was within their backpacks was heavier on their shoulders than the weight alone could create. Once there, they could make out no lights shining through the windows of her house or any of the others which circled them.

"Are we really going to do this?" whispered Johnny. "*Really?*"

"It's not like it's anything we haven't done before," said Biff.

"I don't know about that," said Ron. "Yeah, maybe we did it in games, or saw it in movies, or read about it in comics. But this isn't any of that. This is real life."

"Yes," said Biff, taking the first step forward. "Yes, it is. Now let's do this."

They moved silently to the top of the driveway, and once by the garage, Ron laced his fingers together and gave first Biff, then Johnny, a boost to its roof. Together, the two friends pulled Ron up to join them. They crept along the roofline until they reached the closest second floor window —which was unlocked—and entered.

They tiptoed down a hall which seemed familiar even though they'd never seen it before—the layout of the home was like all the others in the subdivision—and soon located the master bedroom. The door was slightly ajar, and each boy took a turn to peer in through the gap.

"We can't do this," whispered Johnny. "The mother's in there right next to him."

"Change of plans," Biff hissed back. "Now follow my lead."

He waved the others away from him down the hall toward the stairs. As soon as they had dropped out of sight, he pulled the door shut with a slam. He then raced downstairs after them as quietly as he could.

"What was that?" came a loud rumble from the bedroom.

"Probably just the wind," said the wife. "Go back to sleep."

Instead, the man grunted and got out of bed. His feet hitting the floor made the house shake more than any slammed door. He stepped out into the hallway, looked both ways, and just as he spotted the open window at the far end, a thud echoed from below.

"Who's there?" he shouted as he hurried down to see. When he entered the kitchen, the refrigerator door was open, and for an instant, the light blinded him. As he squinted and stepped forward to close the door, Biff emerged from under a table, leapt atop it, and then onto the man's back. Landing, he struck with a hammer on one side of his head. He swung again, and as the man reached back to grab him, but failed, they fell against the refrigerator, which rocked against the wall behind it.

Ron burst out of a cabinet and Johnny from the pantry, and they went after the man's legs, hitting them with their own hammers until he toppled. He tried to push them away, but as one boy was swatted back, the others would take his place. They continued to swing their weapons as long as the man continued to move.

When, breathless, they were done, and dropped their hammers one by one to the floor because they suddenly seemed too heavy to hold, the spatter of blood on their arms and faces was like nothing any of them had ever before seen in the scary stories they loved.

From behind them came a high-pitched scream.

They turned, and there was Mary, in pajamas, one hand to her mouth. There was no bandage on her wrist, no bruises on her face.

"What did you do?" she cried, as she watched the blood

drip from their fingers, and their gazes shifted in horror and disbelief between the unbroken, unblemished spots on her body. "None of it was real. I made it all up. I told you. I told you! I only wanted to scare you. I only wanted you to like me. It was only a story. *It was only a story.*"

NOTES

"Things That Never Happened"

One of the most annoying assumptions readers make about writers is that the characters we share in our fiction have one-to-one analogues in the real world. I know *you* would never make such inferences, no, not you—but there are others out there who do. I've been told a grandfather in one story was surely based on my own, when he was just...a character's grandfather. And that a character who bore the same first name as someone I knew in real life just had to be me making a statement about that real-life acquaintance. But the great mulch pile of the subconscious into which everything I experience gets added and out of which I then draw my stories doesn't work that simply. At least not for me.

So let me get this out of the way before I go on—the mother in "Things That Never Happened" bears no resemblance to my own. Eleanor is an amalgam of others mothers I have known, and I can see them all there, but of my own mother, I can find not a single ingredient. But I can easily find the catalytic moment which caused this story to be.

My mother-in-law was one of the kindest, smartest, most pleasant people I knew, but there came a time when she did not know me. She did not know any of us. She loved us, she enjoyed being around us, and (for this we were all grateful) she was not made anxious by the loss of her memory. And then one Thanksgiving, she uttered the words which I eventually placed in Eleanor's mouth, when she turns to Barb and asks:

"And *you* are?"

Those real-life words eventually had me thinking—what would happen if someone were being haunted, but no longer had the ability to recognize the ghost?

We'd all like to be forgiven, and we all wish we had the capacity to forgive, but what if true forgiveness was an impossibility? Could we still find a way to grant or receive it anyway? So I set up a situation to examine that theme, and came up with a scenario which many of us might someday find ourselves facing, mixed with aspects I hope none will ever have to face anywhere but in the pages of a story.

But, of course, I had to devise someone worthy of being haunted, someone who did not walk through the world as my mother-in-law did. And so I cobbled together bits and pieces of other mothers—including a concentration camp survivor who had gone through such horrors her son was not allowed a moment of sadness, because anything he might be experiencing paled before her past—then threw in a few more attributes entirely out of my imagination.

So while there are subliminal guest appearances by my parents, relatives, friends, acquaintances, and co-workers scattered through my stories, remember—they're not so easy to find, and not hidden in plain sight.

So to paraphrase Stephen King—

It's the tale, not the mother of he who tells it.

Originally published in Postscripts *30/31, November 2013*

"Petrified"

The 2008 World Horror Convention took place in Salt Lake City, Utah, and as an added bonus for attendees that year, the committee decided to publish an accompanying souvenir anthology. A call was put out for stories set in the desert, and because I very much wanted to be a part of the book, I managed to rise to the occasion.

Which was unusual for me.

I tend to find it difficult to deliver when invited to theme anthologies, because I have never been able to write to market. Which might seem odd, considering I started my writing career on comic book scripts for Marvel and DC. But when it comes to prose, I write what I write out of the pure joy of creation, then look around and think...now what? With very few exceptions, I have no market in mind when I sit down to write a story, and one usually doesn't occur to me until after I complete multiple drafts. But this time, for this project, I was willing and able to walk in the desert. Specifically, the Petrified Forest, which I'd visit years earlier, and which seemed the perfect metaphor for a dying relationship.

I think I was able to deliver before the due date because this market intrigued me. I knew copies would be handed out to all of my peers, and I wanted to see if I could come up with something which would please them. I guess I did, because "Petrified" unexpectedly earned me my fourth Bram Stoker Award nomination.

This story would have made a perfect *Twilight Zone* episode, I think, and I was pleased that a number of readers picked up on that and have told me so unprompted.

Originally published in Desolate Souls, *March 2008*
[Bram Stoker Award Finalist: Short Fiction]

"The Hunger of Empty Vessels"

I've already mentioned the difficulty my muse has in being activated by the prompts of theme anthologies. But in addition to that, I have the same problem with hitting word count targets for individual stories. And that pops up in cases where I can't intentionally write stories short or long enough for certain markets. There might be a magazine I'd love to be a part of, but their maximum word length may be 5,000, and no matter how I tried, all of my stories during that period turned out to be 8,000 words or more, because I wrote the story as the story demanded to be written, and wherever it leaves me, that's where I am left.

Conversely, if I hear about a standalone novella or novelette market I'd love to crack, I find myself unable to write at length merely because I wish to. All I can do is write the stories that come to mind, and hope one of them might eventually reach the needed length. Such was the case with this story and Bad Moon Books.

After my pal Gene O'Neill, who I met at the Clarion Science Fiction Writing Workshop we both attended in 1979, informed me editor Roy Robbins was looking for longer works to package as standalones, I wanted to be part of that beautifully packaged line, but there was no way I could create a story deliberately for that company. All I could do was continue to write the stories I felt moved to write, and hope one of them would finish at the right length while the market was still open.

And that's what happened. It came about entirely because of coincidence, not intentionality.

Please note that running one's writing career this way isn't anything I'd recommend. There are many markets which could have published stories by me, but didn't because of the way my muse behaves. But that's the way I'm made.

When published, this story contained a dedication to Thomas M. Disch and Algis Budrys, "two mentors gone too soon," who'd died the previous year, and who I'd first met 30 years previously, two weeks apart, at the same Clarion Workshop where I'd met Gene O'Neill, then a fellow student. I hope they'd have been proud.

Bad Moon Books, April 2009

[Bram Stoker Award Finalist: Long Fiction]

"A TEST OF FAITH FOR A COUPLE OF TRUE BELIEVERS"

I have a soft spot in my heart for *Space & Time* magazine, because my fifth story ever to be published appeared there, way back in 1982. Thirty years after my first publication there—and 29 years after what was then my last—I returned to the pages of one of science fiction's earliest independent magazines.

To learn more about my history with that magazine, check out my comments to "One of the Lucky Ones," also in this volume.

Originally published in Space and Time *#116, Spring 2012*

"IN A STRANGE CITY LYING ALONE"

I've always had a love/hate relationship with the city of my birth, which is why I was so pleased to be a part of editor Luis Ortiz's anthology project, *Why New Yorkers Smoke*, published on September 11, 2011, the 10th anniversary of 9/11.

As Ortiz explains:

"People not there when it all went down seem to have forgotten that it was like a great furnace igniting in hell. It was not much later when I came to realize that I would like to do a book of stories about fear and New Yorkers. As editor I found that unless I wanted a collection of tabloid stories the only way to approach this theme was by embracing fantastika, that is fantasy, horror and science fiction. I was lucky in being able to get some of the top writers working in these genres, many of them New Yorkers themselves, to answer the question: "What is there to fear in New York City?"

This story is my answer to that question.

The title of the story comes from the opening of Edgar Allan Poe's poem "The City in the Sea"—

"Lo! Death has reared himself a throne
In a strange city lying alone.
Far down within the dim West,
Where the good and the bad and the worst and the best
Have gone to their eternal rest."

It seemed apt.

Originally published in Why New Yorkers Smoke, *September 2011*

"BECOMING INVISIBLE, BECOMING SEEN"

If you're the kind of person who reads story notes before reading the story themselves, now's the time to stop…unless you happen to like spoilers. Because I'm about to explain one of my methods for coming up with a story idea, and if you were to read this first, you'd have the conceit blown for you too soon.

I'm often on panels at science fiction, fantasy, and horror conventions on which I join others in pontificating on how to take a story to the next level, and one of the things we often discuss is how to tell the difference between a conceit and a story. Often writers have conceits—for example, a new invention, a societal change, a cosmic event

—but no story, because they've not yet figured out whose story it is.

To whom should that moment matter? Sometimes, that's boiled down to—who hurts?

In this case, I wondered, who would be bothered the most by a world where there's no longer such a thing as the dead? And one of my thoughts was—and I have no idea why I went there, other than it seemed to me to be an obvious answer to my question—a necrophiliac. Because the fetish that scratches his itch cannot exist.

Once I had the conceit, once I had the character, the rest of the story came together quickly. So—

Who hurts? Who's the most changed? Whose life would be altered forever?

Once I feel confident I've correctly answered those questions, I know I have a story worth telling.

Originally published in Dark Discoveries *#30, 2015*

[Bram Stoker Award Finalist: Long Fiction]

"SURVIVAL OF THE FITTEST"

I've told you I find it difficult to write stories for themed anthologies. This was one of the few times I was surprised to find I easily could.

When editor Stephen Jones announced he was assembling an anthology of vacation-themed horror, and was particularly looking for roads less travelled, I thought—hey, I've taken a few vacations like that, including to Antarctica... and the Galapagos Islands.

My wife and I went there back in 2001 having made plans we were going to fulfill that particular lifelong dream as a way to celebrate our 25th anniversary. It was as close as I'm ever going to get to visiting a prehistoric world. I was surrounded by dozens of species that exist nowhere else on

Earth. A number of the scenes from this story as well as all of the details have been snatched from memories of that trip, and I hope to go back again someday to gather new memories, and who knows—inspiration for a future story.

Originally published in Summer Chills, *September 2011*

"THAT PERILOUS STUFF"

Hoarding is personal to me. My Uncle Jack, the man who when I was a kid fed my twin loves of reading and eating by visiting us each weekend bearing bags of science fiction novels and magazines as well as cakes and pies from Ebinger's, died in his hoard, a hoard so toxic that after his death the police would not allow us to enter. Much of who I have become can be traced to those visits, and much of what I have been rescued from can be traced to the manner of his death.

I, too, had hung onto too much clutter for far too long. I had every cancelled check back to my first account as a teen, every utility bill ever sent to me, every magazine I'd ever read whether or not I ever intended to read it again, every…well, you get the idea. When I learned of how he had passed, I was scared straight, and that all changed. I filled 17 shopping bags with scrap paper in the days surrounding his death. And ever since then, I've asked myself the same question my protagonist does in this story, and wondered of each object which enters my house—does this deserve a place in my life?

In fact, I even have a rule that if I head down to our basement, I don't allow myself back up without three items to dispose of, even if that's as simple as three sheets of paper.

So it was inevitable I'd write a story reflecting my desires and fears surrounding owning too much stuff. And I sense this won't end up being the only one.

Originally published in Chiral Mad *3, 2016*

[Bram Stoker Award Finalist: Long Fiction]

"ONE OF THE LUCKY ONES"

This publication in *Space & Time* magazine came 35 years after my first appearance there. Which might seem like a long time, but I'm not the writer with the longest record for having been published there. The title for the writer with the longest run in the magazine belongs to Darrell Schweitzer, who was first published there even earlier than I was.

Traces of my Uncle Jack, whose life and end was part of the inspiration for "That Perilous Stuff," can also be spotted here, though as I mentioned in the first of these story notes, there's never a one-to-one correlation with any friend or family member, and none should be inferred from this piece.

Originally published in Space & Time *#128, 2017*

"A JUDGMENT CALL FOR JUDGMENT DAY"

Editor Mike Heffernan took the title for this WWII horror anthology from the statement made by Winston Churchill on January 22, 1941, about the bleakness of the battles to come:

"Far be it from me to paint a rosy picture of the future. Indeed, I do not think we should be justified in using any but the most sombre tones and colours while our people, our Empire and indeed the whole English-speaking world are passing through a dark and deadly valley."

This is the only story I ever wrote on my phone. When the idea for it came to me, I was on my way to a Worldcon in Glasgow, with the anthology closing immediately on my return. And so whenever I wasn't on programming, in the audience when friends were on programming, or partying, I was writing this story with my thumbs. It's one of only two stories I forced myself to create electronically. I'd prefer if I didn't find myself in such circumstances again. My chosen method is to write longhand, input the text, then print the story out and continue to edit longhand as well.

Can readers tell the difference between stories written in that manner and those created the old-fashioned way? I have no idea. No one's ever pointed out a changed style. Can you tell?

Originally published by A Dark and Deadly Valley, *April 2007*

"HERE CHOOSE I"

This is the least circulated story of mine ever to be published. The only work of mine less read would have to be stories never published in the first place. It appeared as a bonus for those who bought the special lettered edition of *The Hunger of Empty Vessels*. I warned my readers a decade ago that everyone other than those 26 collectors had to wait for it to be reprinted in a future more widely circulated book of mine.

Well, that time is finally here.

The theme brought to life, of one encountering one's future self, is obviously one which fascinated me, because I explored it in the story "I Wish I Knew Where I Was Going" as well, originally published in the 2004 Charles L. Grant tribute anthology *Quietly Now* and late reprinted in my 2018 collection *Tell Me Like You Done Before (and Other Stories Written on the Shoulder of Giants)*. I wonder which handled it best?

It'll be up to readers to tell me. I'm probably not the one best equipped to answer that question.

Originally published by Bad Moon Books, *April 2009*

"The Scariest Story I Know"

After this story was published in the annual anthology *Nemonymous*, I had to wait three months to tell anyone of it, because editor and publisher D.F. Lewis had created an intriguing philosophical experiment. All submissions to the project had to be made anonymously, so that the author's reputation would not affect Lewis' decision to accept or reject each story. Also, the writers would then have to agree to let their stories be published anonymously until some future time, so that readers could also judge the stories on their own merits. Only once Lewis set us free, was I finally able to mention this publication.

Interestingly, this story received some of my best reviews ever, making me think I should publish all of my work anonymously!

Originally published in Nemonymous, *August 2005*

"It's Only a Story"

I end this volume once more proving you should never believe what I say, because this story was born of an anthology invitation, and came easily. I was invited by Alex Scully and B. E. Scully to come up with a story which would celebrate the 200th anniversary of the publication of *Frankenstein*, and I immediately thought of this—a hybrid between *Stranger Things* and that long-ago night when stories were told and The Creature was born.

I don't often say of stories that they were fun to write—I always enjoy writing, but fun isn't the word I'd tend to use—but this one was fun. I liked those kids. I was once one of them. Not that I ended up in the same situation as they did by story's end. But you get the idea.

And in case you think I contradict myself by sharing

with you in this volume so many stories written for themed anthologies, know there are dozens of times I failed to do so. My muse refuses to be saddled...and for that I am forever grateful.

Originally published in Birthing Monsters: Frankenstein's Cabinet of Curiosities and Cruelties, *2018*

ABOUT THE AUTHOR

Scott Edelman has published nearly 100 short stories in magazines such as *Analog, PostScripts, The Twilight Zone, and Dark Discoveries*, and in anthologies such as *Why New Yorkers Smoke, The Solaris Book of New Science Fiction: Volume Three, Crossroads: Southern Tales of the Fantastic, Once Upon a Galaxy, Moon Shots, Mars Probes, and Forbidden Planets.*

His collection of zombie fiction, *What Will Come After*, was published in 2010, and was a finalist for both the Stoker Award and the Shirley Jackson Memorial Award. His science fiction short fiction has been collected in *What We Still Talk About* (2010). His most recent collection was *Tell Me Like You Done Before (and Other Stories Written on the Shoulders of Giants*, which collected stories written to honor the writers who influenced him. He is also the author of the Lambda Award-nominated novel *The Gift* (1990). He has been a Stoker Award finalist eight times, both in the category of Short Story and Long Fiction, and currently holds the record for the most Stoker Award nominations without a win.

He worked as an assistant editor for Marvel Comics in the '70s, writing everything from display copy for superhero Slurpee cups to the famous Bullpen Bulletins pages. While there, he edited the Marvel-produced fan magazine *F.O.O.M.* (Friend of Ol' Marvel). He also wrote trade paperbacks such as *The Captain Midnight Action Book of Sports, Health and Nutrition* and *The Mighty Marvel Fun Book*.

In 1976, he left his staff position to go freelance, and

worked for both Marvel and DC. His scripts appeared in *Captain Marvel, Master of Kung Fu, Omega the Unknown, Time Warp, House of Mystery, Weird War Tales, Welcome Back, Kotter* and other titles. He co-created the character of Dr. Minn-Erva, recently seen portrayed by Gemma Chan in the *Captain Marvel* movie.

Additionally, Edelman worked for the Syfy Channel for more than thirteen years as editor of Science Fiction Weekly, SCI FI Wire, and Blastr. He was the founding editor of *Science Fiction Age*, which he edited during its entire eight-year run. He also edited *SCI FI* magazine, previously known as *Sci-Fi Entertainment*, for more a decade, as well as two other SF media magazines, *Sci-Fi Universe* and *Sci-Fi Flix*. He has been a four-time Hugo Award finalist for Best Editor.